A Master of Craft by W. W. Jacobs

William Wymark Jacobs was born on September 8th, 1863 in the Wapping district of London, England. Jacobs grew up near the docks, where his father was a wharf manager. The docks and river side would be a constant theme of his writing in years to come.

Although surrounded by poverty, he received a formal education in London, first at a private prep school and later at the Birkbeck Literary and Scientific Institute.

His working life began with a less than exciting clerical position at the Post Office Savings Bank. Jacobs put his imagination to good use writing short stories, sketches and articles, many for the Post Office house publication "Blackfriars Magazine."

In 1896 Jacobs published Many Cargoes, a selection of sea-faring yarns, which established him as a popular writer with a knack for authentic dialogue and trick endings.

A year later he published a novelette, The Skipper's Wooing, and in 1898 another collection of short stories; Sea Urchins. These works painted vivid pictures of dockland and seafaring London full of colourful characters.

By 1899, Jacobs was able to quit the post office and write full-time.

He married the noted suffragist Agnes Eleanor Williams (who had been jailed for her protest activities) in 1900. They set up households both in Loughton, Essex and in central London.

The publication in 1902 of At Sunwich Port and Dialstone Lane, in 1904, cemented Jacobs' reputation as one of the leading British authors of the new century.

There followed a string of further successful publications, including Captain's All (1905), Night Watches (1914), The Castaways (1916), and Sea Whispers (1926).

Though Jacobs would create little in the way of new work after 1911, he still wrote and was recognized as a leading humorist, ranked alongside such writers as P. G. Wodehouse.

William Wymark Jacobs died in a North London nursing home in Hornsey Lane, Islington on September 1st, 1943.

Index of Contents

CHAPTER I

A pretty girl stood alone on the jetty of an old-fashioned wharf at Wapping, looking down upon the silent deck of a schooner below. No smoke issued from the soot-stained cowl of the galley, and the fore-scuttle and the companion were both inhospitably closed. The quiet of evening was over everything, broken only by the whirr of the paddles of a passenger steamer as it passed carefully up the centre of the river, or the plash of a lighterman's huge sweep as he piloted his unwieldy craft down on the last remnant of the ebb-tide. In shore, various craft sat lightly on the soft Thames mud: some sheeting a rigid uprightness, others with their decks at various angles of discomfort.

The girl stood a minute or two in thought, and put her small foot out tentatively towards the rigging some few feet distant. It was an awkward jump, and she was still considering it, when she heard footsteps behind, and a young man, increasing his pace as he saw her, came rapidly on to the jetty.

"This is the Foam, isn't it?" enquired the girl, as he stood expectantly. "I want to see Captain Flower."

"He went ashore about half an hour ago," said the other.

The girl tapped impatiently with her foot. "You don't know what time he'll be back, I suppose?" she enquired.

He shook his head. "I think he's gone for the evening," he said, pondering; "he was very careful about his dress."

The ghost of a smile trembled on the girl's lips. "He has gone to call for me," she said. "I must have missed him. I wonder what I'd better do."

"Wait here till he comes back," said the man, without hesitation.

The girl wavered. "I suppose, he'll guess I've come here," she said, thoughtfully.

"Sure to," said the other promptly.

"It's a long way to Poplar," she said, reflectively. "You're Mr. Fraser, the mate, I suppose? Captain Flower has spoken to me about you."

"That's my name," said the other.

"My name's Tyrell," said the girl, smiling. "I daresay you've heard Captain Flower mention it?"

"Must have done," said Fraser, slowly. He stood looking at the girl before him, at her dark hair and shining dark eyes, inwardly wondering why the captain, a fervid admirer of the sex, had not mentioned her.

"Will you come on board and wait?" he asked. "I'll bring a chair up on deck for you if you will."

The girl stood a moment in consideration, and then, with another faint reference to the distance of Poplar from Wapping, assented. The mate sprang nimbly into the ratlins, and then, extending a hand, helped her carefully to the deck.

"How nice it feels to be on a ship again!" said the girl, looking contentedly about her, as the mate brought up a canvas chair from below. "I used to go with my father sometimes when he was alive, but I haven't been on a ship now for two years or more."

The mate, who was watching her closely, made no reply. He was thinking that a straw hat with scarlet flowers went remarkably well with the dark eyes and hair beneath it, and also that the deck of the schooner had never before seemed such an inviting place as it was at this moment.

"Captain Flower keeps his ship in good condition," said the visitor, somewhat embarrassed by his gaze.

"He takes a pride in her," said Fraser; "and it's his uncle's craft, so there's no stint. She never wants for paint or repairs, and Flower's as nice a man to sail under as one could wish. We've had the same crew for years."

"He's very kind and jolly," said the girl.

"He's one of the best fellows breathing," said the mate, warmly; "he saved my life once—went overboard after me when we were doing over ten knots an hour, and was nearly drowned himself."

"That was fine of him," said Miss Tyrell, eagerly. "He never told me anything about it, and I think that's rather fine too. I like brave men. Have you ever been overboard after anybody?"

Fraser shook his head somewhat despondently. "I'm not much of a swimmer," said he.

"But you'd go in for anybody if you saw them drowning?" persisted Miss Tyrell, in a surprised voice.

"I don't know, i'm sure," said Fraser. "I hope I should."

"Do you mean to say," said Miss Tyrell, severely, "that if I fell into the river here, for instance, you wouldn't jump in and try to save me?"

"Of course I should." said Fraser, hotly. "I should jump in after you if I couldn't swim a stroke."

Miss Tyrell, somewhat taken aback, murmured her gratification.

"I should go in after you," continued the mate who was loath to depart from the subject, "if it was blowing a gale, and the sea full of sharks."

"What a blessing it is there are no sharks round our coast," said Miss Tyrell, in somewhat of a hurry to get away from the mate's heroism. "Have you ever seen one?"

"Saw them in the Indian Ocean when I was an apprentice," replied Fraser.

"You've been on foreign-going ships then?" said the girl. "I wonder you gave it up for this."

"This suits me better," said Fraser; "my father's an old man, and he wanted me home. I shall have a little steamer he's got an interest in as soon as her present skipper goes, so it's just as well for me to know these waters."

In this wise they sat talking until evening gave way to night, and the deck of the Foam was obscured in shadow. Lamps were lit on the wharves, and passing craft hung out their side-lights. The girl rose to her feet.

"I won't wait any longer; I must be going," she said.

"He may be back at any moment," urged the mate.

"No, I'd better go, thank you," replied the girl; "it's getting late. I don't like going home alone."

"I'll come with you, if you'll let me," said the mate, eagerly.

"All the way?" said Miss Tyrell, with the air of one bargaining.

"Of course," said Fraser.

"Well, I'll give him another half-hour, then," said the girl, calmly. "Shall we go down to the cabin? It's rather chilly up here now."

The mate showed her below, and, lighting the lamp, took a seat opposite and told her a few tales of the sea, culled when he was an apprentice, and credulous of ear. Miss Tyrell retaliated with some told her by her father, from which Fraser was able to form his own opinion of that estimable mariner. The last story was of a humourous nature, and the laughter which ensued grated oddly on the ear of the sturdy, good-looking seaman who had just come on board. He stopped at the companion for a moment listening in amazement, and then, hastily descending, entered the cabin.

"Poppy!" he cried. "Why, I've been waiting up at the Wheelers' for you for nearly a couple of hours."

"I must have missed you," said Miss Tyrell, serenely. "Annoying, isn't it?"

The master of the Foam said it was, and seemed from his manner to be anxious to do more justice to the subject than that.

"I didn't dream you'd come down here," he said, at length.

"No, you never invited me, so I came without," said the girl softly; "it's a dear little schooner, and I like it very much. I shall come often."

A slight shade passed over Captain Flower's face, but he said nothing.

"You must take me back now," said Miss Tyrell. "Good-bye, Mr. Fraser."

She held out her hand to the mate, and giving a friendly pressure, left the cabin, followed by Flower.

The mate let them get clear of the ship, and then, clambering on to the jetty, watched them off the wharf, and, plunging his hands into his pockets, whistled softly.

"Poppy Tyrell," he said to himself, slowly. "Poppy Tyrell! I wonder why the skipper has never mentioned her. I wonder why she took his arm. I wonder whether she knows that he's engaged to be married."

Deep in thought he paced slowly up and down the wharf, and then wandered listlessly round the piled-up empties and bags of sugar in the open floor beneath the warehouse. A glance through the windows of the office showed him the watchman slumbering peacefully by the light of a solitary gas-jet, and he went back to the schooner and gazed at the dark water and the dim shapes of the neighbouring craft in a vein of gentle melancholy. He walked to the place where her chair had been, and tried to conjure up the scene again; then, becoming uncertain as to the exact spot, went down to the cabin, where, the locker being immovable, no such difficulty presented itself. He gazed his fill, and then, smoking a meditative pipe, turned in and fell fast asleep.

He was awakened suddenly from a dream of rescuing a small shark surrounded by a horde of hungry Poppies, by the hurried and dramatic entrance of Captain Fred Flower. The captain's eyes were wild and his face harassed, and he unlocked the door of his state-room and stood with the handle of it in his hand before he paused to answer the question in the mate's sleepy eyes.

"It's all right, Jack," he said, breathlessly.

"I'm glad of that," said the mate, calmly.

"I hurried a bit," said the skipper.

"Anxious to see me again, I suppose," said the mate; "what are you listening for?"

"Thought I heard somebody in the water as I came aboard," said Flower glibly.

"What have you been up to?" enquired the other, quickly.

Captain Flower turned and regarded him with a look of offended dignity.

"Good heavens! don't look like that," said the mate, misreading it. "You haven't chucked anybody overboard, have you?"

"If anybody should happen to come aboard this vessel," said Flower, without deigning to reply to the question, "and ask questions about the master of it, he's as unlike me, Jack, as any two people in this world can be. D'ye understand?"

"You'd better tell me what you've been up to," urged the mate.

"As for your inquisitiveness, Jack, it don't become you," said Flower, with severity; "but I don't suppose it'll be necessary to trouble you at all."

He walked out of the cabin and stood listening at the foot of the companion-ladder, and the mate heard him walk a little way up. When he reentered the cabin his face had cleared, and he smiled comfortably.

"I shall just turn in for an hour," he said, amiably; "good-night, Jack."

"Good-night," said the curious mate. "I say——" he sat up suddenly in his bunk and looked seriously at the skipper.

"Well?" said the other.

"I suppose," said the mate, with a slight cough—"I suppose it's nothing about that girl that was down here?"

"Certainly not," said Flower, violently. He extinguished the lamp, and, entering his state-room, closed the door and locked it, and the mate, after lying a little while drowsily wondering what it all meant, fell asleep again.

CHAPTER II

While the skipper and mate slumbered peacefully below, the watchman sat on a post at the extreme end of the jetty, yearning for human society and gazing fearfully behind him at the silent, dimly-lit wharf. The two gas-lamps high up on the walls gave but a faint light, and in no way dispelled the deep shadows thrown by the cranes and the piled-up empties which littered the place. He gazed intently at the dark opening of the floor beneath the warehouse, half fancying that he could again discern the veiled apparition which had looked in at him through the office window, and had finally vanished before his horror-struck eyes in a corner the only outlet to which was a grating. Albeit a careful man and tender, the watchman pinched himself. He was awake, and, rubbing the injured part, swore softly.

"If I go down and tell 'em," he murmured softly, in allusion to the crew, "what'll they do? Laugh at me."

He glanced behind him again, and, rising hastily to his feet, nearly fell on to the deck below as a dark figure appeared for a moment at the opening and then vanished again. With more alacrity than might have been expected of a man of his figure, he dropped into the rigging and lowered himself on to the schooner.

The scuttle was open, and the seamen's lusty snores fell upon his ears like sweet music. He backed down the ladder, and groped in the darkness towards the bunks with outstretched hand. One snore stopped instantly.

"Eh!" said a sleepy voice. "Wot! 'Ere, what the blazes are you up to?"

"A' right, Joe," said the watchman, cheerfully.

"But it ain't all right," said the seaman, sharply, "comin' down in the dark an' ketchin' 'old o' people's noses. Give me quite a start, you did."

"It's nothing to the start I've 'ad," said the other, pathetically; "there's a ghost on the wharf, Joe. I want you to come up with me and see what it is.

"Yes, I'm sure to do that," said Joe, turning over in his bunk till it creaked with his weight. "Go away, and let me get to sleep again. I don't get a night's rest like you do, you know."

"What's the matter?" enquired a sleepy voice.

"Old George 'ere ses there's a ghost on the wharf," said Joe.

"I've seen it three times," said the watchman, eager for sympathy.

"I expect it's a death-warning for you, George," said the voice, solemnly. "The last watchman died sudden, you remember."

"So he did," said Joe.

"His 'art was wrong," said George, curtly; "'ad been for years."

"Well, we can't do nothin' for you, George," said Joe, kindly; "it's no good us going up. We sha'n't see it. It isn't meant for us."

"'Ow d'yer know it's a ghost," said a third voice, impatiently; "very likely while you're all jawing about it down 'ere it's a-burglin' the offis."

Joe gave a startled grunt, and, rolling out of his bunk, grabbed his trousers, and began to dress. Three other shadowy forms followed suit, and, hastily dressing, followed the watchman on deck and gained the wharf. They went through the gloomy ground floor in a body, yawning sleepily.

"I shouldn't like to be a watchman," said a young ordinary seaman named Tim, with a shiver; "a ghost might easy do anything with you while you was all alone. P'r'aps it walks up an' down behind you, George, makin' faces. We shall be gorn in another hour, George."

The office, when they reached it, was undisturbed, and, staying only long enough to drink the watchman's coffee, which was heating on a gas-jet, they left it and began to search the wharf, Joe leading with a small lantern.

"Are we all 'ere?" demanded Tim, suddenly.

"I am," said the cook, emphatically.

"'Cos I see su'thing right behind them bags o' sugar," said the youth, clutching hold of the cook on one side and the watchman on the other. "Spread out a bit, chaps."

Joe dashed boldly round with the lantern. There was a faint scream and an exclamation of triumph from the seaman. "I've got it!" he shouted.

The others followed hastily, and saw the fearless Joe firmly gripping the apparition. At the sight the cook furtively combed his hair with his fingers, while Tim modestly buttoned up his jacket.

"Take this lantern, so's I can hold her better," said Joe, extending it.

The cook took it from him, and holding it up, revealed the face of a tall, good-looking woman of some seven or eight and twenty.

"What are you doin' here?" demanded the watchman, with official austerity.

"I'm waiting for a friend of mine," said the visitor, struggling with Joe. "Make this man leave go of me, please."

"Joe," said the watchman, with severity. "I'm ashamed of you. Who is your friend, miss?"

"His name is Robinson," said the lady. "He came on here about an hour ago. I'm waiting for him."

"There's nobody here," said the watchman, shaking his head.

"I'm not sure he didn't go on that little ship," said the lady; "but if he has, I suppose I can wait here till he comes off. I'm not doing any harm."

"The ship'll sail in about an hour's time, miss," said Tim, regretfully, "but there ain't nobody o' the name of Robinson aboard her. All the crew's 'ere, and there's only the skipper and mate on her besides."

"You can't deceive me, young man, so don't try it," said the lady, sharply. "I followed him on here, and he hasn't gone off, because the gate has been locked since."

"I can't think who the lady means," said Joe.

"I ain't seen nobody come aboard. If he did, he's down the cabin."

"Well, I'll go down there," said the lady, promptly.

"Well, miss, it's nothing to do with us," said Joe, "but it's my opinion you'll find the skipper and mate has turned in."

"Well, I'm going down," said the lady, gripping her parasol firmly by the middle; "they can't eat me."

She walked towards the Foam, followed by the perplexed crew, and with the able assistance of five pairs of hands reached the deck. The companion was open, and at Joe's whispered instructions she turned and descended the steps backwards.

It was at first quite dark in the cabin, but as the visitor's eyes became accustomed to it, she could just discern the outlines of a small table, while a steady breathing assured her that somebody was sleeping close by. Feeling her way to the table she discovered, a locker, and, taking a seat, coughed gently. The breathing continuing quite undisturbed, she coughed again, twice.

The breathing stopped suddenly. "Who the devil's that coughing?" asked a surprised voice.

"I beg pardon, I'm sure," said the visitor, "but is there a Mr. Robinson down here?"

The reply was so faint and smothered that she could not hear it. It was evident that the speaker, a modest man, was now speaking from beneath the bedclothes.

"Is Mr. Robinson here?" she repeated loudly.

"Never heard of him," said the smothered voice.

"It's my opinion," said the visitor, hotly, "that you're trying to deceive me. Have you got a match?"

The owner of the voice said that he had not, and with chilly propriety added that he wouldn't give it to her if he had. Whereupon the lady rose, and, fumbling on the little mantel-piece, found a box and struck one. There was a lamp nailed to the bulkhead over the mantel-piece, and calmly removing the chimney, she lit it.

A red, excited face, with the bedclothes fast about its neck, appeared in a small bunk and stared at her in speechless amaze. The visitor returned his gaze calmly, and then looked carefully round the cabin.

"Where does that lead to?" she asked, pointing to the door of the state-room.

The mate, remembering in time the mysterious behaviour of Flower, considered the situation. "That's the pantry," he said, untruthfully.

The visitor rose and tried the handle. The door was locked, and she looked doubtfully at the mate. "I suppose that's a leg of mutton I can hear asleep in there," she said, with acerbity.

"You can suppose what you like," said the mate, testily; "why don't you go away? I'm surprised at you."

"You'll be more surprised before I've done with you," said the lady, with emotion. "My Fred's in there, and you know it."

"Your Fred!" said Fraser, in great surprise.

"Mr. Robinson," said the visitor, correcting herself.

"I tell you there's nobody in there except the skipper," said the mate.

"You said it was the pantry just now," exclaimed the other, sharply.

"The skipper sleeps in the pantry so's he can keep his eye on the meat," explained Fraser.

The visitor looked at him angrily. "What sort of a man is he?" she enquired, suddenly.

"You'll soon know if he comes out," said the mate. "He's the worst-tempered man afloat, I should think. If he comes out and finds you here, I don't know what he'll do."

"I'm not afraid of him," said the other, with spirit. "What do you call him? Skipper?"

The mate nodded, and the visitor tapped loudly at the door. "Skipper!" she cried, "Skipper!"

No answer being vouchsafed, she repeated her cry in a voice louder than before.

"He's a heavy sleeper," said the perturbed Fraser; "better go away, there's a good girl."

The lady, scornfully ignoring him, rapped on the door and again called upon its occupant. Then, despite her assurance, she sprang back with a scream as a reply burst through the door with the suddenness and fury of a thunder-clap.

"Halloa!" it said.

"My goodness," said the visitor, aghast. "What a voice! What a terrible voice!"

She recovered herself and again approached the door.

"Is there a gentleman named Robinson in there?" she asked, timidly.

"Gentleman named who?" came the thunderclap again.

"Robinson," said the lady, faintly.

"No! No!" said the thunder-clap. Then—"Go away," it rumbled. "Go away."

The reverberation of that mighty voice rolled and shook through the cabin. It even affected the mate, for the visitor, glancing towards him, saw that he had nervously concealed himself beneath the bedclothes, and was shaking with fright.

"I daresay his bark is worse than his bite," said the visitor, trembling; "anyway, I'm going to stay here. I saw Mr. Robinson come here, and I believe he's got him in there. Killing him, perhaps. Oh! Oh!"

To the mate's consternation she began to laugh, and then changed to a piercing scream, and, unused to the sex as he was, he realised that this was the much-dreaded hysteria of which he had often heard, and he faced her with a face as pallid as her own.

"Chuck some water over yourself," he said, hastily, nodding at a jug which stood on the table. "I can't very well get up to do it myself."

The lady ignored this advice, and by dint of much strength of mind regained her self-control. She sat down on the locker again, and folding her arms showed clearly her intention to remain.

Half an hour passed; the visitor still sat grimly upright. Twice she sniffed slightly, and, with a delicate handkerchief, pushed up her veil and wiped away the faint beginnings of a tear.

"I suppose you think I'm acting strangely?" she said, catching the mate's eye after one of these episodes.

"Oh, don't mind me," said the mate, with studied politeness; "don't mind hurting my feelings or taking my character away."

"Pooh! you're a man," said the visitor, scornfully; "but character or no character, I'm going to see into that room before I go away, if I sit here for three weeks."

"How're you going to manage about eating and drinking all that time?" enquired Fraser.

"How are you?" said the visitor; "you can't get up while I'm here, you know."

"Well, we'll see," said the mate, vaguely.

"I'm sure I don't want to annoy anybody," said the visitor, softly, "but I've had a lot of trouble, young man, and what's worse, I've been made a fool of. This day three weeks ago I ought to have been married."

"I'm sure you ought," murmured the other.

The lady ignored the interruption.

"Travelling under Government on secret service, he said he was," she continued; "always away: here to-day, China to-morrow, and America the day after."

"Flying?" queried the interested mate.

"I daresay," snapped the visitor; "anything to tell me, I suppose. We were to be married by special license. I'd even got my trousseau ready."

"Got your what ready?" enquired the mate, to whom the word was new, leaning out of his bunk.

"Everything to wear," explained the visitor. "All my relations bought new clothes, too; leastways, those that could afford it did. He even went and helped me choose the cake."

"Well, is that wrong?" asked the puzzled mate.

"He didn't buy it, he only chose it," said the other, having recourse to her handkerchief again. "He went outside the shop to see whether there was one he would like better, and when I came out he had disappeared."

"He must have met with an accident," said the mate, politely.

"I saw him to-night," said the lady, tersely.

"Once or twice he had mentioned Wapping in conversation, and then seemed to check himself. That was my clue. I've been round this dismal heathenish place for a fortnight. To-night I saw him; he came on this wharf, and he has not gone off.... It's my belief he's in that room."

Before the mate could reply the hoarse voice of the watchman came down the company-way. "Ha' past eleven, sir; tide's just on the turn."

"Aye, aye," said the mate. He turned imploringly to the visitor.

"Would you do me the favour just to step on deck a minute?"

"What for?" enquired the visitor, shortly.

"Because I want to get up," said the mate.

"I sha'n't move," said the lady.

"But I've got to get up, I tell you," said the mate; "we're getting under way in ten minutes."

"And what might that be?" asked the lady.

"Why, we make a start. You'd better go ashore unless you want to be carried off."

"I sha'n't move," repeated the visitor.

"Well, I'm sorry to be rude," said the mate. "George."

"Sir," said the watchman from above.

"Bring down a couple o' men and take this lady ashore," said the mate sternly.

"I'll send a couple down, sir," said the watchman, and moved off to make a selection.

"I shall scream 'murder and thieves,'" said the lady, her eyes gleaming. "I'll bring the police up and cause a scandal. Then perhaps I shall see into that room."

In the face of determination like this the mate's courage gave way, and in a voice of much anxiety he called upon his captain for instruction.

"Cast off," bellowed the mighty voice. "If your sweetheart won't go ashore she must come, too. You must pay her passage."

"Well, of all the damned impudence," muttered the incensed mate. "Well, if you're bent on coming," he said, hotly, to the visitor, "just go on deck while I dress."

The lady hesitated a moment and then withdrew. On deck the men eyed her curiously, but made no attempt to interfere with her, and in a couple of minutes the mate came running up to take charge.

"Where are we going?" enquired the lady with a trace of anxiety in her voice.

"France," said Fraser, turning away.

The visitor looked nervously round. At the adjoining wharf a sailing barge was also getting under way, and a large steamer was slowly turning in the middle of the river. She took a pace or two towards the side.

"Cast off," said Fraser, impatiently, to the watchman.

"Wait a minute," said the visitor, hastily, "I want to think."

"Cast off," repeated the mate.

The watchman obeyed, and the schooner's side moved slowly from the wharf. At the sight the visitor's nerve forsook her, and with a frantic cry she ran to the side and, catching the watchman's outstretched hand, sprang ashore.

"Good-bye," sang out the mate; "sorry you wouldn't come to France with us. The lady was afraid of the foreigners, George. If it had been England she wouldn't have minded."

"Aye, aye," said the watchman, significantly, and, as the schooner showed her stern, turned to answer, with such lies as he thought the occasion demanded, the eager questions of his fair companion.

CHAPTER III

Captain Flower, learning through the medium of Tim that the coast was clear, came on deck at Limehouse, and took charge of his ship with a stateliness significant of an uneasy conscience. He noticed with growing indignation that the mate's attitude was rather that of an accomplice than a subordinate, and that the crew looked his way far oftener than was necessary or desirable.

"I told her we were going to France," said the mate, in an impressive whisper.

"Her?" said Flower, curtly. "Who?"

"The lady you didn't want to see," said Fraser, restlessly.

"You let your ideas run away with you, Jack," said Flower, yawning. "It wasn't likely I was going to turn out and dress to see any girl you liked to invite aboard."

"Or even to bawl at them through the speaking-trumpet," said Fraser, looking at him steadily.

"What sort o'looking girl was she?" enquired Flower, craning his neck to see what was in front of him.

"Looked like a girl who meant to find the man she wanted, if she spent ten years over it," said the mate grimly. "I'll bet you an even five shillings, cap'n, that she finds this Mr. Robinson before six weeks are out—whatever his other name is."

"Maybe," said Flower, carelessly.

"It's her first visit to the Foam, but not the last, you mark my words," said Fraser, solemnly. "If she wants this rascal Robinson——"

"What?" interrupted Flower, sharply.

"I say if she wants this rascal Robinson," repeated the mate, with relish, "she'll naturally come where she saw the last trace of him."

Captain Flower grunted.

"Women never think," continued Fraser, judicially, "or else she'd be glad to get rid of such a confounded scoundrel."

"What do you know about him?" demanded Flower.

"I know what she told me," said Fraser; "the idea of a man leaving a poor girl in a cake-shop and doing a bolt. He'll be punished for it, I know. He's a thoughtless, inconsiderate fellow, but one of the best-hearted chaps in the world, and I guess I'll do the best I can for him."

Flower grinned safely in the darkness. "And any little help I can give you, Jack, I'll give freely," he said, softly. "We'll talk it over at breakfast."

The mate took the hint, and, moving off, folded his arms on the taffrail, and, looking idly astern, fell into a reverie. Like the Pharisee, he felt thankful that he was not as other men, and dimly pitied the skipper and his prosaic entanglements, as he thought of Poppy. He looked behind at the dark and silent city, and felt a new affection for it, as he reflected that she was sleeping there.

The two men commenced their breakfast in silence, the skipper eating with a zest which caused the mate to allude impatiently to the last break-fasts of condemned men.

"Shut the skylight, Jack," said the skipper, at length, as he poured out his third cup of coffee.

Fraser complied, and resuming his seat gazed at him with almost indecent expectancy. The skipper dropped some sugar into his coffee, and stirring it in a meditative fashion, sighed gently.

"I've been making a fool of myself, Jack," he said, at length. "I was always one to be fond of a little bit of adventure, but this goes a little too far, even for me."

"But what did you get engaged to her for?" enquired Fraser.

Flower shook his head. "She fell violently in love with me," he said, mournfully. "She keeps the Blue Posts up at Chelsea. Her father left it to her. She manages her step-mother and her brother and everybody else. I was just a child in her hands. You know my easy-going nature."

"But you made love to her," expostulated the mate.

"In a way, I suppose I did," admitted the other. "I don't know now whether she could have me up for breach of promise, because when I asked her I did it this way. I said, 'Will you be Mrs. Robinson?' What do you think?"

"I should think it would make it harder for you," said Fraser. "But didn't you remember Miss Banks while all this was going on?"

"In a way," said Flower, "yes—in a way. But after a man's been engaged to a woman nine years, it's very easy to forget, and every year makes it easier. Besides, I was only a boy when I was engaged to her."

"Twenty-eight," said Fraser.

"Anyway, I wasn't old enough to know my own mind," said Flower, "and my uncle and old Mrs. Banks made it up between them. They arranged everything, and I can't afford to offend the old man.

If I married Miss Tipping—that's the Blue Posts girl—he'd leave his money away from me; and if I marry Elizabeth, Miss Tipping'll have me up for breach of promise—if she finds me."

"If you're not very careful," said Fraser, impressively, "you'll lose both of 'em."

The skipper leaned over the table, and glanced carefully round. "Just what I want to do," he said, in a low voice. "I'm engaged to another girl."

"What?" cried the mate, raising his voice. "Three?"

"Three," repeated the skipper. "Only three," he added, hastily, as he saw a question trembling on the other's lips.

"I'm ashamed of you," said the latter, severely; "you ought to know better."

"I don't want any of your preaching, Jack," said the skipper, briskly; "and, what's more, I won't have it. I deserve more pity than blame."

"You'll want all you can get," said Fraser, ominously. "And does the other girl know of any of the others?"

"Of either of the others—no," corrected Flower. "Of course, none of them know. You don't think I'm a fool, do you?"

"Who is number three?" enquired the mate suddenly.

"Poppy Tyrell," replied the other.

"Oh," said Fraser, trying to speak unconcernedly; "the girl who came here last evening."

Flower nodded. "She's the one I'm going to marry," he said, colouring. "I'd sooner marry her than command a liner. I'll marry her if I lose every penny I'm going to have, but I'm not going to lose the money if I can help it. I want both."

The mate baled out his cup with a spoon and put the contents into the saucer.

"I'm a sort of guardian to her," said Flower. "Her father, Captain Tyrell, died about a year ago, and I promised him I'd look after her and marry her. It's a sacred promise."

"Besides, you want to," said Fraser, by no means in the mood to allow his superior any credit in the matter, "else you wouldn't do it."

"You don't know me, Jack," said the skipper, more in sorrow than in anger.

"No, I didn't think you were quite so bad," said the mate, slowly. "Is—Miss Tyrell—fond of you?"

"Of course she is," said Flower, indignantly; "they all are, that's the worst of it. You were never much of a favourite with the sex, Jack, were you?"

Fraser shook his head, and, the saucer being full, spooned the contents slowly back into the cup again.

"Captain Tyrell leave any money?" he enquired.

"Other way about," replied Flower. "I lent him, altogether, close on a hundred pounds. He was a man of very good position, but he took to drink and lost his ship and his self-respect, and all he left behind was his debts and his daughter."

"Well, you're in a tight place," said Fraser, "and I don't see how you're going to get out of it. Miss Tipping's got a bit of a clue to you now, and if she once discovers you, you're done. Besides, suppose Miss Tyrell finds anything out?"

"It's all excitement," said Flower, cheerfully. "I've been in worse scrapes than this and always got out of 'em. I don't like a quiet life. I never worry about things, Jack, because I've noticed that the things people worry about never happen."

"Well, if I were you, then," said the other, emphasizing his point with the spoon, "I should just worry as much as I could about it. I'd get up worrying and I'd go to bed worrying. I'd worry about it in my sleep."

"I shall come out of it all right," said Flower. "I rather enjoy it. There's Gibson would marry Elizabeth like a shot if she'd have him; but, of course, she won't look at him while I'm above ground. I have thought of getting somebody to tell Elizabeth a lot of lies about me."

"Why, wouldn't the truth do?" enquired the mate, artlessly.

The skipper turned a deaf ear. "But she wouldn't believe a word against me," he said, with mournful pride, as he rose and went on deck. "She trusts me too much."

From his knitted brows, as he steered, it was evident, despite his confidence, that this amiable weakness on the part of Miss Banks was causing him some anxiety, a condition which was not lessened by the considerate behaviour of the mate, who, when any fresh complication suggested itself to him, dutifully submitted it to his commander.

"I shall be all right," said Flower, confidently, as they entered the river the following afternoon and sailed slowly along the narrow channel which wound its sluggish way through an expanse of mud-banks to Seabridge.

The mate, who was suffering from symptoms hitherto unknown to him, made no reply. His gaze wandered idly from the sloping uplands, stretching away into the dim country on the starboard side, to the little church-crowned town ahead, with its out-lying malt houses and neglected, grass-grown quay, A couple of moribund ship's boats lay rotting in the mud, and the skeleton of a fishing-boat completed the picture. For the first time perhaps in his life, the landscape struck him as dull and dreary.

Two men of soft and restful movements appeared on the quay as they approached, and with the slowness characteristic of the best work, helped to make them fast in front of the red-tiled barn which served as a warehouse. Then Captain Flower, after descending to the cabin to make the brief shore-going toilet necessary for Seabridge society, turned to give a last word to the mate.

"I'm not one to care much what's said about me, Jack," he began, by way of preface.

"That's a good job for you," said Fraser, slowly.

"Same time let the hands know I wish 'em to keep their mouths shut," pursued the skipper; "just tell them it was a girl that you knew, and I don't want it talked about for fear of getting you into trouble. Keep me out of it; that's all I ask."

"If cheek will pull you through," said Fraser, with a slight display of emotion, "you'll do. Perhaps I'd better say that Miss Tyrell came to see me, too. How would you like that?"

"Ah, it would be as well," said Flower, heartily. "I never thought of it."

He stepped ashore, and at an easy pace walked along the steep road which led to the houses above. The afternoon was merging into evening, and a pleasant stillness was in the air. Menfolk working in their cottage gardens saluted him as he passed, and the occasional whiteness of a face at the back of a window indicated an interest in his affairs on the part of the fairer citizens of Seabridge. At the gate of the first of an ancient row of cottages, conveniently situated within hail of The Grapes, The Thorn, and The Swan, he paused, and walking up the trim-kept garden path, knocked at the door.

It was opened by a stranger—a woman of early middle age, dressed in a style to which the inhabitants of the row had long been unaccustomed. The practised eye of the skipper at once classed her as "rather good-looking."

"Captain Barber's in the garden," she said, smiling. "He wasn't expecting you'd be up just yet."

The skipper followed her in silence, and, after shaking hands with the short, red-faced man with the grey beard and shaven lip, who sat with a paper on his knee, stood watching in blank astonishment as the stranger carefully filled the old man's pipe and gave him a light. Their eyes meeting, the uncle winked solemnly at the nephew.

"This is Mrs. Church," he said, slowly; "this is my nevy, Cap'n Fred Flower."

"I should have known him anywhere," declared Mrs. Church; "the likeness is wonderful."

Captain Barber chuckled—loudly enough for them to hear.

"Me and Mrs. Church have been watering the flowers," he said. "Give 'em a good watering, we have."

"I never really knew before what a lot there was in watering," admitted Mrs. Church.

"There's a right way and a wrong in doing everything," said Captain Barber, severely; "most people chooses the wrong. If it wasn't so, those of us who have got on, wouldn't have got on."

"That's very true," said Mrs. Church, shaking her head.

"And them as haven't got on would have got on," said the philosopher, following up his train of thought. "If you would just go out and get them things I spoke to you about, Mrs. Church, we shall be all right."

"Who is it?" enquired the nephew, as soon as she had gone.

Captain Barber looked stealthily round, and, for the second time that evening, winked at his nephew.

"A visitor?" said Flower.

Captain Barber winked again, and then laughed into his pipe until it gurgled.

"It's a little plan o' mine." he said, when he had become a little more composed. "She's my housekeeper."

"Housekeeper?" repeated the astonished Flower.

"Bein' all alone here," said Uncle Barber, "I think a lot. I sit an' think until I get an idea. It comes quite sudden like, and I wonder I never thought of it before."

"But what did you want a housekeeper for?" enquired his nephew. "Where's Lizzie?"

"I got rid of her," said Captain Barber. "I got a housekeeper because I thought it was time you got married. Now do you see?"

"No," said Flower, shortly.

Captain Barber laughed softly and, relighting his pipe which had gone out, leaned back in his chair and again winked at his indignant nephew.

"Mrs. Banks," he said, suggestively.

His nephew gazed at him blankly.

Captain Barber, sighing good-naturedly at his dulness, turned his chair a bit and explained the situation.

"Mrs. Banks won't let you and Elizabeth marry till she's gone," said he.

His nephew nodded.

"I've been at her ever so long," said the other, "but she's firm. Now I'm trying artfulness. I've got a good-looking housekeeper—she's the pick o' seventeen what all come here Wednesday morning—and I'm making love to her."

"Making love to her," shouted his nephew, gazing wildly at the venerable bald head with the smoking-cap resting on one huge ear.

"Making love to her," repeated Captain Barber, with a satisfied air. "What'll happen? Mrs. Banks, to prevent me getting married, as she thinks, will give her consent to you an' Elizabeth getting tied up."

"Haven't you ever heard of breach of promise cases?" asked his nephew, aghast.

"There's no fear o' that," said Captain Barber, confidently. "It's all right with Mrs. Church she's a widder. A widder ain't like a young girl she knows you don't mean anything."

It was useless to argue with such stupendous folly; Captain Flower tried another tack.

"And suppose Mrs. Church gets fond of you," he said, gravely. "It doesn't seem right to trifle with a woman's affections like that."

"I won't go too far," said the lady-killer in the smoking-cap, reassuringly.

"Elizabeth and her mother are still away, I suppose?" said Flower, after a pause.

His uncle nodded.

"So, of course, you needn't do much love-making till they come back," said his nephew; "it's waste of time, isn't it?"

"I'll just keep my hand in," said Captain Barber, thoughtfully. "I can't say as I find it disagreeable. I was always one to take a little notice of the sects."

He got up to go indoors. "Never mind about them," he said, as his nephew was about to follow with the chair and his tobacco-jar; "Mrs. Church likes to do that herself, and she'd be disappointed if anybody else did it."

His nephew followed him to the house in silence, listening later on with a gloomy feeling of alarm to the conversation at the supper-table. The rôle of gooseberry was new to him, and when Mrs. Church got up from the table for the sole purpose of proving her contention that Captain Barber looked better in his black velvet smoking-cap than the one he was wearing he was almost on the point of exceeding his duties.

He took the mate into his confidence the next day, and asked him what he thought of it. Fraser said that it was evidently in the blood, and, being pressed with some heat for an explanation, said that he meant Captain Barber's blood.

"It's bad, any way I look at it," said Flower; "it may bring matters between me and Elizabeth to a head, or it may end in my uncle marrying the woman."

"Very likely both," said Fraser, cheerfully. "Is this Mrs. Church good-looking?"

"I can hardly say," said Flower, pondering.

"Well, good-looking enough for you to feel inclined to take any notice of her?" asked the mate.

"When you can talk seriously," said the skipper, in great wrath, "I'll be pleased to answer you. Just at present I don't feel in the sort of temper to be made fun of."

He walked off in dudgeon, and, until they were on their way to London again, treated the mate with marked coldness. Then the necessity of talking to somebody about his own troubles and his uncle's idiocy put the two men on their old footing. In the quietness of the cabin, over a satisfying pipe, he planned out in a kindly and generous spirit careers for both the ladies he was not going to marry. The only thing that was wanted to complete their happiness, and his, was that they should fall in with the measures proposed.

CHAPTER IV

At No. 5 Liston Street, Poppy Tyrell sat at the open window of her room reading The outside air was pleasant, despite the fact that Poplar is a somewhat crowded neighbourhood, and it was rendered more pleasant by comparison with the atmosphere inside, which, from a warm, soft smell not to be described by comparison, suggested washing. In the stone-paved yard beneath the window, a small daughter of the house hung out garments of various hues and shapes, while inside, in the scullery, the master of the house was doing the family washing with all the secrecy and trepidation of one engaged in an unlawful task. The Wheeler family was a large one, and the wash heavy, and besides misadventures to one or two garments, sorted out for further consideration, the small girl was severely critical about the colour, averring sharply that she was almost ashamed to put them on the line.

"They'll dry clean," said her father, wiping his brow with the upper part of his arm, the only part which was dry; "and if they don't we must tell your mother that the line came down. I'll show these to her now."

He took up the wet clothes and, cautiously leaving the scullery, crossed the passage to the parlour, where Mrs. Wheeler, a confirmed invalid, was lying on a ramshackle sofa, darning socks. Mr. Wheeler coughed to attract her attention, and with an apologetic expression of visage held up a small, pink garment of the knickerbocker species, and prepared for the worst.

"They've never shrunk like that?" said Mrs. Wheeler, starting up.

"They have," said her husband, "all by itself," he added, in hasty self-defence.

"You've had it in the soda," said Mrs. Wheeler, disregarding.

"I've not," said Mr. Wheeler, vehemently. "I've got the two tubs there, flannels in one without soda, the other things in the other with soda. It's bad stuff, that's what it is. I thought I'd show you."

"It's management they want," said Mrs. Wheeler, wearily; "it's the touch you have to give 'em. I can't explain, but I know they wouldn't have gone like that if I'd done 'em. What's that you're hiding behind you?"

Thus attacked, Mr. Wheeler produced his other hand, and shaking out a blue and white shirt, showed how the blue had been wandering over the white territory, and how the white had apparently accepted a permanent occupation.

"What do you say to that?" he enquired, desperately.

"You'd better ask Bob what he says," said his wife, aghast; "you know how pertickler he is, too. I told you as plain as a woman could speak, not to boil that shirt."

"Well, it can't be helped," said Mr. Wheeler, with a philosophy he hoped his son would imitate. "I wasn't brought up to the washing, Polly."

"It's a sin to spoil good things like that," said Mrs. Wheeler, fretfully. "Bob's quite the gentleman—he will buy such expensive shirts. Take it away, I can't bear to look at it."

Mr. Wheeler, considerably crestfallen, was about to obey, when he was startled by a knock at the door.

"That's Captain Flower, I expect," said his wife, hastily; "he's going to take Poppy and Emma to a theatre to-night. Don't let him see you in that state, Peter."

But Mr. Wheeler was already fumbling at the strings of his apron, and, despairing of undoing it, broke the string, and pitched it with the other clothes under the sofa and hastily donned his coat.

"Good-evening," said Flower, as Mr. Wheeler opened the door; "this is my mate."

"Glad to see you, sir," said Mr. Wheeler.

The mate made his acknowledgments, and having shaken hands, carefully wiped his down the leg of his trousers.

"Moist hand you've got, Wheeler," said Flower, who had been doing the same thing.

"Got some dye on 'em at the docks," said Wheeler, glibly. "I've 'ad 'em in soak."

Flower nodded, and after a brief exchange of courtesies with Mrs. Wheeler as he passed the door, led the way up the narrow staircase to Miss Tyrell's room.

"I've brought him with me, so that he'll be company for Emma Wheeler," said the skipper, as Fraser shook hands with her, "and you must look sharp if you want to get good seats."

"I'm ready all but my hat and jacket," said Poppy, "and Emma's in her room getting ready, too. All the children are up there helping her."

Fraser opened his eyes at such a toilet, and began secretly to wish that he had paid more attention to his own.

"I hope you're not shy?" said Miss Tyrell, who found his steadfast gaze somewhat embarrassing.

Fraser shook his head. "No, I'm not shy," he said, quietly.

"Because Emma didn't know you were coming," continued Miss Tyrell, "and she's always shy. So you must be bold, you know."

The mate nodded as confidently as he could. "Shyness has never been one of my failings," he said, nervously.

Further conversation was rendered difficult, if not impossible, by one which now took place outside. It was conducted between a small Wheeler on the top of the stairs and Mrs. Wheeler in the parlour below. The subject was hairpins, an article in which it appeared Miss Wheeler was lamentably deficient, owing, it was suggested, to a weakness of Mrs. Wheeler's for picking up stray ones and putting them in her hair. The conversation ended in Mrs. Wheeler, whose thin voice was heard hotly combating these charges, parting with six, without prejudice; and a few minutes later Miss Wheeler, somewhat flushed, entered the room and was introduced to the mate.

"All ready?" enquired Flower, as Miss Tyrell drew on her gloves.

They went downstairs in single file, the builder of the house having left no option in the matter, while the small Wheelers, breathing hard with excitement, watched them over the balusters. Outside the house the two ladies paired off, leaving the two men to follow behind.

The mate noticed, with a strong sense of his own unworthiness, that the two ladies seemed thoroughly engrossed in each other's company, and oblivious to all else. A suggestion from Flower that he should close up and take off Miss Wheeler, seemed to him to border upon audacity, but he meekly followed Flower as that bold mariner ranged himself alongside the girls, and taking two steps on the curb and three in the gutter, walked along for some time trying to think of something to say.

"There ain't room for four abreast," said Flower, who had been scraping against the wall. "We'd better split up into twos."

At the suggestion the ladies drifted apart, and Flower, taking Miss Tyrell's arm, left the mate behind with Miss Wheeler, nervously wondering whether he ought to do the same.

"I hope it won't rain," he said, at last.

"I hope not," said Miss Wheeler, glancing up at a sky which was absolutely cloudless.

"So bad for ladies' dresses," continued the mate.

"What is?" enquired Miss Wheeler, who had covered some distance since the last remark.

"Rain," said the mate, quite freshly. "I don't think we shall have any, though."

Miss Wheeler whose life had been passed in a neighbourhood in which there was only one explanation for such conduct, concluded that he had been drinking, and, closing her lips tightly, said no more until they reached the theatre.

"Oh, they're going in," she said, quickly; "we shall get a bad seat."

"Hurry up," cried Flower, beckoning.

"I'll pay," whispered the mate.

"No, I will," said Flower. "Well, you pay for one and I'll pay for one, then."

He pushed his way to the window and bought a couple of pit-stalls; the mate, who had not consulted him, bought upper-circles, and, with a glance at the ladies, pushed open the swing-doors.

"Come on," he said, excitedly; and seeing several people racing up the broad stone stairs, he and Miss Tyrell raced with them.

"Round this side," he cried, hastily, as he gave up the tickets, and, followed by Miss Tyrell, quickly secured a couple of seats at the end of the front row.

"Best seats in the house almost," said Poppy, cheerfully.

"Where are the others?" said Fraser, looking round.

"Coming on behind, I suppose," said Poppy glancing over her shoulder.

"I'll change places when they arrive," said the other, apologetically; "something's detained them, I should think. I hope they're not waiting for us."

He stood looking about him uneasily as the seats behind rapidly filled, and closely scanned their occupants, and then, leaving his hat on the seat, walked back in perplexity to the door.

"Never mind," said Miss Tyrell, quietly, as he came back. "I daresay they'll find us."

Fraser bought a programme and sat down, the brim of Miss Tyrell's hat touching his face as she bent to peruse it. With her small gloved finger she pointed out the leading characters, and taking no notice of his restlessness, began to chat gaily about the plays she had seen, until a tuning of violins from the orchestra caused her to lean forward, her lips parted and her eyes beaming with anticipation.

"I do hope the others have got good seats," she said, softly, as the overture finished; "that's everything, isn't it?"

"I hope so," said Fraser.

He leaned forward, excitedly. Not because the curtain was rising, but because he had just caught sight of a figure standing up in the centre of the pit-stalls. He had just time to call his companion's attention to it when the figure, in deference to the threats and entreaties of the people behind, sat down and was lost in the crowd.

"They have got good seats," said Miss Tyrell. "I'm so glad. What a beautiful scene."

The mate, stifling his misgivings, gave himself up to the enjoyment of the situation, which in-eluded answering the breathless whispers of his neighbour when she missed a sentence, and helping her to discover the identity of the characters from the programme as they appeared.

"I should like it all over again," said Miss Tyrell, sitting back in her seat, as the curtain fell on the first act.

Fraser agreed with her. He was closely watching the pit-stalls. In the general movement on the part of the audience which followed the lowering of the curtain, the master of the Foam was the first on his feet.

"I'll go down and send him up," said Fraser, rising.

Miss Tyrell demurred, and revealed an unsuspected timidity of character. "I don't like being left here all alone," she remarked. "Wait till they see us."

She spoke in the plural, for Miss Wheeler, who found the skipper exceedingly bad company, had also risen, and was scrutinising the house with a gaze hardly less eager than his own. A suggestion of the mate that he should wave his handkerchief was promptly negatived by Miss Tyrell, on the ground that it would not be the correct thing to do in the upper-circle, and they were still undiscovered when the curtain went up for the second act, and strong and willing hands from behind thrust the skipper back into his seat.

"I expect you'll catch it," said Miss Tyrell, softly, as the performance came to an end; "we'd better go down and wait for them outside. I never enjoyed a piece so much."

The mate rose and mingled with the crowd, conscious of a little occasional clutch at his sleeve whenever other people threatened to come between them. Outside the crowd dispersed slowly, and it was some minutes before they discovered a small but compact knot of two waiting for them.

"Where the—" began Flower.

"I hope you enjoyed the performance, Captain Flower," said Miss Tyrell, drawing herself up with some dignity. "I didn't know that I was supposed to look out for myself all the evening. If it hadn't been for Mr. Fraser I should have been all alone."

She looked hard at Miss Wheeler as she spoke, and the couple from the pit-stalls reddened with indignation at being so misunderstood.

"I'm sure I didn't want him," said Miss Wheeler, hastily. "Two or three times I thought there would have been a fight with the people behind."

"Oh, it doesn't matter," said Miss Tyrell, composedly. "Well, it's no good standing here. We'd better get home."

She walked off with the mate, leaving the couple behind, who realised that appearances were against them, to follow at their leisure. Conversation was mostly on her side, the mate being too much occupied with his defence to make any very long or very coherent replies.

They reached Liston Street at last, and separated at the door, Miss Tyrell shaking hands with the skipper in a way which conveyed in the fullest possible manner her opinion of his behaviour that evening. A bright smile and a genial hand-shake were reserved for the mate.

"And now," said the incensed skipper, breathing deeply as the door closed and they walked up Liston Street, "what the deuce do you mean by it?"

"Mean by what?" demanded the mate, who, after much thought, had decided to take a leaf out of Miss Tyrell's book.

"Mean by leaving me in another part of the house with that Wheeler girl while you and my intended went off together?" growled Flower ferociously.

"Well, I could only think you wanted it," said Fraser, in a firm voice.

"What?" demanded the other, hardly able to believe his ears

"I thought you wanted Miss Wheeler for number four," said the mate, calmly. "You know what a chap you are, cap'n."

His companion stopped and regarded him in speechless amaze, then realising a vocabulary to which Miss Wheeler had acted as a safety-valve all the evening, he turned up a side street and stamped his way back to the Foam alone.

CHAPTER V

The same day that Flower and his friends visited the theatre, Captain Barber gave a small and select tea-party. The astonished Mrs. Banks had returned home with her daughter the day before to find the air full of rumours about Captain Barber and his new housekeeper. They had been watched for hours at a time from upper back windows of houses in the same row, and the professional opinion of the entire female element was that Mrs. Church could land her fish at any time she thought fit.

"Old fools are the worst of fools," said Mrs. Banks, tersely, as she tied her bonnet strings; "the idea of Captain Barber thinking of marrying at his time of life."

"Why shouldn't he?" enquired her daughter.

"Why because he's promised to leave his property to Fred and you, of course," snapped the old lady; "if he marries that hussy it's precious little you and Fred will get."

"I expect it's mostly talk," said her daughter calmly, as she closed the street door behind her indignant parent. "People used to talk about you and old Mr. Wilders, and there was nothing in it. He only used to come for a glass of your ale."

This reference to an admirer who had consumed several barrels of the liquor in question without losing his head, put the finishing touch to the elder lady's wrath, and she walked the rest of the way in ominous silence.

Captain Barber received them in the elaborate velvet smoking-cap with the gold tassel which had evoked such strong encomiums from Mrs. Church, and in a few well-chosen words—carefully rehearsed that afternoon—presented his housekeeper.

"Will you come up to my room and take your things off?" enquired Mrs. Church, returning the old lady's hostile stare with interest.

"I'll take mine off down here, if Captain Barber doesn't mind," said the latter, subsiding into a chair with a gasp. "Him and me's very old friends."

She unfastened the strings of her bonnet, and, taking off that article of attire, placed it in her lap while she unfastened her shawl. She then held both out to Mrs. Church, briefly exhorting her to be careful.

"Oh, what a lovely bonnet," said that lady, in false ecstasy. "What a perfect beauty! I've never seen anything like it before. Never!"

Captain Barber, smiling at the politeness of his housekeeper, was alarmed and perplexed at the generous colour which suddenly filled the old lady's cheeks.

"Mrs. Banks made it herself," he said, "she's very clever at that sort of thing."

"There, do you know I guessed as much," said Mrs. Church, beaming; "directly I saw it, I said to myself: 'That was never made by a milliner. There's too much taste in the way the flowers are arranged.'"

Mrs. Banks looked at her daughter, in a mute appeal for help.

"I'll take yours up, too, shall I?" said the amiable housekeeper, as Mrs. Banks, with an air of defying criticism, drew a cap from a paper-bag and put it on.

"I'll take mine myself, please," said Miss Banks, with coldness.

"Oh, well, you may as well take them all then," said Mrs. Church, putting the mother's bonnet and shawl in her arms. "I'll go and see that the kettle boils," she said, briskly.

She returned a minute or two later with the teapot, and setting chairs, took the head of the table.

"And how's the leg?" enquired Captain Barber, misinterpreting Mrs. Banks' screwed-up face.

"Which one?" asked Mrs. Banks, shortly.

"The bad 'un," said the captain.

"They're both bad," said Mrs. Banks more shortly than before, as she noticed that Mrs. Church had got real lace in her cuffs and was pouring out the tea in full consciousness of the fact.

"Dear, dear," said the Captain sympathetically.

"Swollen?" enquired Mrs. Church, anxiously.

"Swelled right out of shape," exclaimed Captain Barber, impressively; "like pillars almost they are."

"Poor thing," said Mrs. Church, in a voice which made Mrs. Banks itch to slap her. "I knew a lady once just the same, but she was a drinking woman."

Again Mrs. Banks at a loss for words, looked at her daughter for assistance.

"Dear me, how dreadful it must be to know such people," said Mrs. Banks, shivering.

"Yes," sighed the other. "It used to make me feel sorry for her—they were utterly shapeless, you know. Horrid!"

"That's how Mrs. Banks' are," said the Captain, nodding sagely. "You look 'ot, Mrs. Banks. Shall I open the winder a bit?"

"I'll thank you not to talk about me like that, Captain Barber," said Mrs. Banks, the flowers on her hat trembling.

"As you please, ma'am," said Captain Barber, with a stateliness which deserved a better subject. "I was only repeating what Dr. Hodder told me in your presence."

Mrs. Banks made no reply, but created a diversion by passing her cup up for more tea; her feelings, when Mrs. Church took off the lid of the teapot and poured in about a pint of water before helping her, belonging to that kind known as in-describable.

"Water bewitched, and tea begrudged," she said, trying to speak jocularly.

"Well, the fourth cup never is very good, is it," said Mrs. Church, apologetically. "I'll put some more tea in, so that your next cup'll be better."

As a matter of fact it was Mrs. Banks' third cup, and she said so, Mrs. Church receiving the correction with a polite smile, more than tinged with incredulity.

"It's wonderful what a lot of tea is drunk," said Captain Barber, impressively, looking round the table.

"I've heard say it's like spirit drinking," said Mrs. Church; "they say it gets such a hold of people that they can't give it up. They're just slaves to it, and they like it brown and strong like brandy."

Mrs. Banks, who had been making noble efforts, could contain herself no longer. She put down the harmless beverage which had just been handed to her, and pushed her chair back from the table.

"Are you speaking of me, young woman?" she asked, tremulous with indignation.

"Oh, no, certainly not," said Mrs. Church, in great distress. "I never thought of such a thing. I was alluding to the people Captain Barber was talking of—regular tea-drinkers, you know."

"I know what you mean, ma'am," said Mrs. Banks fiercely.

"There, there," said Captain Barber, ill-advisedly.

"Don't you say 'there, there,' to me, Captain Barber, because I won't have it," said the old lady, speaking with great rapidity; "if you think that I'm going to sit here and be insulted by—by that woman, you're mistaken."

"You're quite mistook, Mrs. Banks," said the Captain, slowly. "I've heard everything she said, and, where the insult comes in, I'm sure I don't know. I don't think I'm wanting in common sense, ma'am."

He patted the housekeeper's hand kindly, and, in full view of the indignant Mrs. Banks, she squeezed his in return and gazed at him affectionately. There is nothing humourous to the ordinary person in a teacup, but Mrs. Banks, looking straight into hers, broke into a short, derisive laugh.

"Anything the matter, ma'am?" enquired Cap-tain Barber, regarding her somewhat severely.

Mrs. Banks shook her head. "Only thoughts," she said, mysteriously.

It is difficult for a man to object to his visitors finding amusement in their thoughts, or even to enquire too closely into the nature of them. Mrs. Banks, apparently realising this, laughed again with increased acridity, and finally became so very amused that she shook in her chair.

"I'm glad you're enjoying yourself, ma'am," said Captain Barber, loftily.

With a view, perhaps, of giving his guest further amusement he patted the housekeeper's hand again, whereupon Mrs. Banks' laughter ceased, and she sat regarding Mrs. Church with a petrified stare, met by that lady with a glance of haughty disdain.

"S'pose we go into the garden a bit?" suggested Barber, uneasily. The two ladies had eyed each other for three minutes without blinking, and his own eyes were watering in sympathy.

Mrs. Banks, secretly glad of the interruption, made one or two vague remarks about going home, but after much persuasion, allowed him to lead her into the garden, the solemn Elizabeth bringing up in the rear with a hassock and a couple of cushions.

"It's a new thing for you having a housekeeper," observed Mrs. Banks, after her daughter had returned to the house to assist in washing up.

"Yes, I wonder I never thought of it before," said the artful Barber; "you wouldn't believe how comfortable it is."

"I daresay," said Mrs. Banks, grimly.

"It's nice to have a woman about the house," continued Captain Barber, slowly, "it makes it more homelike. A slip of a servant-gal ain't no good at all."

"How does Fred like it?" enquired Mrs. Banks.

"My ideas are Fred's ideas," said Uncle Barber, somewhat sharply. "What I like he has to like, naturally."

"I was thinking of my darter," said Mrs. Banks, smoothing down her apron majestically. "The arrangement was, I think, that when they were, married they was to live with you?"

Captain Barber nodded acquiescence.

"Elizabeth would never live in a house with that woman, or any other woman, as housekeeper in it," said the mother.

"Well, she won't have to," said the old man; "when they marry and Elizabeth comes here, I sha'n't want a housekeeper—I shall get rid of her."

Mrs. Banks shifted in her chair, and gazed thoughtfully down the garden. "Of course my idea was for them to wait till I was gone," she said at length.

"Just so," replied the other, "and more's the pity."

"But Elizabeth's getting on and I don't seem to go," continued the old lady, as though mildly surprised at Providence for its unaccountable delay; "and there's Fred, he ain't getting younger."

Captain Barber puffed at his pipe. "None of us are," he said profoundly.

"And Fred might get tired of waiting," said Mrs. Banks, ruminating.

"He'd better let me hear him," said the uncle, fiercely; "leastways, o' course, he's tired o' waiting in a sense. He'd like to be married."

"There's young Gibson," said Mrs. Banks in a thrilling whisper.

"What about him?" enquired Barber, surprised at her manner.

"Comes round after Elizabeth," said Mrs. Banks.

"No!" said Captain Barber, blankly.

Mrs. Banks pursed up her lips and nodded darkly.

"Pretends to come and see me," said Mrs. Banks; "always coming in bringing something new for my legs. The worst of it is he ain't always careful what he brings. He brought some new-fangled stuff in a bottle last week, and the agonies I suffered after rubbing it in wouldn't be believed."

"It's like his impudence," said the Captain.

"I've been thinking," said Mrs. Banks, nodding her head with some animation, "of giving Fred a little surprise. What do you think he'd do if I said they might marry this autumn?"

"Jump out of his skin with joy," said Captain Barber, with conviction. "Mrs. Banks, the pleasure you've given me this day is more than I can say."

"And they'll live with you just the same?" said Mrs. Banks.

"Certainly," said the Captain.

"They'll only be a few doors off then," said Mrs. Banks, "and it'll be nice for you to have a woman in the house to look after you."

Captain. Barber nodded softly. "It's what I've been wanting for years," he said, heartily.

"And that huss—husskeeper," said Mrs. Banks, correcting herself—"will go?"

"O' course," said Captain Barber. "I sha'n't want no housekeeper with my nevy's wife in the house. You've told Elizabeth, I s'pose?"

"Not yet," said Mrs. Banks, who as a matter of fact had been influenced by the proceedings of that afternoon to bring to a head a step she had hitherto only vaguely contemplated.

Elizabeth, who came down the garden again, a little later, accompanied by Mrs. Church, received the news stolidly. A feeling of regret, that the attention of the devoted Gibson must now cease, certainly occurred to her, but she never thought of contesting the arrangements made for her, and accepted the situation with a placidity which the more ardent Barber was utterly unable to understand.

"Fred'll stand on his.'ed with joy," the unsophisticated mariner declared, with enthusiasm.

"He'll go singing about the house," declared Mrs. Church.

Mrs. Banks regarded her unfavourably.

"He's never said much," continued Uncle Barber, in an exalted strain; "that ain't Fred's way. He takes arter me; he's one o' the quiet ones, one o' the still deep waters what always feels the most. When I tell 'im his face'll just light up with joy."

"It'll be nice for you, too," said Mrs. Banks, with a side glance at the housekeeper; "you'll have somebody to look after you and take an interest in you, and strangers can't be expected to do that even if they're nice."

"We shall have him standing on his head, too," said Mrs. Church, with a bright smile; "you're turning everything upside down, Mrs. Banks."

"There's things as wants altering," said the old lady, with emphasis. "There's few things as I don't see, ma'am."

"I hope you'll live to see a lot more," said Mrs. Church, piously.

"She'll live to be ninety," said Captain Barber, heartily.

"Oh, easily," said Mrs. Church.

Captain Barber regarding his old friend saw her face suffused with a wrath for which he was utterly unable to account. With a hazy idea that something had passed which he had not heard, he caused a diversion by sending Mrs. Church indoors for a pack of cards, and solemnly celebrated the occasion with a game of whist, at which Mrs. Church, in partnership with Mrs. Banks, either through sheer wilfulness or absence of mind, contrived to lose every game.

CHAPTER VI

As a result of the mate's ill-behaviour at the theatre, Captain Fred Flower treated him with an air of chilly disdain, ignoring, as far as circumstances would permit, the fact that such a person existed. So far as the social side went the mate made no demur, but it was a different matter when the skipper acted as though he were not present at the breakfast table, and being chary of interfering with the other's self-imposed vow of silence, he rescued a couple of rashers from his plate and put them on his own. Also, in order to put matters on a more equal footing, he drank three cups of coffee in rapid succession, leaving the skipper to his own reflections and an empty coffee-pot. In this sociable fashion they got through most of the day, the skipper refraining from speech until late in the afternoon, when, both being at work in the hold, the mate let a heavy case fall on his foot.

"I thought you'd get it," he said, calmly, as Flower paused to take breath; "it wasn't my fault."

"Whose was it, then?" roared Flower, who had got his boot off and was trying various tender experiments with his toe to see whether it was broken or not.

"If you hadn't been holding your head in the air and pretending that I wasn't here, it wouldn't have happened," said Fraser, with some heat.

The skipper turned his back on him, and meeting a look of enquiring solicitude from Joe, applied to him for advice.

"What had I better do with it?" he asked.

"Well, if it was my toe, sir," said Joe regarding it respectfully, "I should stick it in a basin o' boiling water and keep it there as long as I could bear it."

"You're a fool," said the skipper, briefly. "What do you think of it, Ben? I don't think it's broken."

The old seaman scratched his head. "Well, if it belonged to me," he said, slowly, "there's some ointment down the fo'c's'le which the cook 'ad for sore eyes. I should just put some o' that on. It looks good stuff."

The skipper, summarising the chief points in Ben's character, which, owing principally to the poverty of the English language, bore a remarkable likeness to Joe's and the mate's, took his sock and boot in his hand, and gaining the deck limped painfully to the cabin.

The foot was so painful after tea that he could hardly bear his slipper on, and he went ashore in his working clothes to the chemist's, preparatory to fitting himself out for Liston Street. The chemist, leaning over the counter, was inclined to take a serious view of it, and shaking his head with much solemnity, prepared a bottle of medicine, a bottle of lotion and a box of ointment.

"Let me see it again as soon as you've finished the medicine," he said, as he handed the articles over the counter.

Flower promised, and hobbling towards the door turned into the street. Then the amiable air which he had worn in the shop gave way to one of unseemly hauteur as he saw Fraser hurrying towards him.

"Look out," cried the latter, warningly.

The skipper favoured him with a baleful stare.

"All right," said the mate, angrily, "go your own way, then. Don't come to me when you get into trouble, that's all."

Flower passed on his way in silence. Then a thought struck him and he stopped suddenly.

"You wish to speak to me?" he asked, stiffly.

"No, I'm damned if I do," said the mate, sticking his hands into his pockets.

"If you wish to speak to me," said the other, trying in vain to conceal a trace of anxiety in his voice, "it's my duty to listen. What were you going to say just now?"

The mate eyed him wrathfully, but as the pathetic figure with its wounded toe and cargo of remedies stood there waiting for him to speak, he suddenly softened.

"Don't go back, old man," he said, kindly, "she's aboard."

Eighteen pennyworth of mixture, to be taken thrice daily from tablespoons, spilled over the curb, and the skipper, thrusting the other packets mechanically into his pockets, disappeared hurriedly around the corner.

"It's no use finding fault with me," said Fraser, quickly, as he stepped along beside him, "so don't try it. They came down into the cabin before I knew they were aboard, even."

"They?" repeated the distressed Flower. "Who's they?"

"The young woman that came before and a stout woman with a little dark moustache and earrings. They're going to wait until you come back to ask you a few questions about Mr. Robinson. They've been asking me a few. I've locked the door of your state-room and here's the key."

Flower pocketed it and, after a little deliberation thanked him.

"I did the best I could for you," said the other, with a touch of severity. "If I'd treated you as some men would have done, I should have just let you walk straight into the trap."

Flower gave an apologetic cough. "I've had a lot of worry lately, Jack," he said, humbly; "come in and have something. Perhaps it will clear my head a bit."

"I told 'em you wouldn't be back till twelve at least," said the mate, as Flower rapidly diagnosed his complaint and ordered whisky, "perhaps not then, and that when you did turn up you'd sure to be the worse for liquor. The old lady said she'd wait all night for the pleasure of seeing your bonny face, and as for you being drunk, she said she don't suppose there's a woman in London that has had more experience with drunken men than she has."

"Let this be a warning to you, Jack," said the skipper, solemnly, as he drained his glass and put it thoughtfully on the counter.

"Don't you trouble about me," said Fraser; "you've got all you can do to look after yourself. I've come out to look for a policeman; at least, that's what I told them."

"All the police in the world couldn't do me any good," sighed Flower. "Poppy's got tickets for a concert to-night, and I was going with her. I can't go like this."

"Well, what are you going to do?" enquired the other.

Flower shook his head and pondered. "You go back and get rid of them the best way you can," he said, at length, "but whatever you do, don't have a scene. I'll stay here till you come and tell me the coast is clear."

"And suppose it don't clear?" said Fraser.

"Then I'll pick you up at Greenwich in the morning," said Flower.

"And suppose they're still aboard?" said Fraser.

"I won't suppose any such thing," said the other, hotly; "if you can't get rid of two women between now and three in the morning, you're not much of a mate. If they catch me I'm ruined, and you'll be responsible for it."

The mate, staring at him blankly, opened his mouth to reply, but being utterly unable to think of anything adequate to the occasion, took up his glass instead, and, drinking off the contents, turned to the door. He stood for a moment at the threshold gazing at Flower as though he had just discovered points about him which had hitherto escaped his notice, and then made his way back to the wharf.

"They're still down below, sir," said Joe, softly, as he stepped aboard, "and making as free and as comfortable as though they're going to stay a month."

Fraser shrugged his shoulders and went below. The appearance of the ladies amply confirmed Joe's remark.

"Never can find one when you want him, can you?" said the elder lady, in playful allusion to the police.

"Well, I altered my mind," said Fraser, amiably, "I don't like treating ladies roughly, but if the cap'n comes on board and finds you here it'll be bad for me, that's all."

"What time do you expect him?" enquired Miss Tipping.

"Not before we sail at three in the morning." said the mate, glibly; "perhaps not then. I often have to take the ship out without him. He's been away six weeks at a stretch before now."

"Well, we'll stay here till he does come," said the elder lady. "I'll have his cabin, and my step-daughter'll have to put up with your bed."

"If you're not gone by the time we start, I shall have to have you put off," said Fraser.

"Those of us who live longest'll see the most," said Mrs. Tipping, calmly.

An hour or two passed, the mate sitting smoking with a philosophy which he hoped the waiting mariner at the "Admiral Cochrane" would be able to imitate. He lit the lamp at last, and going on deck, ordered the cook to prepare supper.

Mother and daughter, with feelings of gratitude, against which they fought strongly, noticed that the table was laid for three, and a little later, in a somewhat awkward fashion, they all sat down to the meal together.

"Very good beef," said Mrs. Tipping, politely.

"Very nice," said her daughter, who was ex-changing glances with the mate. "I suppose you're very comfortable here, Mr. Fraser?"

The mate sighed. "It's all right when the old man's away," he said, deceitfully. "He's got a dreadful temper."

"I hope you didn't get into trouble through my coming aboard the other night," said Miss Tipping, softly.

"Don't say anything about it," replied the mate, eyeing her admiringly. "I'd do more than that for you, if I could."

Miss Tipping, catching her mother's eye, bestowed upon her a glance of complacent triumph.

"You don't mind us coming down here, do you?" she said, languishingly.

"I wish you'd live here," said the unscrupulous Fraser; "but of course I know you only come here to try and see that fellow Robinson," he added, gloomily.

"I like to see you, too," was the reply. "I like you very much, as a friend."

The mate in a melancholy voice thanked her, and to the great annoyance of the cook, who had received strict orders from the forecastle to listen as much as he could, sat in silence while the table was cleared.

"What do you say to a hand at cards?" he said, after the cook had finally left the cabin.

"Three-handed cribbage," said Mrs. Tipping, quickly; "it's the only game worth playing."

No objection being raised, the masterful lady drew closer to the table, and concentrating energies of no mean order on the game, successfully played hands of unvarying goodness, aided by a method of pegging which might perhaps be best described as dot and carry one.

"You haven't seen anything of this Mr. Robinson since you were here last, I suppose?" said Fraser, noting with satisfaction that both ladies gave occasional uneasy glances at the clock.

"No, an' not likely to," said Mrs. Tipping; "fifteen two, fifteen four, fifteen six, and a pair's eight."

"Where's the fifteen six?" enquired Fraser, glancing oven

"Eight and seven," said the lady, pitching the cards with the others and beginning to shuffle for the next deal.

"It's very strange behaviour," said the mate; "Robinson, I mean. Do you think he's dead?"

"No, I don't," said Mrs. Tipping, briefly. "Where's that captain of yours?"

Fraser, whose anxiety was becoming too much for his play, leaned over the table as though about to speak, and then, apparently thinking better of it, went on with the game.

"Eh?" said Mrs. Tipping, putting her cards face downwards on the table and catching his eye. "Where?"

"O, nowhere," said Fraser, awkwardly. "I don't want to be dragged into this, you know. It isn't my business."

"If you know where he is, why can't you tell us?" asked Mrs. Tipping, softly. "There's no harm in that."

"What's the good?" enquired Fraser, in a low voice; "when you've seen the old man you won't be any forwarder—he wouldn't tell you anything even if he knew it."

"Well, we'd like to see him," said Mrs. Tipping, after a pause.

"You see, you put me in a difficulty," said Fraser; "if the skipper doesn't come aboard, you're going with us, I understand?"

Mrs. Tipping nodded. "Exactly," she said, sharply.

"That'll get me into trouble, if anything will," said the mate, gloomily. "On the other hand, if I tell you where he is now, that'll get me into trouble, too."

He sat back and drummed on the table with his fingers. "Well, I'll risk it," he said, at length; "you'll find him at 17, Beaufort Street, Bow."

The younger woman sprang excitedly to her feet, but Mrs. Tipping, eyeing the young man with a pair of shrewd, small eyes, kept her seat.

"And while we're going, how do we know the capt'n won't come back and go off with the ship?" she enquired.

Fraser hesitated. "Well, I'll come with you, if you like," he said, slowly.

"And suppose they go away and leave you, behind?" objected Mrs. Tipping.

"Oh, well, you'd better stay then," said the mate, wearily, "unless we take a couple of the hands with us. How would that suit you? They can't sail with half a crew."

Mrs. Tipping, who was by no means as anxious for a sea voyage as she tried to make out, carefully pondered the situation. "I'm going to take an arm of each of 'em and Matilda'll take yours," she said, at length.

"As you please," said Fraser, and in this way the procession actually started up the wharf, and looking back indignantly over its shoulder saw the watchman and Ben giving way to the most unseemly mirth, while the cook capered joyously behind them. A belated cab was passing the gate as they reached it, and in response to the mate's hail pulled sharply up.

Mrs. Tipping, pushing her captives in first, stepped heavily into the cab followed by her daughter, while the mate, after a brief discussion, clambered onto the box.

"Go on," he said, nodding.

"Wot, ain't the rest of you comin'?" enquired the cabman, eyeing the crowd at the gate, in pained surprise.

"No. 17, Beaufort Street, Bow," said Mrs. Tipping, distinctly, as she put her head out of the window.

"You could sit on 'er lap," continued the cabman, appealingly.

No reply being vouchsafed to this suggestion, he wrapped himself up in various rugs and then sat down suddenly before they could unwind themselves. Then, with a compassionate "click" to his horse, started up the road. Except for a few chance wayfarers and an occasional coffee-stall, the main streets were deserted, but they were noisy compared with Beaufort Street. Every house was in absolute darkness as the cab, with instinctive deference to slumber, crawled slowly up and down looking for No. 17.

It stopped at last, and the mate, springing down, opened the door, and handing out the ladies, led the way up a flight of steps to the street door.

"Perhaps you won't mind knocking," he said to Mrs. Tipping, "and don't forget to tell the cap'n I've done this to oblige you because you insisted upon it."

Mrs. Tipping, seizing the knocker, knocked loud and long, and after a short interval repeated the performance. Somebody was heard stirring upstairs, and a deep voice cried out that it was coming, and peremptorily requested them to cease knocking.

"That's not Flower's voice," said Fraser.

"Not loud enough," said Miss Tipping.

The bolts were drawn back loudly and the chain grated; then the door was flung open, and a big, red-whiskered man, blinking behind a candle, gruffly enquired what they meant by it.

"Come inside," said Mrs. Tipping to her following.

"Ain't you come to the wrong house?" demanded the red-whiskered man, borne slowly back by numbers.

"I don't think so," said Mrs. Tipping, suavely; "I want to see Captain Flower."

"Well, you've come to the wrong house," said the red-whiskered man, shortly, "there's no such name here."

"Think," said Mrs. Tipping.

The red-whiskered man waved the candle to and fro until the passage was flecked with tallow.

"Go away directly," he roared; "how dare you come disturbing people like this?"

"You may just as well be pleasant over it," said Mrs. Tipping, severely; "because we sha'n't go away until we have seen him. After all, it's got nothing to do with you."

"We don't want anything to say to you," affirmed her daughter.

"Will—you—get—out—of—my—house?" demanded the owner, wildly.

"When we've seen Capt'n Flower," said Mrs. Tipping, calmly, "and not a moment before. We don't mind your getting in a temper, not a bit. You can't frighten us."

The frenzied and reckless reply of the red-whiskered man was drowned in the violent slamming of the street-door, and he found himself alone with the ladies. There was a yell of triumph outside, and the sounds of a hurried scramble down the steps. Mrs. Tipping, fumbling wildly at the catch of the door, opened it just in time to see the cabman, in reply to the urgent entreaties of the mate, frantically lashing his horse up the road.

"So far, so good," murmured the mate, as he glanced over his shoulder at the little group posing on the steps. "I've done the best I could, but I suppose there'll be a row."

The watchman, with the remainder of the crew, in various attitudes of expectant curiosity, were waiting to receive them at the wharf. A curiosity which increased in intensity as the mate, slamming the gate, put the big bar across and turned to the watchman.

"Don't open that to anybody till we're off," he said, sharply. "Cap'n Flower has not turned up yet, I suppose?"

"No, sir," said Ben.

They went aboard the schooner again, and the mate, remaining on deck, listened anxiously for the return of the redoubtable Mrs. Tipping, occasionally glancing over the side in expectation of being boarded from the neighbouring stairs; but with the exception of a false alarm caused by two maddened seamen unable to obtain admittance, and preferring insulting charges of somnolency against the watchman, the time passed quietly until high water. With the schooner in midstream slowly picking her way through the traffic, any twinges of remorse that he might have had for the way he had treated two helpless women left him, and he began to feel with his absent commander some of the charm which springs from successful wrong-doing.

CHAPTER VII

He brought up off Greenwich in the cold grey of the breaking day. Craft of all shapes and sizes were passing up and down, but he looked in vain for any sign of the skipper. It was galling to him as a seaman to stay there with the wind blowing freshly down the river; but over an hour elapsed before a yell from Tim, who was leaning over the bows, called his attention to a waterman's skiff, in the stern of which sat a passenger of somewhat dejected appearance. He had the air of a man who had been up all night, and in place of returning the hearty and significant greeting of the mate, sat down in an exhausted fashion on the cabin skylight, and eyed him in stony silence until they were under way again.

"Well," he said at length, ungraciously.

Chilled by his manner, Fraser, in place of the dramatic fashion in which he had intended to relate the events of the preceding night, told him in a few curt sentences what had occurred. "And you can finish this business for yourself," he concluded, warmly; "I've had enough of it."

"You've made a pretty mess of it," groaned the other; "there'll be a fine set-out now. Why couldn't you coax 'em away? That's what I wanted you to do. That's what I told you to do."

"Well, you'll have plenty of opportunities of coaxing yourself so far as I can see," retorted Fraser, grimly. "Then you'll see how it works. It was the only way of getting rid of them."

"You ought to have sent round to me and let me know what you were doing," said Flower. "I sat in that blamed pub till they turned me out at twelve, expecting you every minute. I'd only threepence left by then, and I crossed the water with that, and then I had to shuffle along to Greenwich as best I could with a bad foot. What'll be the end of it all, I don't know."

"Well, you're all right at present," said Fraser, glancing round; "rather different to what you'd have been if those two women had come to Ipswich and seen Cap'n Barber."

The other sat for a long time in thought. "I'll lay up for a few weeks with this foot," he said, slowly, "and you'll have to tell the Tipping family that I've changed into another trade. What with the worry I've had lately, I shall be glad of a rest."

He made his way below, and turning in slept soundly after his fatigue until the cook aroused him a few hours later with the information that breakfast was ready.

A wash and a change, together with a good breakfast, effected as much change in his spirits as in his appearance. Refreshed in mind and body, he slowly paced the deck, his chest expanding as he sniffed the fresh air, and his soul, encouraged by the dangers he had already passed through, bracing itself for fresh encounters.

"I 'ope the foot is goin' on well, sir," said Tim, breaking in upon his meditations, respectfully.

"Much easier this morning," said the skipper, amiably.

Tim, who was lending the cook a hand, went back into the galley to ponder. As a result of a heated debate in the fo'c's'le, where the last night's proceedings and the mysterious appearance of the skipper off Greenwich had caused a great sensation, they had drawn lots to decide who was to bell the cat, and Tim had won or lost according as the subject might be viewed.

"You don't want to walk about on it much, sir," he said, thrusting his head out again.

The skipper nodded.

"I was alarmed last night," said Tim. "We was all alarmed," he added, hastily, in order that the others might stand in with the risk, "thinking that perhaps you'd walked too far and couldn't get back."

The master of the Foam looked at him, but made no reply, and Tim's head was slowly withdrawn. The crew, who had been gazing over the side with their ears at the utmost tension, gave him five minutes' grace and then, the skipper having gone aft again, walked up to the galley.

"I've done all I could," said the wretched youth.

"Done all ye could?" said Joe, derisively, "why you ain't done nothin' yet."

"I can't say anything more," said Tim. "I dassent. I ain't got your pluck, Joe."

"Pluck be damned!" said the seaman, fiercely; "why there was a chap I knew once, shipwrecked he was, and had to take to the boats. When the grub give out they drew lots to see who should be killed and eaten. He lost. Did 'e back out of it? Not a bit of it; 'e was a man, an' 'e shook 'ands with 'em afore they ate 'im and wished 'em luck."

"Well, you can kill and eat me if that's what you want," said Tim, desperately. "I'd sooner 'ave that."

"Mind you," said Joe, "till you've arsked them questions and been answered satisfactorily—none of us'll 'ave anything to do with you, besides which I'll give you such a licking as you've never 'ad before."

He strolled off with Ben and the cook, as the skipper came towards them again, and sat down in the bows. Tim, sore afraid of his shipmates' con. tempt, tried again.

"I wanted to ask your pardon in case I done wrong last night, sir," he said, humbly.

"All right, it's granted," replied the other, walking away.

Tim raised his eyes to heaven, and then lowering them, looked even more beseechingly at his comrades.

"Go on," said Ben, shaping the words only with his mouth.

"I don't know, sir, whether you know what I was alloodin' to just now," said Tim, in trembling accents, as the skipper came within earshot again. "I'm a-referring to a cab ride."

"And I told you that I've forgiven you," said Flower, sternly, "forgiven you freely—all of you."

"It's a relief to my mind, sir," faltered the youth, staring.

"Don't mix yourself up in my business again, that's all," said the skipper; "you mightn't get off so easy next time."

"It's been worrying me ever since, sir," persisted Tim, who was half fainting. "I've been wondering whether I ought to have answered them ladies' questions, and told 'em what I did tell 'em."

The skipper swung round hastily and confronted him. "Told them?" he stuttered, "told them what?"

"I 'ardly remember, sir," said Tim, alarmed at his manner. "Wot with the suddenness o' the thing, an' the luckshury o' riding in a cab, my 'ead was in a whirl."

"What did they ask you?" demanded the shipper.

"They asked me what Cap'n Flower was like an' where 'e lived," said Tim, "an' they asked me whether I knew a Mr. Robinson."

Captain Flower, his eyes blazing, waited.

"I said I 'adn't got the pleasure o' Mr. Robinson's acquaintance," said Tim, with a grand air. "I was just goin' to tell 'em about you when Joe 'ere gave me a pinch."

"Well?" enquired the skipper, stamping with impatience.

"I pinched 'im back agin," said Tim, smiling tenderly at the reminiscence.

"Tim's a fool, sir," said Joe, suddenly, as the overwrought skipper made a move towards the galley. "'E didn't seem to know wot 'e was a sayin' of, so I up and told 'em all about you."

"You did, did you? Damn you," said Flower, bitterly.

"In answer to their questions, sir," said Joe, "I told 'em you was a bald-headed chap, marked with the small-pox, and I said when you was at 'ome, which was seldom, you lived at Aberdeen."

The skipper stepped towards him and laid his hand affectionately on his shoulder. "You ought to have been an admiral, Joe," he said, gratefully, without intending any slur on a noble profession.

"I also told George, the watchman, to tell 'em the same thing, if they came round again worrying," said Joe, proudly.

The skipper patted him on the shoulder again.

"One o' these days, Joe," he remarked, "you shall know all about this little affair; for the present it's enough to tell you that a certain unfortunate young female has took a fancy to a friend o' mine named Robinson, but it's very important, for Robinson's sake, that she shouldn't see me or get to know anything about me. Do you understand?"

"Perfectly," said Joe, sagely.

His countenance was calm and composed, but the cook's forehead had wrinkled itself into his hair in a strong brain effort, while Ben was looking for light on the deck, and not finding it. Flower, as a sign that the conversation was now ended, walked aft again, and taking the wheel from the mate, thoughtfully suggested that he should go below and turn in for five minutes.

"I'll get through this all right, after all," he said, comfortably. "I'll lay up at Seabridge for a week or two, and after that I'll get off the schooner at Greenwich for a bit and let you take her up to London. Then I'll write a letter in the name of Robinson and send it to a man I know in New York to post from there to Miss Tipping."

His spirits rose and he slapped Fraser heartily on the back. "That disposes of one," he said, cheerily. "Lor', in years to come how I shall look back and laugh over all this!"

"Yes, I think it'll be some time before you do any laughing to speak of," said Fraser.

"Ah, you always look on the dark side of things," said Flower, briskly.

"Of course, as things are, you're going to marry Miss Banks," said Fraser, slowly.

"No, I'm not," said the other, cheerfully; "it strikes me there's plenty of time before that will come to a head, and that gives me time to turn round. I don't think she's any more anxious for it than I am."

"But suppose it does come to a head," persisted Fraser, "what are you going to do?"

"I shall find a way out of it," said the skipper, confidently. "Meantime, just as an exercise for your wits, you might try and puzzle out what would be the best thing to do in such a case."

His good spirits lasted all the way to Seabridge, and, the schooner berthed, he went cheerfully off home. It was early afternoon when he arrived, and, Captain Barber being out, he had a comfortable tête à tête with Mrs. Church, in which he was able to dilate pretty largely upon the injury to his foot. Captain Barber did not return until the tea was set, and then shaking hands with his nephew, took a seat opposite, and in a manner more than unusually boisterous, kept up a long conversation.

It was a matter of surprise to Flower that, though the talk was by no means of a sorrowful nature, Mrs. Church on three separate occasions rose from the table and left the room with her handkerchief to her eyes. At such times his uncle's ideas forsook him, and he broke off not only in the middle of a sentence, but even in the middle of a word. At the third time Flower caught his eye, and with a dumb jerk of his head toward the door enquired what it all meant.

"Tell you presently," said his uncle, in a frightened whisper, "Hush! Don't take no notice of it. Not a word."

"What is it?" persisted Flower.

Captain Barber gave a hurried glance towards the door and then leaned over the table "Broken 'art," he whispered, sorrowfully.

Flower whistled, and, full of the visions which this communication opened up, neglected to join in the artificial mirth which his uncle was endeavouring to provoke upon the housekeeper's return. Finally he worked up a little mirth on his own account, and after glancing from his uncle to the housekeeper, and from the housekeeper back to his uncle again, smothered his face in his handkerchief and rushed from the room.

"Bit on a bad tooth," he said, untruthfully, when he came back.

Captain Barber eyed him fiercely, but Mrs. Church regarded him with compassionate interest, and, having got the conversation upon such a safe subject, kept it there until the meal was finished.

"What's it all about?" enquired Flower, as, tea finished, Captain Barber carried his chair to the extreme end of the garden and beckoned his nephew to do likewise.

"You're the cause of it," said Captain Barber, severely.

"Me?" said Flower, in surprise.

"You know that little plan I told you of when you was down here?" said the other.

His nephew nodded.

"It came off," groaned Captain Barber. "I've got news for you as'll make you dance for joy."

"I've got a bad foot," said Flower, paling.

"Never mind about your foot," said his uncle, regarding him fixedly. "Your banns are up."

"Up! Up where?" gasped Flower.

"Why—in the church," said the other, staring at him; "where do you think? I got the old lady's consent day before yesterday, and had 'em put up at once."

"Is she dead, then?" enquired his nephew, in a voice the hollowness of which befitted the question.

"How the devil could she be?" returned his uncle, staring at him.

"No, I didn't think of that," said Flower; "of course, she couldn't give her consent, could she—not if she was dead, I mean."

Captain Barber drew his chair back and looked at him. "His joy has turned his brain," he said, with conviction.

"No, it's my foot," said Flower, rallying. "I've had no sleep with it. I'm delighted! Delighted! After all these years."

"You owe it to me," said his uncle, with a satisfied air. "I generally see my way clear to what I want, and generally get it, too. I've played Mrs. Banks and Mrs. Church agin one another without their knowing it. Both 'elpless in my hands, they was."

"But what's the matter with Mrs. Church?" said his depressed nephew.

"Oh, that's the worst of it," said Uncle Barber, shaking his head. "While I was in play, that pore woman must have thought I was in earnest. She don't say nothing. Not a word, and the efforts she makes to control her feelings is noble."

"Have you told her she has got to go then?" enquired Flower.

Captain Barber shook his head. "Mrs. Banks saved me that trouble," he said, grimly.

"But she can't take notice from Mrs. Banks," said Flower, "it'll have to come from you."

"All in good time," said Captain Barber, wiping his face. "As I've done all this for you, I was going to let you tell her."

"Me!" said Flower, with emphasis.

"Certainly," said Captain Barber, with more emphasis still. "Just get her to yourself on the quiet and allude to it casual. Then after that bring the subject up when I'm in the room. As it's to make room for you and your wife, you might fix the date for 'er to go. That'll be the best way to do it."

"It seems to me it is rather hard on her," said his nephew, compassionately; "perhaps we had better wait a little longer."

"Certainly not," said Captain Barber, sharply; "don't I tell you your banns are up. You're to be asked in church first time next Sunday, You'll both live with me as agreed, and I'm going to make over three o' the cottages to you and a half-share in the ship. The rest you'll have to wait for. Why don't you look cheerful? You ought to."

"I'm cheerful enough," said Flower, recovering himself. "I'm thinking of you."

"Me?" said his uncle.

"You and Mrs. Church," said his nephew. "So far as I can see, you've committed yourself."

"I can manage," said Uncle Barber. "I've always been master in my own house. Now you'd better step round and see the bride that is to be."

"Well, you be careful," said his nephew, warningly.

"I'm coming, too," said Captain Barber, with some haste; "there's no need to stay and wait for trouble. When you go into the house, come back as though you'd forgotten something, and sing out to me that you want me to come too—hard enough for 'er to hear, mind."

CHAPTER VIII

The bewildered master of the Foam spent the remainder of the time at Seabridge in a species of waking nightmare.

A grey-haired dressmaker and a small apprentice sat in the Banks' best parlour, and from a chaos of brown paper patterns stuck over with pins a silk dress of surpassing beauty began slowly to emerge. As a great concession Flower was allowed to feel the material, and even to rub it between his finger and thumb in imitation of Captain Barber, who was so prone to the exercise that a small piece was cut for his especial delectation. A colour of unwonted softness glowed in the cheek of Elizabeth and an air of engaging timidity tempered her interview with Flower, who had to run the gauntlet of much friendly criticism on the part of his fair neighbours.

Up to the time of sailing for London again the allusion to Mrs. Church's departure, desired by Captain Barber, had not been made by the younger man. The housekeeper was still in possession, and shook hands with him at the front door as he limped slowly off with Miss Banks and his uncle to go down to the schooner. His foot was still very bad, so bad that he stumbled three times on the way to the quay despite the assistance afforded by the arm of his betrothed.

"Seems to be no power in it," he said smiling faintly; "but I daresay it'll be all right by the time. I get back."

He shook hands with Captain Barber and, as a tribute to conventionality, kissed Miss Banks. The last the two saw of him, he was standing at the wheel waving his handkerchief. They waved their own in return, and as the Foam drew rapidly away gave a final farewell and departed.

"What's the game with the foot?" enquired the mate, in a low voice.

"Tell you by-and-by," said the skipper; "it's far from well, but even if it wasn't I should pretend it was bad. I suppose that doesn't suggest anything to you?"

The mate shook his head.

"Can you see any way out of it?" enquired the other. "What would you do if you were in my place?"

"Marry the girl I wanted to marry," said the mate, sturdily, "and not trouble about anything else."

"And lose thirteen cottages and this ship and my berth in the bargain," said the skipper. "Now you try and think of some other way, and if you haven't thought of it by dinner-time, I'll tell you what I'm going to do."

No other scheme having suggested itself to the mate by the time that meal arrived, he prepared to play the part of listener. The skipper, after carefully closing both the door and the skylight, prepared to speak.

"I'm in a desperate fix, Jack, that you'll admit," he said, by way of preparation.

The mate cordially agreed with him.

"There's Poppy down at Poplar, Matilda at Chelsea, and Elizabeth at Seabridge," continued Flower, indicating various points on the table with his finger as he spoke. "Some men would give up in despair, but I've thought of a way out of it. I've never got into a corner I couldn't get out of yet."

"You want a little help though sometimes," said Fraser.

"All part of my plans," rejoined Flower, airily. "If it hadn't been for my uncle's interference I should have been all right. A man's no business to be so officious. As it is, I've got to do something decided."

"If I were you," interrupted Fraser, "I should go to Captain Barber and tell him straight and plain how the thing stands. You needn't mention anything about Miss Tipping. Tell him about the other, and that you intend to marry her. It'll be beat in the long run, and fairer to Miss Tyrell, too."

"You don't know my uncle as well as I do," retorted the skipper. "He's as obstinate an old fool as ever breathed. If I did as you say I should lose everything. Now, I'll tell you what I'm going to do:— To-night, during your watch, I shall come up on deck and stand on the side of the ship to look at something in the water, when I shall suddenly hear a shout."

The mate, who had a piece of dumpling on his fork, half-way to his mouth, put it down again and regarded him open-mouthed.

"My foot," continued the skipper, in surprisingly even tones, answering his subject, "will then give way and I shall fall overboard."

The mate was about to speak, but the skipper, gazing in a rapt manner before him, waved him into silence.

"You will alarm the crew and pitch a life-belt overboard," he continued; "you will then back sails and lower the boat."

"You'd better take the lifebelt with you, hadn't you?" enquired the mate, anxiously.

"I shall be picked up by a Norwegian barque, bound for China," continued the skipper, ignoring the interruption; "I shall be away at least six months, perhaps more, according as things turn out."

The mate pushed his scarcely tasted dinner from him, and got up from the table. It was quite evident to him that the skipper's love affairs had turned his brain.

"By the time I get back, Matilda'll have ceased from troubling, anyway," said the skipper, "and I have strong hopes that Elizabeth'll take Gibson. I shall stay away long enough to give her a fair chance, anyway."

"But s'pose you get drowned before anything can pick you up!" suggested the mate, feebly.

"Drowned?" repeated the skipper. "Why, you didn't think I was really going overboard, did you? I shall be locked up in my state-room."

The mate's brow cleared and then darkened again, suddenly. "I see, some more lies for me to tell, I suppose," he said, angrily.

"After you've raised the alarm and failed to recover the body," said the skipper, with relish, "you'll lock my door and put the key in your pocket. That would be the proper thing to do if I really did go overboard, you know, and when we get to London I'll just slip quietly ashore."

The mate came back to his dinner and finished it in silence, while the skipper kept up a rambling fire of instructions for his future guidance.

"And what about Miss Tyrell?" said the mate, at length. "Is she to know?"

"Certainly not," said Flower, sharply. "I wouldn't have her know for anything. You're the only person to know, Jack. You'll have to break the news to 'em all, and mind you do it gently, so as not to cause more grief than you can help."

"I won't do it at all," said the mate.

"Yes, you will," said Flower, "and if Matilda or her mother come down again, show it to 'em in the paper. Then they'll know it'll be no good worrying Cap'n Flower again. If they see it in the paper they'll know it's true; it's sure to be in the local papers, and in the London ones, too, very likely. I should think it would; the master of a vessel!"

Fraser being in no mood to regard this vanity complacently, went up on deck and declined to have anything to do with the matter. He maintained this attitude of immovable virtue until tea-time, by which time Flower's entreaties had so won upon him that he was reluctantly compelled to admit that it seemed to be the only thing possible in the circumstances, and more reluctantly still to promise his aid to the most unscrupulous extent possible.

"I'll write to you when I'm fixed up," said the skipper, "giving you my new name and address. You're the only person I shall be able to keep touch with. I shall have to rely upon you for everything. If it wasn't for you I should be dead to the world."

"I know what you'll do as well as possible," said Fraser; "you've got nothing to do for six months, and you'll be getting into some more engagements."

"I don't think you have any call to say that, Jack," remarked Flower, with some dignity.

"Well, I wish it was well over," said the mate, despondently. "What are you going to do for money?"

"I drew out £40 to get married with—furniture and things," said Flower; "that'll go overboard with me, of course. I'm doing all this for Poppy's sake more than my own, and I want you to go up and see her every trip, and let me know how she is. She mightn't care what happened to her if she thinks I'm gone, and she might marry somebody else in desperation."

"I don't care about facing her," said Fraser, bitterly; "it's a shady business altogether."

"It's for her sake," repeated Flower, calmly, "Take on old Ben as mate, and ship another hand forward."

The mate ended the subject by going to his bunk and turning in; the skipper, who realised that he himself would have plenty of time for sleep, went on deck and sat silently smoking. Old Ben was at the wheel, and the skipper felt a glow of self-rightousness as he thought of the rise in life he was about to give the poor fellow.

At eight o'clock the mate relieved Ben, and the skipper with a view of keeping up appearances announced his intention of turning in for a bit.

The sun went down behind clouds of smoky red, but the light of the summer evening lasted for some time after. Then darkness came down over the sea, and it was desolate except for the sidelights of distant craft. The mate drew out his watch and by the light of the binnacle-lamp, saw that it was ten minutes to ten. At the same moment he heard somebody moving about forward.

"Who's that for'ard?" he cried, smartly.

"Me, sir," answered Joe's voice. "I'm a bit wakeful, and it's stiflin' 'ot down below."

The mate hesitated, and then, glancing at the open skylight, saw the skipper, who was standing on the table.

"Send him below," said the latter, in a sharp whisper.

"You'd better get below, Joe," said the mate.

"W'y, I ain't doin' no 'arm, sir," said Joe, in surprise.

"Get below," said the mate, sharply. "Do you hear?—get below. You'll be sleeping in your watch if you don't sleep now."

The sounds of a carefully modulated grumble came faintly aft, then the mate, leaning away from the wheel to avoid the galley which obstructed his view, saw that his order had been obeyed.

"Now," said the skipper, quietly, "you must give a perfect scream of horror, mind, and put this on the deck. It fell off as I went over, d'ye see?"

He handed over the slipper he had been wearing, and the mate took it surlily.

"There ought to be a splash," he murmured. "Joe's awake."

The skipper vanished, to reappear a minute or two later with a sack into which he had hastily thrust a few lumps of coal and other rubbish. The mate took it from him, and, placing the slipper on the deck, stood with one hand holding the wheel and the other the ridiculous sack.

"Now," said the skipper.

The sack went overboard, and, at the same moment, the mate left the wheel with an ear-splitting yell and rushed to the galley for the life-belt which hung there. He crashed heavily into Joe, who had rushed on deck, but, without pausing, ran to the side and flung it overboard.

"Skipper's overboard," he yelled, running back and putting the helm down.

Joe put his head down the fore-scuttle and yelled like a maniac; the others came up in their night-gear, and in a marvellously short space of time the schooner was hove to and the cook and Joe had tumbled into the boat and were pulling back lustily in search of the skipper.

Half an hour elapsed, during which those on the schooner hung over the stern listening intently. They could hear the oars in the rowlocks and the shouts of the rowers. Tim lit a lantern and dangled it over the water.

"Have you got 'im?" cried Ben, as the boat came over the darkness and the light of the lantern shone on the upturned faces of the men.

"No," said Joe, huskily.

Ben threw him a line, and he clambered silently aboard, followed by the cook.

"Better put about," he said to the mate, "and cruise about until daylight. We ain't found the belt either, and it's just possible he's got it."

The mate shook his head. "It's no good," he said, confidently; "he's gone."

"Well, I vote we try, anyhow," said Joe, turning on him fiercely. "How did it happen?"

"He came up on deck to speak to me," said the mate, shortly. "He fancied he heard a cry from the water and jumped up on the side with his hand on the rigging to see. I s'pose his bad foot slipped and he went over before I could move."

"We'll cruise about a bit," said Joe, loudly, turning to the men.

"Are you giving orders here, or am I?" said the mate sternly.

"I am," said Joe, violently. "It's our duty to do all we can." There was a dead silence. Joe, pushing himself in between Ben and the cook, eyed the men eagerly.

"What do you mean by that?" said the mate at last.

"Wot I say," said Joe, meeting him eye to eye, and thrusting his face close to his.

The mate shrugged his shoulders and walked slowly aft; then, with a regard for appearances which the occasion fully warranted, took the schooner for a little circular tour in the neighbourhood of the skipper's disappearance.

At daybreak, not feeling the loss quite as much as the men, he went below, and, having looked stealthily round, unlocked the door of the state-room and peeped in. It was almost uncanny, considering the circumstances, to see in the dim light the skipper sitting on the edge of his bunk.

"What the blazes are you doing, dodging about like this?" he burst out, ungratefully.

"Looking for the body," said the mate. "Ain't you heard us shouting? It's not my fault—the crew say they won't leave the spot while there's half a chance."

"Blast the crew," said the skipper, quite untouched by this devotion. "Ain't you taking charge o' the ship?"

"Joe's about half mad," said the mate. "It's wonderful how upset he is."

The skipper cursed Joe separately, and the mate, whose temper was getting bad, closed the interview by locking the door.

At five o'clock, by which time they had cleared three masses of weed and a barnacle-covered plank, they abandoned the search and resumed the voyage. A gloom settled on the forecastle, and the cook took advantage of the occasion to read Tim a homily upon the shortness of life and the suddenness of death. Tim was much affected, but not nearly so much as he was when he discovered that the men were going to pay a last tribute to the late captain's memory by abstaining from breakfast. He ventured to remark that the excitement and the night air had made him feel very hungry, and was promptly called an unfeeling little brute by the men for his pains. The mate, who, in deference to public opinion, had to keep up appearances the same way, was almost as much annoyed as Tim, and, as for the drowned man himself, his state of mind was the worst of all. He was so ungrateful that the mate at length lost his temper and when dinner was served allowed a latent sense ot humour to have full play.

It consisted of boiled beef, with duff, carrots, and potatoes, and its grateful incense filled the cabin.

The mate attacked it lustily listening between mouthfuls for any interruption from the state-room. At length, unable to endure it any longer, the prisoner ventured to scratch lightly on the door.

"Hist!" said the mate, in a whisper.

The scratching ceased, and the mate, grinning broadly, resumed his dinner. He finished at last, and lighting his pipe sat back easily in the locker watching the door out of the corner of his eye.

With hunger at his vitals the unfortunate skipper, hardly able to believe his ears, heard the cook come down and clear away. The smell of dinner gave way to that of tobacco, and the mate, having half finished his pipe, approached the door.

"Are you there?" he asked, in a whisper.

"Of course I am, you fool!" said the skipper, wrathfully; "where's my dinner?"

"I'm very sorry," began the mate, in a whisper.

"What?" enquired the skipper, fiercely.

"I've mislaid the key," said the mate, grinning fiendishly, "an', what's more, I can't think what I've done with it."

At this intelligence, the remnants of the skipper's temper vanished, and every bad word he had heard of, or read of, or dreamt of, floated from his hungry lips in frenzied whispers.

"I can't hear what you say," said the mate. "What?"

The prisoner was about to repeat his remarks with a few embellishments, when the mate stopped him with one little word. "Hist!" he said, quietly.

At the imminent risk of bursting, or going mad, the skipper stopped short, and the mate, addressing a remark to the cook, who was not present, went up on deck.

He found the key by tea-time, and, his triumph having made him generous, passed the skipper in a large hunk of the cold beef with his tea. The skipper took it and eyed him wanly, having found an empty stomach very conducive to accurate thinking.

"The next thing is to slip ashore at Wapping, Jack," he said, after he had finished his meal; "the whar'll be closed by the time we get there."

"The watchman's nearly sure to be asleep," said Fraser, "and you can easily climb the gate. If he's not, I must try and get him out of the way somehow."

The skipper's forebodings proved to be correct. It was past twelve by the time they reached Wapping, but the watchman was wide awake and, with much bustle, helped them to berth their craft. He received the news of the skipper's untimely end with well-bred sorrow, and at once excited the wrath of the sensitive Joe by saying that he was not surprised.

"I 'ad a warning," he said solemnly, in reply to the indignant seaman. "Larst night exactly as Big Ben struck ten o'clock the gate-bell was pulled three times."

"I've pulled it fifty times myself before now," said Joe, scathingly, "and then had to climb over the gate and wake you up."

"I went to the gate at once," continued George, addressing himself to the cook; "sometimes when I'm shifting a barge, or doing any little job o' that sort, I do 'ave to keep a man waiting, and, if he's drunk, two minutes seems like ages to 'im."

"You ought to know wot it seems like," muttered Joe.

"When I got to the gate an' opened it there was nobody there," continued the watchman, impressively, "and while I was standing there I saw the bell-pull go up an' down without 'ands and the bell rung agin three times."

The cook shivered. "Wasn't you frightened, George?" he asked, sympathetically.

"I knew it was a warning," continued the vivacious George. "W'y 'e should come to me I don't know. One thing is I think 'e always 'ad a bit of a fancy for me."

"He 'ad," said Joe; "everybody wot sees you loves you, George. They can't help theirselves."

"And I 'ave 'ad them two ladies down agin asking for Mr. Robinson, and also for poor Cap'n Flower," said the watchman; "they asked me some questions about 'im, and I told 'em the lies wot you told me to tell 'em, Joe; p'r'aps that's w'y I 'ad the warning."

Joe turned away with a growl and went below, and Tim and the cook after greedily waiting for some time to give the watchman's imagination a further chance, followed his example. George left to himself took his old seat on the post at the end of the jetty, being, if the truth must be told, somewhat alarmed by his own fertile inventions.

Three times did the mate, in response to the frenzied commands of the skipper, come stealthily up the companion-way and look at him. Time was passing and action of some kind was imperative.

"George," he whispered, suddenly.

"Sir," said the watchman.

"I want to speak to you," said Fraser, mysteriously; "come down here."

George rose carefully from his seat, and lowering himself gingerly on board, crept on tiptoe to the galley after the mate.

"Wait in here till i come back," said the latter, in a thrilling whisper; "I've got something to show you. Don't move, whatever happens."

His tones were so fearful, and he put so much emphasis on the last sentence, that the watchman burst hurriedly out of the galley.

"I don't like these mysteries," he said, plainly.

"There's no mystery," said the mate, pushing him back again; "something I don't want the crew to see, that's all. You're the only man I can trust."

He closed the door and coughed, and a figure which had been lurking on the companion-ladder, slipped hastily on deck and clambered noiselessly onto the jetty. The mate clambered up beside it, and hurrying with it to the gate helped it over, and with much satisfaction heard it alight on the other side.

"Good-night, Jack," said Flower. "Don't forget to look after Poppy."

"Good-night," said the mate. "Write as soon as you're fixed."

He walked back leisurely to the schooner and stood in some perplexity, eyeing the galley which contained the devoted George, He stood for so long that his victim lost all patience, and, sliding back the door, peered out and discovered him.

"Have you got it?" he asked, softly.

"No," replied Fraser; "there isn't anything. I was only making a fool of you, George. Good-night."

He walked aft, and stood at the companion watching the outraged George as he came slowly out of the galley and stared about him.

"Good-night, George," he repeated.

The watchman made no reply to the greeting, but, breathing heavily, resumed his old seat on the post; and, folding his arms across his panting bosom, looked down with majestic scorn upon the schooner and all its contents. Long after the satisfied mate had forgotten the incident in sleep, he sat there striving to digest the insult of which he had been the victim, and to consider a painful and fitting retribution.

CHAPTER IX

The mate awoke next morning to a full sense of the unpleasant task before him, and, after irritably giving orders for the removal of the tarpaulin from the skylight, a substitution of the ingenious cook's for the drawn blinds ashore, sat down to a solitary breakfast and the composition of a telegram to Captain Barber. The first, a beautiful piece of prose, of which the key-note was resignation, contained two shillings' worth of sympathy and fourpence-halfpenny worth of religion. It was too expensive as it stood, and boiled down, he was surprised to find that it became unfeeling to the verge of flippancy. Ultimately he embodied it in a letter, which he preceded by a telegram, breaking the sad news in as gentle a form as could be managed for one-and-three.

The best part of the day was spent in relating the sad end of Captain Fred Flower to various enquirers. The deceased gentleman was a popular favourite, and clerks from the office and brother skippers came down in little knots to learn the full particulars, and to compare the accident with others in their experience. It reminded one skipper, who invariably took to drink when his feelings were touched, of the death of a little nephew from whooping-cough, and he was so moved over a picture he drew of the meeting of the two, that it took four men to get him off the schooner without violence.

The mate sat for some time after tea striving to summon up sufficient courage for his journey to Poplar, and wondering whether it wouldn't perhaps be better to communicate the news by letter. He even went so far as to get the writing materials ready, and then, remembering his promise to the skipper, put them away again and prepared for his visit. The crew who were on deck eyed him stolidly as he departed, and Joe made a remark to the cook, which that worthy drowned in a loud and troublesome cough.

The Wheeler family were at home when he arrived, and received him with some surprise, Mrs. Wheeler, who was in her usual place on the sofa, shook hands with him in a genteel fashion, and calling his attention to a somewhat loudly attired young man of unpleasant appearance, who was making a late tea, introduced him as her son Bob.

"Is Miss Tyrell in?" enquired Fraser, shaking his head as Mr. Wheeler dusted a small Wheeler off a chair and offered it to him.

"She's upstairs," said Emma Wheeler; "shall I go and fetch her?"

"No, I'll go up to her," said the mate quietly. "I think I'd better see her alone. I've got rather bad news for her."

"About the captain?" enquired Mrs. Wheeler, sharply.

"Yes," said Fraser, turning somewhat red. "Very bad news."

He fixed his eyes on the ground, and, in a spasmodic fashion, made perfect by practice, recited the disaster.

"Pore feller," said Mrs. Wheeler, when he had finished. "Pore feller, and cut down suddenly like that. I s'pose he 'adn't made any preparation for it?"

"Not a bit," said the mate, starting, "quite unprepared."

"You didn't jump over after him?" suggested Miss Wheeler, softly.

"I did not," said the mate, firmly; whereupon Miss Wheeler, who was fond of penny romance, sighed and shook her head.

"There's that pore gal upstairs," said Mrs. Wheeler, sorrowfully, "all innocent and happy, probably expecting him to come to-night and take her out. Emma'd better go up and break it to 'er."

"I will," said Fraser, shortly.

"Better to let a woman do it," said Mrs. Wheeler. "When our little Jemmy smashed his finger we sent Emma down to break it to his father and bring 'im 'ome. It was ever so long before she let you know the truth, wasn't it, father?"

"Made me think all sorts of things with her mysteries," said the dutiful Mr. Wheeler, in triumphant corroboration. "First of all she made me think you was dead; then I thought you was all dead—give me such a turn they 'ad to give me brandy to bring me round. When I found out it was only Jemmy's finger, I was nearly off my 'ed with joy."

"I'll go and tell her," interrupted Mr. Bob Wheeler, delicately, using the inside edge of the table-cloth as a serviette. "I can do it better than Emma can. What she wants is comforting; Emma would go and snivel all over her."

Mrs. Wheeler, raising her head from the sofa, regarded the speaker with looks of tender admiration, and the young man, after a lengthy glance in the small pier-glass ornamented with coloured paper, which stood on the mantel-piece, walked to the door.

"You needn't trouble," said Fraser, slowly; "I'm going to tell her."

Mrs. Wheeler's dull eyes snapped sharply. "She's our lodger," she said, aggressively.

"Yes, but I'm going to tell her," rejoined the mate; "the skipper told me to."

A startled silence was broken by Mr. Wheeler's chair, which fell noisily.

"I mean," stammered Fraser, meeting the perturbed gaze of the dock-foreman, "that he told me once if anything happened to him that I was to break the news to Miss Tyrell. It's been such a shock to me I hardly know what I am saying."

"Yes, you'll go and frighten her," said Bob Wheeler, endeavouring to push past him.

The mate blocked the doorway.

"Are you going to try to prevent me going out of a room in my own house?" blustered the young man.

"Of course not," said Fraser, and, giving way, ascended the stairs before him. Mr. Wheeler, junior, after a moment's hesitation, turned back and, muttering threats under his breath, returned to the parlour.

Miss Tyrell, who was sitting by the window reading, rose upon the mate's entrance, and, observing that he was alone, evinced a little surprise as she shook hands with him. It was the one thing necessary to complete his discomfiture, and he stood before her in a state of guilty confusion.

"Cap'n Flower couldn't come," he stammered.

The girl said nothing, but with her dark eyes fixed upon his flushed face waited for him to continue.

"It's his misfortune that he couldn't come," con-tinued Fraser, jerkily.

"Business, I suppose?" said the girl, after another wait. "Won't you sit down?"

"Bad business," replied Fraser. He sat down, and fancied he saw the way clear before him.

"You've left him on the Foam, I suppose?" said Poppy, seeing that she was expected to speak.

"No; farther back than that," was the response.

"Seabridge?" queried the girl, with an air of indifference.

Fraser regarded her with an expression of studied sadness. "Not so far back as that," he said, softly.

Miss Tyrell manifested a slight restlessness. "Is it a sort of riddle?" she demanded.

"No, it's a tale," replied Fraser, not without a secret admiration of his unsuspected powers of breaking bad news; "a tale with a bad ending."

The girl misunderstood him. "If you mean that Captain Flower doesn't want to come here, and sent you to say so—" she began, with dignity.

"He can't come," interrupted the mate, hastily.

"Did he send you to tell me?" she asked

Fraser shook his head mournfully. "He can't come," he said, in a low voice; "he had a bad foot—night before last he was standing on the ship's side—when he lost his hold—"

He broke off and eyed the girl nervously, "and fell overboard," he concluded.

Poppy Tyrell gave a faint cry and, springing to her feet, stood with her hand on the back of her chair regarding him. "Poor fellow," she said, softly—"poor fellow."

She sat down again by the open window and nervously plucked at the leaves of a geranium. Her face was white and her dark eyes pitiful and tender. Fraser, watching her, cursed his resourceful skipper and hated himself.

"It's a terrible thing for his friends," said Poppy, at length. "And for you," said Fraser, respectfully.

"I am very grieved," said Poppy, quietly; "very shocked and very grieved."

"I have got strong hopes that he may have got picked up," said Fraser, cheerfully; "very strong hopes, I threw him a life-belt, and though we got the boat out and pulled about, we couldn't find either of them. I shouldn't be at all surprised if he has been picked up by some vessel outward bound. Stranger things have happened."

The girl shook her head. "You didn't go overboard after him?" she asked, quietly.

"I did not," said the mate, who was somewhat tired of this tactless question; "I had to stand by the ship, and besides, he was a much better swimmer than I am—I did the best I could."

Miss Tyrell bowed her head in answer. "Yes," she said, softly.

"If there's anything I can do," said Fraser, awkwardly, "or be of use to you in any way, I hope you'll let me know—Flower told me you were all alone, and—"

He broke off suddenly as he saw the girl's lips quiver. "I was very fond of my father," she said, in extenuation of this weakness.

"I suppose you've got some relatives?" said Fraser.

The girl shook her head.

"No cousins?" said Fraser, staring. He had twenty-three himself.

"I have some in New Zealand," said Poppy, considering. "If I could, I think I should go out there."

"And give up your business here?" enquired the mate, anxiously.

"It gave me up," said Poppy, with a little tremulous laugh. "I had a week's pay instead of notice the day before yesterday. If you know anybody who wants a clerk who spells 'impatient' with a 'y' and is off-hand when they are told of it, you might let me know."

The mate stared at her blankly. This was a far more serious case than Captain Flower's. "What are you going to do?" he asked.

"Try for another berth," was the reply.

"But if you don't get it?"

"I shall get it sooner or later," said the girl.

"But suppose you don't get one for a long time?" suggested Fraser.

"I must wait till I do," said the girl, quietly.

"You see," continued the mate, twisting his hands, "it might be a long job, and I—I was wondering—what you would do in the meantime. I was wondering whether you could hold out."

"Hold out?" repeated Miss Tyrell, very coldly.

"Whether you've got enough money," blurted the mate.

Miss Tyrell turned upon him a face in which there was now no lack of colour. "That is my business," she said, stiffly.

"Mine, too," said Fraser, gazing steadily at the pretty picture of indignation before him. "I was Flower's friend as well as his mate, and you are only a girl." The indignation became impatience. "Little more than a child," he murmured, scrutinising her.

"I am quite big enough to mind my own business," said Poppy, reverting to chilly politeness.

"I wish you would promise me you won't leave here or do anything until I have seen you again," said Fraser, who was anxious to consult his captain on this new phase of affairs.

"Certainly not," said Miss Tyrell, rising and standing by her chair, "and thank you for calling."

Fraser rubbed his chin helplessly.

"Thank you for calling," repeated the girl, still standing.

"That is telling me to go, I suppose?" said, Fraser, looking at her frankly. "I wish I knew how to talk to you. When I think of you being here all alone, without friends and without employment, it seems wrong for me to go and leave you here."

Miss Tyrell gave a faint gasp and glanced anxiously at the door. Fraser hesitated a moment, and then rose to his feet.

"If I hear anything more, may I come and tell you?" he asked.

"Yes," said Poppy, "or write; perhaps it would be better to write; I might not be at home. Goodbye."

The mate shook hands, and, blundering down the stairs, shouted good-night to a segment of the Wheeler family visible through the half-open door, and passed out into the street. He walked for some time rapidly, gradually slowing down as he collected his thoughts.

"Flower's a fool," he said, bitterly; "and, as for me, I don't know what I am. It's so long since I told the truth I forget what it's like, and I'd sooner tell lies in a church than tell them to her."

CHAPTER X

He looked expectantly on the cabin table for a letter upon his return to the ship, but was disappointed, and the only letter yielded by the post next morning came from Captain Barber. It was couched in terms of great resignation, and after bemoaning the unfortunate skipper's untimely demise in language of great strength, wound up with a little Scripture and asked the mate to act as master and sail the schooner home.

"You'll act as mate, Ben, to take her back," said the new skipper, thrusting the letter in his pocket.

"Aye, aye, sir," said Ben, with a side glance at Joe, "but I'll keep for'ard, if you don't mind."

"As you please," said Fraser, staring.

"And you're master, I s'pose?" said Joe, turning to Fraser.

Fraser, whose manner had already effected the little change rendered necessary by his promotion from mate to master, nodded curtly, and the crew, after another exchange of looks, resumed their work without a word. Their behaviour all day was docile, not to say lamb-like, and it was not until evening that the new skipper found it necessary to enforce his authority.

The exciting cause of the unpleasantness was Mr. William Green, a slim, furtive-eyed young man, whom Fraser took on in the afternoon to fill the vacancy caused by Ben's promotion. He had not been on board half an hour before trouble arose from his attempt to introduce the manners of the drawing-room into the forecastle.

"Mr. Will-yum Green," repeated Joe, when the new arrival had introduced himself; "well, you'll be Bill 'ere."

"I don't see why, if I call you Mr. Smith, you shouldn't call me Mr. Green," said the other.

"Call me wot?" enquired Joe, sternly; "you let me 'ear you callin' me mister anythink, that's all; you let me 'ear you."

"I'm sure the cook 'ere don't mind me callin' 'im Mr. Fisher," said the new seaman.

"Cert'nly not," said the gratified cook; "only my name's Disher."

The newcomer apologised with an urbanity that rendered Joe and old Ben speechless. They gazed at each other in silent consternation, and then Ben rose.

"We don't want no misters 'ere," he said, curtly, "an' wot's more, we won't 'ave 'em. That chap's name's Bob, but we calls 'im Slushy. If it's good enough for us, it's good enough for a ordinary seaman wot's got an A. B. discharge by mistake. Let me 'ear you call 'im Slushy. Go on now."

"I've no call to address 'im at all just now," said Mr. Green, loftily.

"You call 'im Slushy," roared Joe, advancing upon him; "call 'im Slushy till I tell you to stop."

"Slushy," said Mr. Green, sullenly, and avoiding the pained gaze of the cook; "Slushy, Slushy, Slushy, Slushy, Sl——"

"That'll do," said the cook, rising, with a scowl. "You don't want to make a song abart it."

Joe, content with his victory, resumed his seat on the locker and exchanged a reassuring glance with Ben; Mr. Green, with a deprecatory glance at the cook, sat down and offered him a pipe of tobacco.

"Been to sea long?" enquired the cook, accepting it

"Not long," said the other, speaking very distinctly.

"I was brought up for something quite different. I'm just doing this till something better turns up. I find it very difficult to be a gentleman at sea."

The cook, with an eye on Joe, ventured on a gentle murmur of sympathy, and said that he had experienced the same thing.

"I 'ad money," continued Mr. Green, musingly, "and I run through it; then I 'ad more money, and I run through that."

"Ben," said Joe, suddenly, "pass me over that boot o' yours."

"Wha' for?" enquired Ben, who had just taken it off.

"To chuck at that swab there," said the indignant seaman.

Ben passed it over without a word, and his irritated friend, taking careful aim, launched it at Mr. Green and caught him on the side of the head with it. Pain standing the latter in lieu of courage, he snatched it up and returned it, and the next moment the whole forecastle was punching somebody else's head, while Tim, in a state of fearful joy, peered down on it from his bunk.

Victory, rendered cheap and easy by reason of the purblindness of the frantic cook, who was trying to persuade Mr. Green to raise his face from the floor so that he could punch it for him, remained with Joe and Ben, who, in reply to the angry shouts of the skipper from above, pointed silently to the combatants. Explanations, all different and all ready to be sworn to if desired, ensued, and Fraser, after curtly reminding Ben of his new position and requesting him to keep order, walked away.

A silence broken only by the general compliments of the much gratified Tim, followed his departure, although another outbreak nearly occurred owing to the cook supplying raw meat for Mr. Green's eye and refusing it for Joe's. It was the lack of consideration and feeling that affected Joe, not for the want of the beef, that little difficulty being easily surmounted by taking Mr. Green's. The tumult was just beginning again, when it was arrested by the sound of angry voices above. Tim, followed by Joe, sprang up the ladder, and the couple with their heads at the opening listened with appreciative enjoyment to a wordy duel between Mrs. Tipping and daughter and the watchman.

"Call me a liar, then," said old George, in bereaved accents.

"I have," said Mrs. Tipping.

"Only you're so used to it you don't notice it," remarked her daughter, scathingly.

"I tell you he's drownded," said the watchman, raising his voice; "if you don't believe me, go and ask Mr. Fraser. He's skipper in his place now."

He waved his hand in the direction of Fraser, who, having heard the noise, was coming on deck to see the cause of it. Mrs. Tipping, compressing her lips, got on board, followed by her daughter, and marching up to him eyed him severely.

"I wonder you can look us in the face after the trick you served us the other night," she said, fiercely.

"You brought it on yourselves," said Fraser, calmly. "You wouldn't go away, you know. You can't always be coming here worrying."

"We shall come whenever we choose," said Mrs. Tipping. "In the first place, we want to see Mr. Robinson; anyway we intend to see Captain Flower, so you can save that fat old man the trouble of telling us lies about him."

"Captain Flower fell overboard night before last, if that's what you mean," said Fraser, gravely.

"I never saw such a man in all my life," exclaimed Mrs. Tipping, wrathfully. "You're a perfect—what's the man's name in the Scriptures?" she asked, turning to her daughter.

Miss Tipping, shaking her head despondently, requested her parent not to worry her.

"Well, it doesn't signify. I shall wait here till he comes," said Mrs. Tipping.

"What, Ananias?" cried Fraser, forgetting himself.

Mrs. Tipping, scorning to reply, stood for some time gazing thoughtfully about her. Then, in compliance with her whispered instructions, her daughter crossed to the side and, brushing aside the outstretched hand of the watchman, reached the jetty and walked into the office. Two of the clerks were still working there, and she came back hastily to her mother with the story of the captain's death unmistakably confirmed.

Mrs. Tipping, loath to accept defeat, stood for some time in consideration. "What had Captain Flower to do with Mr. Robinson?" she asked at length, turning to Fraser.

"Can't say," was the reply.

"Have you ever seen Mr. Robinson?" enquired the girl.

"I saw him one night," said the other, after some deliberation. "Rather good-looking man, bright blue eyes, good teeth, and a jolly laugh."

"Are you likely to see him again?" enquired Miss Tipping, nodding in confirmation of these details.

"Not now poor Flower's gone," replied Fraser. "I fancy we shipped some cases of rifles for him one night. The night you first came. I don't know what it all was about, but he struck me as being rather a secretive sort of man."

"He was that," sighed Miss Tipping, shaking her head.

"I heard him say that night," said the mate, forgetful of his recent longings after truth, "that he was off abroad. He said that something was spoiling his life, I remember, but that duty came first."

"There, do you hear that, mother?" said Miss Tipping.

"Yes, I hear," said the other, with an aggressive sniff, as she moved slowly to the side. "But I'm not satisfied that the captain is dead. They'd tell us anything. You've not seen the last of me, young man, I can tell you."

"I hope not," said Fraser, cordially. "Any time the ship's up in London and you care to come down, I shall be pleased to see you."

Mrs. Tipping, heated with the climb, received this courtesy with coldness, and having enquired concerning the fate of Captain Flower of six different people, and verified their accounts from the landlord of the public-house at the corner, to whom she introduced herself with much aplomb as being in the profession, went home with her daughter, in whom depression, in its most chronic form, had settled in the form of unfilial disrespect.

Two hours later the Foam got under way, and, after some heated language owing to the watchman mistaking Mr. Green's urbanity for sarcasm, sailed slowly down the river. The hands were unusually quiet, but their behaviour passed unnoticed by the new skipper, who was too perturbed by the falsehoods he had told and those he was about to tell to take much heed of anything that was passing.

"I thought you said you preferred to keep for-'ard?" he said to Ben, as that worthy disturbed his meditations next morning by bustling into the cabin and taking his seat at the breakfast table.

"I've changed my mind; the men don't know their place," said the mate, shortly.

Fraser raised his eyebrows.

"Forget who I am," said Ben, gruffly. "I was never one to take much count of such things, but when it comes to being patted on the back by an A. B., it's time to remind 'em."

"Did they do that?" said Fraser, in a voice of horror.

"Joe did," said Ben. "'E won't do it ag'in, I don't think. I didn't say anything, but I think 'e knows my feelings."

"There's your berth," said Fraser, indicating it with a nod.

Ben grunted in reply, and being disinclined for conversation, busied himself with the meal, and as soon as he had finished went up on deck.

"Wot yer been down there for, Bennie?" asked Joe, severely, as he appeared; "your tea's all cold."

"I've 'ad my breakfast with the skipper," said Ben, shortly.

"You was always fond of your stummick, Bennie," said Joe, shaking his head, sorrowfully. "I don't think much of a man wot leaves his old mates for a bit o' bacon."

The new mate turned away from him haughtily, "Tim," he said, sharply.

"Yes, Ben," said the youth. "Why, wot's the matter? Wot are you looking like that for? Ain't you well?" "Wot did you call me?" demanded the new mate.

"I didn't call you anything," said the startled Tim.

"Let me 'ear you call me Ben ag'in and you'll hear of it," said the other, sharply. "Go and clean the brasswork."

The youth strolled off, gasping, with an envious glance at the cook, who, standing just inside the galley, cheerfully flaunted a saucepan he was cleaning, as though defying the mate to find him any work to do.

"Bill," said the mate.

"Sir," said the polite seaman.

"Help Joe scrub paintwork," was the reply.

"Me!" broke in the indignant Joe.

"Scrub—Look 'ere, Ben."

"Pore old Joe," said the cook, who had not forgiven him for the previous night's affair. "Pore old Joe."

"Don't stand gaping about," commanded the new mate. "Liven up there."

"It don't want cleaning. I won't do it," said Joe, fiercely.

"I've give my orders," said the new mate, severely; "if they ain't attended to, or if I 'ear any more about not doing 'em, you'll hear of it. The idea o' telling me you won't do it. The idea o' setting such an example to the young 'uns. The idea—Wot are you making that face for?"

"I've got the earache," retorted Joe, with bitter sarcasm.

"I thought you would 'ave, Joe," said the vengeful cook, retiring behind a huge frying-pan, "when I 'eard you singing this morning."

Fraser, coming on deck, was just in time to see a really creditable imitation of a famous sculpture as represented by Joe, Tim, and Ben, but his criticism was so sharp and destructive that the group at once broke and never re-formed. Indeed, with a common foe in the person of Ben, the crew adjusted their own differences, and by the time Seabridge was in sight were united by all the fearful obligations of a secret society of which Joe was the perpetual president.

Captain Barber, with as much mourning as he could muster at such short notice, was waiting on the quay. His weather-beaten face was not quite so ruddy as usual, and Fraser, with a strong sense of shame, fancied, as the old man clambered aboard the schooner, that his movements were slower than of yore.

"This is a dreadful business, Jack," he said, giving him a hearty grip, when at length he stood aboard the schooner.

"Shocking," said Fraser, reddening.

"I've spoken to have the coast-guards look out for him," said the old man. "He may come ashore, and I know he'd be pleased to be put in the churchyard decent."

"I'm sure he would," said Fraser. "I suppose there's no chance of his having been picked up. I slung a life-belt overboard."

Captain Barber shook his head. "It's a mysterious thing," he said slowly; "a man who'd been at sea all his life to go and tumble overboard in calm weather like that."

"There's a lot that's mysterious about it, sir," said Joe, who had drawn near, followed by the others. "I can say that, because I was on deck only a few minutes before it happened."

"Pity you didn't stay up," said Captain Barber, ruefully.

"So I thought, sir," said Joe, "but the mate saw me on deck and made me go below. Two minutes afterwards I heard a splash, and the skipper was overboard."

There was a meaning in his words that there was no mistaking. The old man, looking round at the faces, saw that the mate's was very pale.

"What did he make you go below for?" he asked, turning to Joe.

"Better ask him, sir," replied the seaman. "I wanted to stay up on deck, but I 'ad to obey orders. If I 'ad stayed on deck, he wouldn't have been cap'n."

Captain Barber turned and regarded the mate fixedly; the mate, after a vain attempt to meet his gaze, lowered his eyes to the deck.

"What do you say to all this?" enquired Barber, slowly.

"Nothing," replied the mate. "I did send Joe below and the skipper fell overboard a minute or two afterwards. It's quite true."

"Fell?" enquired Captain Barber.

"Fell," repeated the other, and looked him squarely in the eyes.

For some time Captain Barber said nothing, and the men, finding the silence irksome, shuffled uneasily.

"Fred saved your life once," said Barber, at length.

"He did," replied Fraser.

The old man turned and paced slowly up and down the deck.

"He was my sister's boy," he said, halting in front of the mate, "but he was more like my son. His father and mother were drownded too, but they went down fair and square in a gale. He stuck by his ship, and she stuck by him, God bless her."

Fraser nodded.

"I'm obliged to you for bringing my ship from London," said Barber, slowly. "I sha'n't want you to take 'er back. I sha'n't want you to stay in 'er at all. I don't want to see you again."

"That's as you please," said Fraser, trying to speak unconcernedly. "It's your ship, and it's for you to do as you like about her. I'll put my things together now."

"You don't ask for no reason?" asked Barber, eyeing him wistfully.

The other shook his head. "No," he said, simply, and went below.

He came up some little time later with his belongings in a couple of chests, and, the men offering no assistance, put them ashore himself, and hailing a man who was sitting in a cart on the quay, arranged with him to convey them to the station.

"Is 'e to be let go like this?" said Joe, hotly.

"Will you stop me?" demanded Fraser, choking with rage, as he stepped aboard again.

"Joe," said Ben, sharply.

The seaman glared at him offensively.

"Go for'ard," said the new mate, peremptorily, "go for'ard, and don't make yourself so busy."

The seaman, helpless with rage, looked to Captain Barber for guidance, and, the old man endorsing the new mate's order, went forward, indulging in a soliloquy in which Ben as a proper noun was mixed up in the company of many improper adjectives.

Fraser, clambering into the cart, looked back at the Foam. The old man was standing with his hands clasped behind his back looking down on the deck, while the hands stood clumsily by. With an idea that the position had suddenly become intolerable he sat silent until they reached the station, and being for the first time for many months in the possession of a holiday, resolved for various reasons to pay a dutiful visit to his father at Bittlesea.

CHAPTER XI

Captain Barber walked to his house in thoughtful mood, and sighed as he thought of the uncertainty of life and the futility of earthly wishes. The blinds at his windows were all decently drawn, while the Union Jack drooped at half-mast in the front garden. He paused at the gate, with a strong distaste for encountering the subdued gloom and the wealth of womanly love which awaited him indoors, and bethinking himself of the masterless state of his craft, walked slowly back and entered the Thorn Inn.

"No news, I suppose, Captain Barber?" said the landlady, regarding him with great sympathy.

The captain shook his head, and exchanging greetings with a couple of neighbours, ordered something to drink.

"It's wonderful how you bear up, I'm sure," said the landlady. "When my poor dear died I cried every day for five weeks. I came down to skin and bone almost."

"Well, if I was you—" said the old man, irritably, and regarding the lady's ample proportions with an unfavourable eye.

"What?" enquired the other, pausing with her fingers on the whisky-tap.

"If I was you," repeated Captain Barber, slowly, in order to give time for full measure, "I should go an' cry for five months all day and all night."

The landlady put the glass in front of him sharply, and after giving him his change without looking at him, thoughtfully wiped down the counter.

"Mrs. Church quite well?" she enquired, with studied artlessness.

"Quite well," replied the captain, scenting danger.

The landlady, smiling amiably, subsided into a comfortable Windsor-chair, and shook her head at him so severely that, against his better sense, he felt compelled to demand an explanation.

"There, there," replied the landlady, "get along with you, do! Innocence!"

"It's no good, Cap'n Barber," said one of the customers, with the best intentions in the world.

"It struck me all of a heap," said the landlady.

"So it did me," said the other man.

"My missus knew it all along," said the first man; "she said she knew it by the way they looked at one another."

"Might I ask who you're talking of?" demanded the incensed Barber, who had given up the effort to appear unconscious as being beyond his powers.

"A young engaged couple," said the landlady.

The captain hesitated. "What have you been shaking your head at me and telling me it's no good for, then?" he demanded.

"At your pretending not to have heard of it," said the landlady.

"I have not 'eard of it," said Captain Barber, fiercely, as he took up his glass and walked towards the parlour. "I've got something better to do than talk about my neighbours' affairs."

"Yes, of course you have," said the landlady. "We know that."

The indignant Barber closed the door behind him with a bang, and, excited with the controversy, returned with a short and suspicious nod the greeting of a small man of shrunken and forlorn aspect who was sitting at the other side of the room.

"Mornin', Cap'n Nibletts," he growled.

"Mornin, sir," said Nibletts; "how's things?"

Captain Barber shook his head. "Bad as bad can be," he replied, slowly; "there's no hope at all. I'm looking for a new master for my vessel."

Nibletts looked up at him eagerly, and then looked away again. His last command had hoisted the green flag at the mouth of the river in a position which claimed attention, respect, and profanity from every craft which passed, its master having been only saved from the traditional death of the devoted shipmaster by the unpardonable conduct of the mate, who tore him from his craft by the scruff of his neck and the seat of his trousers.

"What about Harris?" he suggested.

"I don't like Harris's ways," said Barber, slowly.

"Well, what about Fletcher?" said Nibletts.

"Fletcher's ways are worse than wot Harris's ways are," commented Captain Barber.

"I can understand you being careful," said Captain Nibletts; "she's the prettiest little craft that ever sailed out of Seabridge. You can't be too careful.".

"If things 'ad been different," said the gratified owner, rolling his whisky round his mouth and swallowing it gently, "I'd have liked you to have 'ad her."

"Thankee," said Nibletts, quietly.

There was a pause, during which both men eyed the noble specimens of fish which are preserved for tavern parlours. Captain Barber took another sip of whisky.

"I'm going to use my own judgment, Nibletts," he said slowly. "I've always rose superior to the opinions of other people. There's nobody you know would give you a ship. I'm going to give you the Foam!"

Captain Nibletts, rising from his seat, crossed over, and taking his hand, thanked him in broken accents for this overpowering expression of confidence in him. Then he walked back, and taking his whisky from the table, threw it on the floor.

"I've had enough of that," he said briefly. "When am I to take her over, Cap'n Barber?"

"So soon as ever you please," said his benefactor. "Old Ben'll stay on as mate; Fraser's gone."

Captain Nibletts thanked him again, and, clapping on his hard hat, passed hastily into the bar, his small visage twisted into a smile, to which it had long been a stranger. With the customers in the bar he exchanged remarks of so frivolous a nature in passing that the landlady nearly dropped the glass she was wiping, and then, crimson with indignation, as the door swung behind him, realised that the melancholy and usually respectful Nibletts had thought fit to publicly address her as "Gertie."

In the same high spirits the new master swung hastily down the road to his new command. Work had already commenced, and the energetic Ben, having been pushed over once by a set of goods in the slings owing to the frantic attempts of the men at the hand-crane to keep pace with his demands, was shouting instructions from a safe distance. He looked round as Nibletts stepped aboard, and, with a wary eye on the crane, bustled towards him.

"Wot can we do for you, Cap'n Nibletts?" he enquired, with a patronising air.

"I'm to be master," replied the other, quietly.

"You?" said Ben, with offensive astonishment, as he saw the death of his own ambitious hopes in that quarter. "You to be master?"

Nibletts nodded and coloured. "Cap'n Barber just gave me the berth," he remarked.

Ben sighed and shook his head. "He'll never be the same man ag'in," he affirmed, positively; "'e went away: from 'ere dazed, quite dazed. 'Ow was 'e when you saw 'im?"

"He was all right," was the reply.

Ben shook his head as one who knew better. "I 'ope he won't get no more shocks," he observed, gravely. "It'll be nice for you to get to sea ag'in, Cap'n."

Captain Nibletts raised his weather-beaten countenance and sniffed the air with relish.

"You'll be able to see the Diadem as we go by," continued the sorely-aggravated Ben. "There's just her masts showing at 'igh water."

A faint laugh rose from somebody in the hold, and Nibletts, his face a dull red, stole quietly below and took possession of his new quarters. In the course of the day he transferred his belongings to the schooner, and, as though half fearful that his new command might yet slip through his fingers, slept on board.

On the way back to London a sum in simple proportion, set by Joe, helped to exercise the minds of the crew in the rare intervals which the new mate allowed them for relaxation: "If Ben was bad on the fust v'y'ge, and much wuss on the second, wot 'ud he be like on the tenth?" All agreed that the answer would require a lot of working. They tarred the rigging, stropped the blocks, and in monkey-like attitudes scraped the masts. Even the cook received a little instruction in his art, and estranged the affections of all hands by a "three-decker," made under Ben's personal supervision.

The secret society discussed the matter for some time in vain. The difficulty was not so much in inventing modes of retaliation as in finding some bold spirit to carry them out. In vain did the president allot tasks to his admiring followers, preceded by excellent reasons why he should not perform them himself. The only one who showed any spirit at all was Tim, and he, being ordered to spill a little tar carelessly from aloft, paid so much attention to the adverb that Joe half killed him when he came down again.

Then Mr. William Green, having learnt that the mate was unable to read, did wonders with a piece of chalk and the frying pan, which he hung barometer fashion outside the galley when the skipper was below, the laughter of the delighted crew bearing witness to the success of his efforts, laughter which became almost uncontrollable as the mate, with as stately an air as he could assume, strode towards the galley and brought up in front of the frying-pan.

"Wot's all that, cook?" he demanded, pointing to the writing.

"Wot, sir?" asked the innocent.

"On the frying-pan," replied Ben, scowling.

"That's chalk-marks," explained the cook, "to clean it with."

"It looks to me like writing," snapped the mate.

"Lor, no, sir," said the cook, with a superior smile.

"I say it does," said Ben, stamping.

"Well, o' course you know best, sir," said the cook, humbly. "I ain't nothing of a scholard myself. If it's writing, wot does it say, please?"

"I don't say it is writing," growled the old man. "I say it looks like it."

"I can assure you you're mistook, sir," said the cook, blandly; "you see, I clean the sorsepans the same way. I only 'eard of it lately. Look 'ere."

He placed the articles in question upside down in a row on the deck, and Tim, reading the legends inscribed thereon, and glancing from them to the mate, was hastily led below in an overwrought condition by the flattered Mr. Green.

"Cook," said the mate, ferociously.

"Sir," said the other.

"I won't 'ave the sorsepans cleaned that way.

"No, sir," said the cook, respectfully, "it does make 'em larf, don't it, sir, though I can't see wot they're larfing at any more than wot you can."

The mate walked off fuming, and to his other duties added that of inspector of pots and pans, a condition of things highly offensive to the cook, inasmuch as certain culinary arrangements of his, only remotely connected with cleanliness, came in for much unskilled comment.

The overworked crew went ashore at the earliest possible moment after their arrival in London, in search of recuperative draughts. Ben watched them a trifle wistfully as they moved off, and when Nibletts soon after followed their example without inviting him to join him in a social glass of superior quality, smiled mournfully as he thought of the disadvantages of rank.

He sat for some time smoking in silence, monarch of all he surveyed, and then, gazing abstractedly at the silent craft around him, fell into a pleasant dream, in which he saw himself in his rightful position as master of the Foam, and Nibletts, cashiered for drunkenness, coming to him for employment before the mast. His meditations were disturbed by a small piece of coal breaking on the deck, at which he looked lazily, until, finding it followed by two other pieces, he reluctantly came to the conclusion that they were intended for him. A fourth piece, better aimed, put the matter beyond all reasonable doubt, and, looking up sharply, he caught the watchman in the act of launching the fifth.

"Hullo, old 'un," said George, cheerfully, "I thought you was asleep."

"You thought wrong, then," said the mate, sourly; "don't you do that ag'in."

"Why, did I 'urt you?" said the other, surprised at his tone.

"Next time you want to chuck coal at anybody," continued Ben, with dignity, "pick out one o' the 'ands; mates don't like 'aving coal chucked at 'em by watchmen."

"Look who we are," gasped the petrified George. "Look who we are," he repeated, helplessly. "Look who we are."

"Keep your place, watchman," said the mate, severely; "keep your place, and I'll keep mine."

The watchman regarded him for some time in genuine astonishment, and then, taking his old seat on the post, thrust his hands in his pockets, and gave utterance to this shocking heresy, "Mates ain't nothing."

"You mind your business, watchman," said the nettled Ben, "and I'll mind mine."

"You don't know it," retorted the other, breathing heavily; "be—sides, you don't look like a mate. I wouldn't chuck coal at a real mate."

He said no more, but sat gazing idly up and down the river with a face from which all expression had been banished, except when at intervals his gaze rested upon the mate, when it lit up with an expression of wonder and joy which made the muscles ache with the exercise.

He was interrupted in this amusement by the sound of footsteps and feminine voices behind him; the indefatigable Tippings were paying another of their informal visits, and, calmly ignoring his presence, came to the edge of the jetty and discussed ways and means of boarding the schooner.

"Mr. Fraser's gone," said the watchman, politely and loudly, "there's a new skipper now, and that tall, fine, 'andsome, smart, good-looking young feller down there is the new mate."

The new mate, looking up fiercely, acknowledged the introduction with an inhospitable stare, a look which gave way to one of anxiety as Mrs. Tipping, stepping into the rigging, suddenly lost her nerve, and, gripping it tightly, shook it in much the same fashion as a stout bluebottle shakes the web of a spider.

"Hold tight, mar," cried her daughter, excitedly.

The watchman stepped into the rigging beside her, and patted her soothingly on the back; the mate, coming to the side, took her foot and assisted her to reach the deck. Miss Tipping followed, and the elder lady, after recovering from the shock caused by her late peril, fell to discussing the eternal subject of Mr. Robinson with the new mate.

"No, I never see 'im," said Ben, thoughtfully; "I never heard of him till you come asking arter 'im.

"You must make up your mind he's gone," said Mrs. Tipping, turning to her daughter, "that's what I keep telling you. I never was so tired of anything in my life as tramping down here night after night. It ain't respectable."

"You needn't come," said the other, dutifully. "He was last heard of on this ship, and where else am I to look for him? You said you'd like to find him yourself."

"I should," said Mrs. Tipping, grimly; "I should. Me an' him are to have a little talk, if ever we do meet."

"If he ever comes aboard this ship," said the mate, firmly, "I'll tackle him for you."

"Find out where he lives," said Mrs. Tipping, eagerly.

"And let us know," added her daughter, giving him a card; "that's our address, and any time you're up our way we shall be very pleased to see you, Mr.——"

"Brown," said the mate, charmed with their manners. "Mr. Brown."

"Ben," cried a voice from the wharf.

The new mate gazed austerely at the small office-boy above.

"Letter for the mate," said the youth, who was unversed in recent history; "catch."

He pitched it to the deck and walked off whistling. There was only one mate in Ben's world, and he picked the letter up and put it in his pocket.

"Don't mind us, if you want to read it," said Mrs. Tipping, kindly.

"Only business, I expect," said Ben, grandly.

He took it from his pocket, and, tearing the envelope, threw it aside and made a feint of reading the contents.

"Not bad news, I hope?" said Mrs. Tipping, noticing his wrinkled brow.

"I can't read without my glasses," said the mate, with a measure of truth in the statement. He looked at Mrs. Tipping, and saw a chance of avoiding humiliation.

"P'r'aps you'd just look at it and see if it's important," he suggested.

Mrs. Tipping took the letter from him, and, after remarking on the strangeness of the handwriting, read aloud:—

"Dear Jack:—If you want to see Mr. Norton, come to 10, John Street, Walworth, and be careful nobody sees you."

"Jack," said the mate, stooping for the envelope.

"Why it must be meant for Mr.—for Jack Fraser."

"Careful nobody sees you," murmured Miss Tipping, excitedly, as she took the envelope from the mate; "why, the address is printed by hand."

Mother and daughter looked at each other. It was evident that their thoughts were similar, and that one could have known them without the expenditure of the proverbial penny.

"I'll give it to him when I see him," remarked Ben, thrusting the letter in his pocket. "It don't seem to be important. He ain't in London, at present, I don't think."

"I shouldn't think it was important at all," said Mrs. Tipping, soothingly.

"Not at all," echoed her daughter, whose cheek was burning with excitement. "Good-night, Mr. Brown."

Ben bade them good-night, and in his capacity of host walked up the wharf with them and saw them depart.

"Nice little thing, ain't she?" said the watchman who was standing there, after Mrs. Tipping had bidden the mate good-bye; "be careful wot you're a-doin' of, Ben. Don't go and spile yourself by a early marriage, just as you're a-beginning to get on in life. Besides, a mate might do better than that, and she'd only marry you for your persition."

CHAPTER XII

In happy ignorance of the changes caused by his sudden and tragic end, Captain Flower sat at the open window of his shabby Walworth lodging, smoking an after-breakfast pipe, and gazing idly into the dismal, littered yard beneath. Time—owing to his injured foot, which, neatly bandaged at a local dispensary, rested upon a second chair—hung rather heavily upon his hands as he sat thinking of ways and means of spending the next six months profitably and pleasantly. He had looked at the oleographs on the walls until he was tired, and even the marvels of the wax fruit under a cracked glass shade began to pall upon him.

"I'll go and stay in the country a bit," he muttered; "I shall choke here."

He took a slice of bread from the tray, and breaking it into small pieces, began to give breakfast to three hens which passed a precarious existence in the yard below.

"They get quite to know you now," said the small but shrewd daughter of the house, who had come in to clear the breakfast things away. "How'd you like your egg?"

"Very good," said Flower.

"It was new laid," said the small girl.

She came up to the window and critically inspected the birds. "She laid it," she said, indicating one of the three.

"She's not much to look at," said Flower, regarding the weirdest-looking of the three with some interest.

"She's a wonderful layer," said Miss Chiffers, "and as sharp as you make 'em. When she's in the dust-bin the others 'ave to stay outside. They can go in when she's 'ad all she wants."

"I don't think I'll have any more eggs," said Flower, casually. "I'm eating too much. Bacon'll do by itself."

"Please yourself," said Miss Chiffers, turning from the window. "How's your foot?"

"Better," said Flower.

"It's swelled more than it was yesterday," she said, with ill-concealed satisfaction.

"It feels better," said the captain.

"That's 'cos it's goin' dead," said the damsel; "then it'll go black all up your leg, and then you'll 'ave to 'ave it orf."

Flower grinned comfortably.

"You may larf," said the small girl, severely; "but you won't larf when you lose it, an' all becos you won't poultice it with tea leaves."

She collected the things together on a tea tray of enormous size, and holding it tightly pressed to her small waist, watched with anxious eyes as the heavy articles slowly tobogganed to the other end. A knife fell outside the door, and the loaf, after a moment's hesitation which nearly upset the tray, jumped over the edge and bounded downstairs.

Flower knocked the ashes out of his pipe, and slowly refilling it, began to peruse the morning paper, looking in vain, as he had looked each morning, for an account of his death.

His reading was interrupted by a loud knock at the street door, and he threw down the paper to be ready to receive the faithful Fraser. He heard the door open, and then the violent rushing upstairs of Miss Chiffers to announce his visitor.

"Somebody to see you, Mr. Norton," she panted, bursting into the room.

"Well, show him up," said Flower.

"All of 'em?" demanded Miss Chiffers.

"Is there more than one?" enquired Flower in a startled voice.

"Three," said Miss Chiffers, nodding; "two gentlemen and a lady."

"Did they say what their names were?" enquired the other, turning very pale.

Miss Chiffers shook her head, and then stooped to pick up a hairpin. "One of 'em's called Dick," she said, replacing the pin.

"Tell them I'm not at home," said Flower, hastily, "but that I shall be back at twelve o'clock, See?"

He produced a shilling, and the small girl, with an appreciative nod, left the room, and closed the door behind her. Flower, suffering severely from nervous excitement, heard a discussion in the passage below, and then sounds of a great multitude coming upstairs and opening various doors on its way, in spite of the indignant opposition afforded by the daughter of the house.

"What's in here?" enquired a well-known voice, as a hand was placed on his door handle.

"Nothing," said Miss Chiffers; "'ere, you go away, that's my bedroom. Go away, d'you 'ear?"

There was the sound of a diminutive scuffle outside, then the door opened and a smartly-dressed young man, regardless of the fair form of Miss Chiffers, which was coiled round his leg, entered the room.

"Why, Dick," said the skipper, rising, "Dick! Thank goodness it's you."

"I've no doubt you're delighted," said Mr. Tipping, coldly. "What are you doing with that knife?"

"I thought it was somebody else," said Flower, putting it down. "I thought it was another attempt on my life."

Mr. Tipping coughed behind his hand and murmured something inaudibly as his sister entered the room, followed by the third member of the party.

"Oh, Fred!" she said, wildly, "I wonder you can look me in the face. Where have you been all this time? Where have you been?"

"Give the man time to think," said her brother, exchanging a glance with the other man.

"I've been everywhere," said Flower, facing them defiantly. "I've been hunted all over the country."

"But where did you go when you left me that day?" enquired Miss Tipping.

"It's a long story," said Flower, slowly. "But you got the letter I wrote you?"

Miss Tipping shook her head.

"You didn't get it?" said Flower, in surprise. "I can't think what you must have thought of me."

"I'll tell you what I thought of you, if you'd like to know," interrupted Mr. Tipping, eagerly.

"I wrote to you to explain," said Flower, glibly "I went abroad suddenly, called away at a moment's notice."

"Special trains and all that sort o' thing, I s'pose," said Mr. Tipping, with interest.

"Dick," said Miss Tipping, fiercely.

"Well," said Dick, gruffly.

"Hold your tongue."

"I've not had any real sleep since," said Flower, pathetically, "what with the danger and thinking of you."

"Why didn't you write again?" enquired Miss Tipping.

"I asked you to write to a certain address in that letter I sent you," said Flower, "and when I came back to England and found there was no letter, I concluded that you couldn't forgive me."

Miss Tipping looked at him reproachfully, but Mr. Tipping, raising his eyes, gasped for air.

"But who are these enemies?" asked Miss Tipping, tenderly drawing closer to Flower.

"A man in the Government service——" began the captain.

He broke off disdainfully until such time as Mr. Tipping should have conquered a somewhat refractory cough.

"In the secret service," continued Flower, firmly, "has got enemies all round him."

"You'll have to get something else to do when we are married, Fred," said Miss Tipping, tearfully.

"You've forgiven me, then?" said Flower, hoping that he had concealed a nervous start.

"I'd forgive you anything, Fred," said Miss Tipping, tenderly; "you'll have to give up this job at once."

Captain Flower shook his head and smiled mournfully, thereby intimating that his services were of too valuable a nature for any Government to lightly dispense with.

"May I come round and see you to-morrow?" he enquired, putting his arm about the lady's waist.

"Come round to-morrow?" repeated Miss Tipping, in surprise; "why, you don't think I'm going to leave you here surrounded by dangers? You're coming home with us now."

"No, to-morrow," said the unhappy mariner, in a winning voice.

"You don't go out of my sight again," said Miss Tipping, firmly. "Dick, you and Fred shake hands."

The two gentlemen complied. Both were somewhat proud of their grip, and a bystander might have mistaken their amiable efforts to crush each other's fingers for the outward and visible signs of true affection.

"You'd better settle up here now, Fred," said Miss Tipping.

Flower, putting the best face he could upon it, assented with a tender smile, and, following them downstairs, held a long argument with Mrs. Chiffers as to the amount due, that lady having ideas upon the subject which did more credit to her imagination than her arithmetic.

The bill was settled at last, and the little party standing on the steps waited for the return of Miss Chiffers, who had been dispatched for a four-wheeler.

"Oh, what about your luggage, Fred?" enquired Miss Tipping, suddenly.

"Haven't got any," said Flower, quickly. "I managed to get away with what I stand up in, and glad to do that."

Miss Tipping squeezed his arm and leaned heavily upon his shoulder.

"I was very lucky to get off as I did," continued the veracious mariner. "I wasn't touched except for a rap over my foot with the butt-end of a revolver. I was just over the wall in time."

"Poor fellow," said Miss Tipping, softly, as she shivered and looked up into his face. "What are you grinning at, Dick?"

"I s'pose a fellow may grin if he likes," said Mr. Tipping, suddenly becoming serious.

"This is the first bit of happiness I've had since I saw you last," murmured Flower.

Miss Tipping squeezed his arm again.

"It seems almost too good to be true," he continued. "I'm almost afraid I shall wake up and find it all a dream."

"Oh, you're wide-awake enough," said Mr. Tipping.

"Wide-awake ain't the word for it," said the other gentleman, shaking his head.

"Uncle," said Miss Tipping, sharply.

"Yes, my dear," said the other, uneasily.

"Keep your remarks for those that like them," said his dutiful niece, "or else get out and walk."

Mr. Porson, being thus heckled, subsided into defiant mutterings, intended for Dick Tipping's ear alone, and the remainder of the drive to Chelsea passed almost in silence. Arrived at the Blue Posts, Flower got out with well-simulated alacrity, and going into the bar, shook hands heartily with Mrs. Tipping before she quite knew what he was doing.

"You've got him, then," she said, turning to her daughter, "and now I hope you're satisfied. Don't stand in the bar; I can't say what I want to say here—come in the parlour and shut the door."

They followed the masterful lady obediently into the room indicated.

"And now, Mr. Robinson," she said, with her hands on her hips, "now for your explanation."

"I have explained to Matilda," said Flower, waving his hand.

"That's quite right, mar," said Miss Tipping, nodding briskly.

"He's had a dreadful time, poor feller," said Dick Tipping, unctuously. "He's been hunted all over England by—who was it, Mister Robinson?"

"The parties I'm working against," said Flower, repressing his choler by a strong effort.

"The parties he's working against," repeated Mr. Tipping.

"Somebody ought to talk to them parties," said Mr. Porson, speaking with much deliberation, "that is, if they can find 'em."

"They want looking after, that's what they want," said Dick Tipping, with a leer.

"It's all very well for you to make fun of it," said Mrs. Tipping, raising her voice. "I like plain, straightforward dealing folk myself. I don't under-stand nothing about your secret services and Governments and all that sort of thing. Mr. Robinson, have you come back prepared to marry my daughter? Because, if you ain't, we want to know why not."

"Of course I have," said Flower, hotly. "It's the dearest wish of my life. I should have come before, only I thought when she didn't answer my letter that she had given me up."

"Where 'ave you been, and what's it all about?" demanded Mrs. Tipping.

"At present," said Flower, with an appearance of great firmness, "I can't tell you. I shall tell Matilda the day after we're married—if she'll still trust me and marry me—and you shall all know as soon as we think it's safe."

"You needn't say another word, mar," said Miss Tipping, warningly.

"I'm sure," said the elder lady, bridling. "Perhaps your uncle would like to try and reason with you."

Mr. Porson smiled in a sickly fashion, and cleared his throat.

"You see, my dear—" he began.

"Your tie's all shifted to one side," said his niece, sternly, "and the stud's out of your buttonhole. I wish you'd be a little tidier when you come here, uncle; it looks bad for the house."

"I came away in a hurry to oblige you," said Mr. Porson. "I don't think this is a time to talk about button-holes."

"I thought you were going to say something," retorted Miss Tipping, scathingly, "and you might as well talk about that as anything else."

"It ain't right," said Mrs. Tipping, breaking in, "that you should marry a man you don't know anything about; that's what I mean. That's only reasonable, I think."

"It's quite fair," said Flower, trying hard to speak reluctantly. "Of course, if Matilda wishes, I'm quite prepared to go away now. I don't wish her to tie herself up to a man who at present, at any rate, has to go about wrapped in a mystery."

"All the same," said Mrs. Tipping, with a gleam in her eyes, "I'm not going to have anybody playing fast and loose with my daughter. She's got your ring on her finger. You're engaged to be married to her, and you mustn't break it off by running away or anything of that kind. If she likes to break it off, that's a different matter."

"I'm not going to break it off," said Miss Tipping, fiercely; "I've made all the arrangements in my own mind. We shall get married as soon as we can, and I shall put Dick in here as manager, and take a nice little inn down in the country somewhere."

"Mark my words," said Mrs. Tipping, solemnly, "you'll lose him again."

"If I lose him again," said Miss Tipping, dramatically, "if he's spirited away by these people, or anything happens to him, Dick won't be manager here. Uncle Porson will have as much drink and as many cigars as he pays for, and Charlie will find another berth."

"Nobody shall hurt a hair of his head," said Mr. Tipping, with inimitable pathos.

"He must be protected against hisself," said Mr. Porson, spitefully; "that's the 'ardest part. He's a man what if 'e thinks it's his dooty 'll go away just as 'e did before."

"Well if he gets away from Charlie," said Mr. Tipping, "he'll be cute. There's one thing, Mr. Robinson: if you try to get away from those who love you and are looking after you, there'll be a fight first, then there'll be a police court fuss, and then we shall find out what the Government mean by it."

Captain Flower sat down in an easy posture as though he intended a long stay, and in a voice broken with emotion murmured something about home, and rest, and freedom from danger.

"That's just it," said Mrs. Tipping, "here you are, and here you'll stay. After you're married, it'll be Matilda's affair; and now let's have some tea."

"First of all, mar, kiss Fred," said Miss Tipping, who had been eyeing her parent closely.

Mrs. Tipping hesitated, but the gallant captain, putting a good face on it, sprang up and, passing his arm about her substantial waist, saluted her, after which, as a sort of set-off, he kissed Miss Tipping.

"I can only say," he said truthfully, "that this kindness hurts me. The day I'm married I'll tell you all."

CHAPTER XIII

In happy ignorance that the late master of the Foam had secured a suite of rooms at the Blue Posts Hotel, the late mate returned to London by train with a view of getting into communication with him as soon as possible. The delay occasioned by his visit to Bittlesea was not regretted, Mr. Fraser senior having at considerable trouble and expense arranged for him to take over the Swallow at the end of the week.

Owing to this rise in his fortune he was in fairly good spirits, despite the slur upon his character, as he made his way down to the wharf. The hands had knocked off work for the day, and the crew of the schooner, having finished their tea, were sprawling in the bows smoking in such attitudes of unstudied grace as best suited the contours of their figures. Joe looked up as he approached, and removing his pipe murmured something inaudible to his comrades.

"The mate's down below, sir," said Mr. William Green in reply to Fraser. "I shall be pleased to fetch him."

He walked aft and returned shortly, followed by Ben, who, standing stiffly before his predecessor, listened calmly to his eager enquiry about his letter.

"No, there's been nothing for you," he said, slowly. He had dropped the letter overboard as the simplest way of avoiding unpleasantness. "Was you expecting one?"

Fraser, gazing blankly at him, made no reply, being indeed staggered by the thoroughness with which he imagined the wily Flower was playing his part.

"He's going to be lost his full six months, that's evident," he thought, in consternation. "He must have seen the way I should be affected; it would serve him right to tell the whole thing right away to Captain Barber."

"If anything does come I'll send it on to you," said Ben, who had been watching him closely.

"Thanks," said Fraser, pondering, and walked away with his eyes on the ground. He called in at the office as he passed it; the staff had gone, but the letter-rack which stood on the dusty, littered mantel-piece was empty, and he went into the street again.

His programme for the evening thus suddenly arrested, he walked slowly up Tower Hill into the Minories, wondering what to do with himself. Something masquerading as a conscience told him severely that he ought to keep his promise to the errant Flower and go and visit Poppy; conscience without any masquerading at all told him he was a humbug, and disclaimed the responsibility. In the meantime, he walked slowly in the direction of Poplar, and having at length made up a mind which had been indulging in civil war all the way, turned up Liston Street and knocked at the Wheelers' door.

A murmur of voices' from the sitting-room stopped instantly. A double knock was a rare occurrence on that door, and was usually the prelude to the sudden disappearance of the fairer portion of the family, while a small boy was told off to answer it, under dire penalties if he officiated too soon.

This evening, however, the ladies had made their toilet, and the door was opened after a delay merely sufficient to enable them to try and guess the identity of the guest before the revelation. Poppy Tyrell opened it, and turned upon him eyes which showed the faintest trace of surprise.

"Good evening," said Fraser, holding out his hand.

"Good evening," said the girl.

"Fine weather we're having," said the embarrassed ex-mate, "for June," he added, in justification of the remark.

Miss Tyrell assented gravely, and stood there waiting.

It is probable that two members at least of the family would have been gratified by the disappearance of the caller then and there, but that Mr. Wheeler, a man of great density and no tact whatever, came bustling out into the passage, and having shaken hands in a hearty fashion, told him to put his hat on a nail and come in.

"No news of the cap'n, I suppose?" he asked, solemnly, after Fraser was comfortably seated.

"Not a word," was the reply.

The dock-foreman sighed and shook his head as he reflected on the instability of human affairs. "There's no certainty about anything," he said, slowly. "Only yesterday I was walking down the Commercial Road, and I slipped orf the curb into the road before you could say Jack Robinson."

"Nearly run over?" queried Fraser.

Mr. Wheeler shook his head. "No," he said, quietly.

"Well, what of it?" enquired his son.

"It might just as well have been the edge of the dock as the curb; that's what I mean," said Mr. Wheeler, with a gravity befitting his narrow escape.

"I'm alwis telling you not to walk on the edge, father," said his wife, uneasily.

The dock-foreman smiled faintly. "Dooty must be done," he said, in a firm voice. "I'm quite prepared, my life's insured, and I'm on the club, and some o' the children are getting big now, that's a comfort."

A feeling of depression settled on all present, and Augustus Wheeler, aged eight, having gleaned from the conversation that his sire had received instructions, which he intended promptly to obey, to fall into the dock forthwith, suddenly opened his mouth and gave vent to his affection and despair in a howl so terrible that the ornaments on the mantelpiece shook with it.

"Don't scold 'im," said the dock-foreman, tenderly, as Mrs. Wheeler's thin, shrill voice entered into angry competition with the howl; "never mind, Gussie, my boy, never mind."

This gentleness had no effect, Gussie continuing to roar with much ardour, but watching out of the corner of one tear-suffused eye the efforts of his eldest sister to find her pocket.

"Hold your noise and I'll give you a ha'penny," she said, tartly.

Gussie caught his breath with a sob, but kept steam up, having on some similar occasions been treated with more diplomacy than honesty. But to-day he got the half-penny, together with a penny from the visitor, and, having sold his concern in his father for three halfpence, gloated triumphantly in a corner over his envious peers.

"Death," said Mr. Wheeler, slowly, after silence had been restored, "is always sudden. The most sudden death I knew 'appened to a man who'd been dying for seven years. Nobody seemed to be able to believe he'd gone at last."

"It's a good job he wasn't married," said Mrs. Wheeler, raising herself on her elbow; "sailors 'ave no right to marry at all. If I thought that one 'o my gals was goin' to marry a sailor, I don't know what I shouldn't do. Something steady on shore is the thing."

"I don't know," said the tactless Mr. Wheeler. "I think if I was a gal I should like to marry a sailor; there's something romantic about them. I often wish I'd been a sailor."

"Then you wouldn't 'ave 'ad me," said the lady from the sofa, grimly.

Mr. Wheeler sighed, but whether at the thought of what he might have lost or what he had gained, cannot be safely determined. Still in a morbid mood, he relapsed into silence, leaving Fraser to glance anxiously to where Poppy, pale and pretty, sat listening to the clumsy overtures of Mr. Bob Wheeler.

"I might 'ave 'ad two or three sailors if I'd liked," continued Mrs. Wheeler, musingly, "but I wouldn't."

Fraser murmured his admiration at her firmness.

"There was Tom Rogers, 'e was the first," said Mrs. Wheeler; "you remember 'im, father?"

"Chap with bow legs and a squint, wasn't he?" said the dock-foreman, anxious to please.

"I never saw 'im squint," said his wife, sharply. "Then there was Robert Moore—he was number two, I think."

"'Ad a wife a'ready," said Mr. Wheeler, turning to the visitor; "'e was a bright lot, 'e was."

"I don't know what they saw in me, I'm sure," said Mrs. Wheeler, with a little modest laugh; "it wasn't my good looks, I'm sure."

"You 'ad something better than good looks, my dear," said the dock-foreman, affectionately, "something what's wore better."

Mrs. Wheeler turned on the sofa, and detecting Gussie in the act of using his mouth as a moneybox, upbraided him shrilly and sent him into a corner. She then brought sundry charges of omission and commission against the other children, until the air was thick with denials and explanations, in the midst of which Fraser turned towards Poppy.

"I want to have a few minutes' talk with you, Miss Tyrell," he said, nervously.

The girl looked up at him. "Yes," she said, gravely.

"I mean alone," continued the other, marvelling at his hardihood; "it's private."

He lowered his voice from a shout to its normal tone as Emma Wheeler in self-defence opened the door and drove the small fry out.

"I've not got my rooms now," said the girl, quietly.

"Well, my dear—" began the dock-foreman.

"Don't interfere, father," said Mrs. Wheeler somewhat sharply. "I'm sure Mr. Fraser needn't mind saying anything before us. It's nothing he's ashamed of, I'm sure."

"Certainly not," said Fraser, sternly, "but it's quite private for all that. Will you put your hat on and come out a little way, Miss Tyrell?"

"That I'm sure she won't," said the energetic Mrs. Wheeler. "She's that particular she won't even go out with Bob, and they're like brother and sister almost. Will she, Bob?"

Mr. Bob Wheeler received the appeal somewhat sullenly, and in a low voice requested his parent not to talk so much. Fraser, watching Poppy closely, saw with some satisfaction a tinge of colour in her cheek, and what in any other person he would have considered a very obstinate appearance about her shapely chin.

"I'll get my hat on, if you'll wait a minute," she said, quietly.

She rose and went upstairs, and Fraser with a cheerful glance at Mrs. Wheeler entered into conversation with her husband about overside work in the docks, until the door was pushed open a little to reveal Miss Tyrell ready for walking.

They walked on for some little time in silence. The sun had set, and even in the close streets of Poplar the evening air was cool and refreshing. When this fact had thoroughly impressed itself on Mr. Fraser's mind he communicated it to Miss Tyrell.

"It's very pleasant," she answered, briefly. "What was it you wanted to talk to me about?"

"About a lot of things," said Fraser. "What a tremendous lot of children there are about here."

Miss Tyrell coldly admitted an obvious fact, and stepping out into the road to avoid spoiling a small maiden's next move at "hop scotch," returned to the pavement to listen to a somewhat lengthy dissertation upon the game in question.

"What did you want to say to me?" she asked at length, turning and regarding him.

"In the first place," said Fraser, "I wanted to tell you that, though nothing has been heard of Captain Flower, I feel certain in my own mind that he has not been drowned."

Miss Tyrell shook her head slowly.

"Then I ought to tell you that I have left the Foam" continued the other. "I think that there is some idea that I knocked Flower overboard to get his place."

The girl turned quickly, and her face flushed. "How absurd," she said, indignantly, and her manner softened.

"Thank you," said Fraser. "If you don't believe it, I don't care what anybody else thinks."

Miss Tyrell, looking straight in front of her, stole a glance at this easily satisfied young man from the corner of her eye. "I should never expect to hear of you doing anything wicked," she said. Fraser thanked her again, warmly. "Or venturesome," added Miss Tyrell, thoughtfully. "You're not the kind."

They walked on in silence; indignant silence on the part of the ex-mate.

"Then you are out of a berth?" said Poppy, not unkindly.

Fraser shook his head and explained. "And I told my father about you," he added, nervously. "He knew Flower very well, and he told me to say that he would be very pleased and proud if you would come down and stay with him at Bittlesea for a time."

"No, thank you," said Miss Tyrell.

"The air would do you good," persisted Fraser; "you could come down by train or come down with me on the Swallow next week."

Miss Tyrell repeated her refusal. "I must stay in London and get something else to do," she said, quietly.

"What do you think of doing?" enquired Fraser.

"Anything I can get," was the reply.

"And in the meantime——" he began, nervously.

"In the meantime I'm living on the Wheelers," said the girl, pressing her lips together; "that was what you were going to say, wasn't it?"

"I was not going to say anything of the kind," said Fraser, warmly. "I was not thinking of it."

"Well, it's true," said Poppy, defiantly.

"It isn't true," said Fraser, "because you will pay them back."

"Shall we turn back?" said the girl.

Fraser turned and walked beside her, and, glancing furtively at the pale, proud face, wondered how to proceed.

"I should be delighted if you would come to Bittlesea," he said, earnestly, "and I'm sure if Flower should ever turn up again, he would say it was the best thing you could have done."

"Thank you, but I prefer to stay here," was the reply, "and I don't wish to be ungrateful, but I wish that people would not trouble me with their charity."

She walked on in silence, with her face averted, until they reached Liston Street, and, stopping at the door, turned to bid him good-bye. Her face softened as she shook hands, and in the depths of her dark eyes as they met his he fancied that he saw a little kindness. Then the door opened, and, before he could renew his invitation, closed behind her as rapidly as Mr. Bob Wheeler could perform the feat.

CHAPTER XIV

When the tide is up and the sun shining, Sea-bridge has attractions which make the absence of visitors something of a marvel to the inhabitants. A wandering artist or two, locally known as "painter-chaps," certainly visit it, but as they usually select subjects for their canvases of which the progressive party of the town are heartily ashamed, they are regarded as spies rather than visitors, and are tolerated rather than welcomed. To a citizen who has for a score of years regretted the decay of his town, the spectacle of a stranger gloating over its ruins and perpetuating them on canvas is calculated to excite strong doubts as to his mental capacity and his fitness to be at large.

On a summer's evening, when the tide is out and the high ground the other side of the river is assuming undefinable shadows, the little town has other charms to the meditative man. Such life as there is, is confined to the taverns and the two or three narrow little streets which comprise the town. The tree-planted walk by the river is almost deserted, and the last light of the dying day is reflected in the pools and mud left by the tide.

Captain Nibletts, slowly pacing along and smoking his pipe in the serenity of the evening, felt these things dimly. His gaze wandered from a shadowy barge crawling along in mid-channel to the cheery red blind of Boatman's Arms, and then to the road in search of Captain Barber, for whom he had been enquiring since the morning. A stout lady stricken in years sat on a seat overlooking the river, and the mariner, with a courteous salutation, besought her assistance.

"I've been looking for him myself," said Mrs. Banks, breathlessly, "and now my Elizabeth's nowhere to be found. She's been out since two o'clock this afternoon."

Nibletts pointed up the road with his pipe. "I see her only ten minutes ago with young Gibson," he said, slowly.

"Which way was they going?" demanded the old lady, rising.

"I don't know," said Nibletts. "I don't think they knew either an' what's more, I don't think they cared."

The old lady resumed her seat, and, folding her hands in her lap, gazed in a troubled fashion across the river, until the figure of another woman coming along the walk brought her back to every-day affairs.

"Why, it's Mrs. Church," said Nibletts. "He's nowhere to be found," he shouted, before she reached them.

"He?" said the widow, slowly. "Who?"

"Cap'n Barber," replied the mariner.

"Oh, indeed," she said, politely. "Good evening, Mrs. Banks."

Mrs. Banks returned the courtesy. "It looks as though Cap'n Barber has run away," she said, with attempted jocularity.

Mrs. Church smiled a superior smile. "He is not far off," she said, quietly.

"Resting, I suppose," said Mrs. Banks, with intent.

Mrs. Church took higher ground. "Of course this sad affair has upset him terribly," she said, gravely. "His is a faithful nature, and he can't for-get. How is Miss Banks bearing up?"

Mrs. Banks, looking up suspiciously, said, "Wonderful, considering," and relapsed into silence until such time as her foe should give her an opening. Mrs. Church took a seat by her side, and Nibletts, with a feeling of something strained in the atmosphere, for which he could not account, resumed his walk.

He was nearly up to Captain Barber's house when he saw a figure come out of the lane by the side, and after glancing furtively in all directions make silently for the door. The watching Nibletts quickening his pace, reached it at almost the same moment.

"Mrs. Banks is looking for you," he said, as he followed him into the parlour.

Captain Barber turned on him a weary eye, but made no reply.

"And Mrs. Church, too; at least, I think so,' continued the other.

"Cap'n Nibletts," said the old man, slowly, "I 'ope you'll never live long enough to be run arter in the way I'm run arter."

The astonished mariner murmured humbly that he didn't think it was at all likely, and also that Mrs. Nibletts would probably have a word or two to say in the matter.

"From the moment I get up to the moment I get to bed, I'm run arter," continued the hapless Barber. "Mrs. Church won't let me go out of 'er sight if she can help it, and Mrs. Banks is as bad as she is. While they was saying nice things to each other this morning in a nasty way I managed to slip out."

"Well, why not get rid o' Mrs. Church?" said the simple Nibletts.

"Rid o' Mrs. Church!" repeated Captain Barber, aghast; "why don't you get rid o' your face, Nibletts?" he asked, by way of comparison merely.

"Because I don't want to," replied the other, flushing.

"Because you can't" said Captain Barber, emphatically. "And no more can't I get rid of 'er. You see, I 'appened to take a little notice of 'er."

"Oh, well," said the other, and sighed and shook his head discouragingly.

"I took a little notice of 'er," repeated Captain Barber, "and then to spare her feelings I 'ad to sort o' let 'er know that I could never marry for Fred's sake, d'ye see? Then on top of all that poor Fred goes and gets drownded."

"But have you promised to marry her?" asked Nibletts, with a cunning look.

"Of course I've not," rejoined Captain Barber, testily; "but when you know as much about wimmen as I do, you'll know that that's got nothing to do with it. It gets took for granted. Mrs. Church's whole manner to me now is that of a engaged young person. If she was sitting here now she'd put 'er hand on top o' mine."

"Not before me?" said Nibletts, in a shocked voice.

"Before the Prince of Wales and all the Royal Family," replied Captain Barber, with conviction. "You've no idea how silly and awkward it makes me feel."

"Here she comes," said Nibletts, in a low voice, "and Mrs. Banks and her daughter, too."

Captain Barber coughed and, sitting upright, strove to look unconcerned as the three ladies came into the room and expressed their pleasure at seeing him.

"I couldn't think what 'ad happened to you," said Mrs. Banks, as she sank panting into a chair, and, unfastening her bonnet-strings, sat regarding him with her hands on her knees.

"I knew he was all right," said Mrs. Church, folding her hands and regarding him with her head on one side; "if anything happened to him I should know if he was a hundred miles away."

She sat down by Captain Barber, and laying her hand upon his, pressed it affectionately. The captain, a picture of misery, exchanged a significant glance with Nibletts, and emitted an involuntary groan.

"Don't take on so," said Mrs. Banks, compassionately. "Do you know, I've got a feeling that poor Fred has been saved!"

"That's my feeling, too," said Captain Barber, in a firm voice.

"It's very likely," said Captain Nibletts, slowly.

"What's easier than for him to have been picked up by a passing vessel, and carried off goodness knows where?" enquired Mrs. Banks, with a glance evenly distributed between her daughter and the housekeeper.

"I heard of a man once who fell overboard," said Captain Nibletts, softly, "and he turned up safe and sound twenty years arter."

"Married man?" enquired Miss Banks, softly.

"He was," said the captain, with the doggedness of a witness under cross-examination.

Mrs. Church turned her eyes upwards. "Fancy the joyful meeting of husband and wife," she said, sentimentally.

"She died just two days afore he turned up," said Captain Nibletts, simply.

There was a frigid silence during which the three ladies, sinking for a time their differences, eyed him with every sign of strong disapprobation, Mrs. Banks giving vent to a sniff which disparaged the whole race of man.

"As for men who fall overboard and get picked up and turn up months afterwards," continued the faithful Nibletts, "why, every sailorman knows scores of 'em."

"I knowed seven," said Captain Barber, with the exactness of untruth. "They didn't seem to think much of it, didn't seem to think it anything unusual, I mean."

"It ain't," said Nibletts, stoutly.

The room relapsed into silence, and Captain Nibletts, finding Mrs. Church's gaze somewhat trying got up to admire a beautiful oil painting on glass in a black frame which hung over the mantelpiece, and after a few encomiums on his host's taste, bade him good-bye.

"I'm coming with you," said Barber, rising; "I've got some business to talk about."

"What, out again," said Mrs. Church, tenderly, "after being on your poor feet all day?"

Captain Barber murmured something inaudible in reply, and taking his hat from the sideboard went out with Nibletts, For a time they trudged along in silence until the latter, who wanted to go to his own home, ventured to ask where they were going.

"All places are alike to me," replied the old man, dismally. "I only want to get away, that's all. She an' Mrs. Banks are sure to have a turn and try and drag me into it."

He clasped his hands behind his back, and, pausing at a turn of the road, looked down upon the little quay below. Out in the river two or three small craft rode at anchor, while a bauble of cheerful voices from a distant boat only served to emphasise the stillness of the evening.

"Looks quiet," said Captain Nibletts, after watching him for some time.

"I'm thinking of my nevy," said Captain Barber, slowly. "I remember me an' my sister bringing 'im here when he was three year old, and I 'ad to carry him all the way back. He put his arms round my neck, and I can smell peppermint-ball now."

Captain Nibletts, who did not quite follow him, attributed the outrage to a young couple who had just passed.

"I'm all alone now," continued Captain Barber, unheeding, "but I don't want to marry. Why not? 'Cos I'm too old, and because it's like beginning where other people leave off."

"Well, make up your mind and tell her so," said the other.

"It wouldn't do any good," said Barber, dolefully.

"Tell her to-night," said Nibletts, "Come into the Thorn and have a glass, just so as to warm you up to it, and then get it over."

Captain Barber made no reply, but turning round led the way slowly back to the inn, and after acknowledging the respectful salutations of the crew of the schooner who were in the bar by ordering the landlady to fill their pots again, led the way into the parlour and began to charge himself for the interview.

That he did not underestimate the difficulties of the ordeal was evident by the extent of his orders, and Captain Nibletts noted with satisfaction as the evening wore on that the old man's spirits were improving considerably. Twice he sent out instructions to the bar to have the men's mugs replenished, a proceeding which led to Mr. William Green being sent by the grateful crew to express their feelings in a neat little speech.

"A very nice-spoken young fellow," said Captain Barber, approvingly.

He had some more whisky, and at the sounds of a step-dance on the brick floor of the adjoining taproom, took up his glass, and, followed by Nibletts, watched the proceedings from the doorway. Mr. William Green, who worshipped wealth and position, sidled up to him, and with much deference discussed the dancing.

He made such a favourable impression that Cap-tain Barber, who was in a semi-maudlin mood, took him by the arm to the now deserted parlour, and ensconcing him in a corner, told him all his troubles and warned him of the pitfalls which beset the feet of good-looking bachelors. Mr. Green was sympathy itself, and for some time sat silently evolving various schemes for the deliverance of his patron.

Captain Nibletts returning to the parlour a little later found them in close consultation. A ray of hope illuminated the somewhat heavy features of the old man, and, catching sight of the captain, he beckoned him to his side.

"Me an' this young man have thought of something," he said, in a voice rendered husky with excitement.

Nibletts waited.

"He's goin' to call at my place," continued the other, "and tell Mrs. Church that I've been took unwell at the Cauliflower at Mapleden, and want to see her, and he's to bring her there at once. Arter they've started I go in and get to bed, and earthquakes wouldn't wake me, let alone a knock at the door. D'ye see?"

"What good's that goin' to do?" enquired the astonished listener.

"Next day," said Barber, in thrilling tones, as he placed his forefinger on the other's arm, "I refuse to believe her story. Green, here, denies of it too, and sez 'e saw her at the gate and asked her to go for a walk with him."

Captain Nibletts fingered his beard. "It don't seem to be the sort of trick to play on a woman," he expostulated, "an' it's four miles to Mapleden. What's she goin' to do?"

"That's 'er lookout," observed Captain Barber, with much composure, "all I know is she won't wake me. I daresay she'll come on to your place. Wimmen wot sets their caps at men wot don't want 'em set at 'em must put up with the consequences."

"You give me half an hour, sir," said Mr. Green, impressively, "and then you can come on as soon as you like. You'll find the coast clear by then."

He bit off the end of the cigar presented by Captain Barber, and, thanking him effusively as he struck a match for him, quitted the inn. The two captains waited restlessly for the time specified, and then, finishing their drinks, went outside, and, standing in the light which streamed from the windows and doorway of the Thorn, gazed at the dark road beyond.

"It looks all right," said Barber, shaking hands. "Good-night."

"Good luck," said Nibletts.

The other, not without a little trepidation, walked towards his house, and opening the door, after a little difficulty, stood safely inside. The house was quiet and in darkness, except for the lamp which stood on the parlour-table, and after a moment's survey he proceeded to shut up for the night.

As a rule he was careless about such matters, but to-night no gaoler saw to his bolts and bars more carefully than he did. He returned to the parlour, having made all secure, and lighting his pipe for a few final whiffs before retiring, winked at himself solemnly in the glass. Then fearful that the housekeeper might return sooner than was expected, he blew out the lamp and smoked in the dark.

He knocked out his pipe at last, and walked slowly and ponderously upstairs. He grinned again as he passed the door of the housekeeper's room, and then, with a catch in his breath, clutched heavily at the banister as a soft female voice bade him "Good-night."

Captain Barber, surprised beyond all measure, was unable to speak.

"I thought you'd got lost again," said the voice, playfully. "Good-night."

"Good-night," rejoined the other, in hollow tones. "Mrs. Banks stay long?" he enquired, pausing at his door.

"She went just about half an hour before you came in," replied the housekeeper. "Elizabeth went soon after you did, but her mother stopped on. She went very suddenly when she did go, and was very mysterious about it. Not that I want to know her business."

"Mysterious?" faltered the captain.

"Some young man came to the door," continued the innocent woman, "and they were talking in a low voice. I don't know who it was, because Mrs. Banks let me see quite plainly that she didn't want me to know. Then she just called out 'Goodnight,' and went off as fast as you please."

Captain Barber supported himself for a moment by the handle of his door, and then in a dazed way blundered into his room. He was a good-hearted man in a way, and pushing open the little casement he thrust out his head and sighed with genuine feeling as he thought of his poor old friend plodding slowly to Mapleden. Incidentally he felt a little bit sorry for Mr. William Green.

He was awaked next morning after a somewhat restless night by the sounds of an unwonted noise downstairs, and lay in amazement listening to a hum of excited voices below. Knuckles rapped on his door and the voice of Mrs. Church, much agitated, requested him to rise and attire himself.

He was out of bed at that and looking from the window. A small group of children stood in the road outside the house, while Joe and the cook with their arms on the fence were staring hard at his parlour window, occasionally varying the proceedings by a little conversation with the people next door, who were standing in their front garden. In a state of considerable agitation he hurriedly dressed himself and went downstairs.

His sitting-room was full. Mrs. Banks, looking very tired, was sitting in the arm-chair taking smelling-salts at intervals, and staring fiercely at Mr. William Green, who was huddled in a corner smiling sheepishly behind Captain Nibletts and Ben.

"What's all this?" demanded Captain Barber, in a trembling voice, as his eye met Mr. Green's.

Several of Mrs. Banks's relatives began speaking at once, assisted by some of the neighbours. The substance of their remarks was that a man. whose polite tongue hid the falseness of his heart, had lured Mrs. Banks for a four-mile walk to Mapleden late the preceding night under the pretence that Captain Barber, who was evidently hale and hearty, was lying ill at the Cauliflower. They demanded his immediate dismissal from the ship and his exemplary punishment by the law.

"What 'ave you got to say to this?" demanded Captain Barber of the villain, in tones of righteous indignation tempered by fear.

"It isn't true, sir," said Mr. Green, respectfully. "I didn't say anything of the kind."

"Wot did you say, then?" enquired Captain Barber, in a voice which the company thought far too mild for the occasion.

"She was standing at the door as I passed," said Mr. Green, nervously, "and I asked her to go for a walk with me."

"Lawk-a-mussy me!" screamed the horrified Mrs. Banks.

"We went for a nice little stroll," continued the graceless Mr. Green, "and then I s'pose she found it was later than she thought, and she began to make a fuss."

"Me, at my time o' life?" demanded the indignant Mrs. Banks of the audience.

"You did make a fuss," said Mr. Green.

"O' course I made a fuss when I found out how I had been deceived. You were here when he came, Mrs. Church, weren't you?"

"I would rather not say anything about it," said the housekeeper, freezingly.

"I insist upon your speaking," said the old lady, getting very red in the face.

"Well, I don't know much about it," said the housekeeper, looking round appealingly. "I heard you speaking to somebody at the door in a low voice."

"It wasn't a low voice," interrupted Mrs. Banks, sharply.

"Well, I couldn't hear what you were saying, and then when you went outside and I asked you whether you were going home you said 'yes,' didn't you?"

"Are you sure she said she was going home?" said Mrs. Banks's brother-in-law, in an awful voice, as the old lady sank back in her chair.

"Yes," said Mrs. Church, with a fine show of reluctance.

There was a dead silence, during which they all heard the smelling-salts drop.

"If this man said Captain Barber was ill at Mapleden, why didn't you tell me?" continued Mrs. Church, in a mildly aggrieved voice. "I think if anybody ought to have known, it should have been me."

"It's all a fuss about nothing," said Mr. Green, brazenly. "She stayed out a bit too late, and then wanted to put it all on to me."

A good Samaritan picked up the smelling-salts and held them to the victim's nose, while her scandalized relatives discussed the situation in hurried whispers. The brother-in-law eyed her with bewildered disapproval, and in the disjointed accents peculiar to surprise was heard to make use of the words "friskiness" and "gallivanting" and "old enough to know better."

Her relatives' remarks, however, caused Mrs. Banks comparatively little pain. Her attention was fully taken up by the housekeeper, in whose satisfied smile she saw a perfect recognition of the reasons for her action of the previous evening. She got up from her chair, and with a stateliness which her brother-in-law thought somewhat misplaced, took her daughter's arm, and slowly left the room, her departure being the signal for a general breakup. By twos and threes the company drifted slowly up the road in her wake, while Captain Barber, going in the other direction, accompanied Captain Nibletts and party as far as the schooner, in order that he might have the opportunity of saying a few well-chosen words to Mr. Green on the subject of precipitancy.

"If it 'adn't been for me tipping 'im the wink, so as to let him know what line 'e was to go on when I came down, where should I 'ave been?" he demanded of Captain Nibletts.

And that astonished mariner, with a helpless shake of his head, gave it up.

CHAPTER XV

The Blue Posts, Chelsea, is an old-time public-house pleasantly situated by the river, with an extensive connection amongst gentlemen's servants, 'busmen, and other skilled judges of good beer, the subtle and delicate perfume of which liquor pervades the place from cellar to basement, and has more than once taken the policeman on duty to the back door, under the impression that something wanted looking into.

To some men imprisonment in such a place would have been little short of ecstasy. In the heat of summer they would have sat in the cool cellar amid barrels of honest beer; in winter, they would have led the conversation cosily seated around the taproom fire. For exercise, profitable employment at the beer-engine in the bar; for intellectual exercise, the study of practical chemistry in the cellar.

To Captain Fred Flower none of these things appealed. He had visited the cellar certainly—in search of subterranean exits; he had sat in the tap-room—close to the open window; but his rabid desire to get away from the place and never see it again could not have been surpassed by the most bitter teetotaler that ever breathed.

His greatest trouble was with Porson, whose limpet-like qualities were a source of never-failing concern to the unfortunate mariner. Did he ascend to the drawing-room and gaze yearningly from the windows at the broad stream of Father Thames and the craft dropping down on the ebb-tide to the sea, Uncle Porson, sallow of face and unclean of collar, was there to talk beery romance of the ocean. Did he retire to the small yard at the rear of the premises and gaze from the back door at the passing life of a Chelsea by-street, Uncle Porson was looking over his shoulder, pointing out milkmen with histories, and cabmen with a past.

The second week of his stay was drawing to a close before he fully realised the horror of his position. His foot, which had been giving him considerable trouble, was getting much better, though it was by no means well enough to give him a chance in a foot-race with Mr. Porson or Charles, and as the family at the Blue Posts realised the improvement, the attentions of his personal attendants were redoubled. The key of his bed-room door was turned every night after he had retired, a discovery he had made the first night after carefully dressing for flight and spending an hour over the composition of a farewell note to Miss Tipping. There was no chance of reaching the roof from his bed-room window, and the pavement below offered him his choice between a wedding and a funeral.

And amid all this the fiction was maintained of preserving him from his lawless foes and his own inconvenient devotion to duty. A struggle for escape was not to be thought of, as the full measure of his deceitfulness would transpire in the event of failure, and the wedding drew nearer day by day, while his active brain was still casting about in vain for any means of escape.

"Next Tuesday," said Mrs. Tipping to her stepdaughter, as they sat in the much decorated drawing-room one afternoon, "you'll be Mrs. Robinson."

Miss Tipping, who was sitting next to the skipper, looked at him languishingly, and put her head on his shoulder.

"I can hardly believe it," she said, coyly.

Flower, who was in the same predicament, patted her head tenderly, as being easier than replying.

"And I must say," said Mrs. Tipping, regarding the pair, "I'm a plain woman, and I speak my mind, that if it was me, I should want to know more about him first."

"I'm quite satisfied, mar," said Miss Tipping, without raising her head.

"There's your relations to be satisfied, Matilda," said Uncle Porson, in an important voice.

Miss Tipping raised her head and favoured the interrupter with a baleful stare, whereupon Mr. Porson, scratching his neck feebly, glanced at Mrs. Tipping for support.

"Our relations needn't come to see us," said his niece, at length. "He's marrying me, not my relations."

"He's making me his uncle, at any rate," said Mr. Porson, with a sudden access of dignity.

"You don't mind, Fred, do you?" asked Miss Tipping, anxiously.

"I'd put up with more than that for your sake," said Flower. "I needn't tell people."

"That's all very fine," said Mrs. Tipping, taking up the cudgels for the speechless and glaring victim of these pleasantries, "but there's no mystery about your uncle; everybody knows him. He doesn't disappear just as he is going to get married, and be brought back in a cab months afterwards. He isn't full of secrets he mustn't tell people who ought to know."

"Never kep' a secret in my life," agreed Uncle Porson, whose head was buzzing under this unaccustomed praise.

"I know quite eno'ugh about Fred," said Miss Tipping, tenderly; "when I want your opinion, mar, I'll ask you for it."

Mrs. Tipping's reply was interrupted by the entrance of a young man from the jeweller's with four brooches for Flower to present to the bridesmaids. Mrs. Tipping had chosen them, and it did not take the hapless skipper long to arrive at the conclusion that she was far fonder of bridesmaids than he was. His stock of money was beginning to dwindle, and the purchase of a second wedding suit within a month was beginning to tell even upon his soaring spirits.

"There's another thing about Fred I don't quite like," said Mrs. Tipping, as she sat with the brooches ranged upon her capacious lap; "he's extravagant. I don't like a mean man, but one who flings his money away is almost as bad. These 'ere brooches are very pretty, and they do him credit, but I can't say but what something cheaper wouldn't 'ave done as well."

"I thought you liked them," said the indignant Flower.

"I like them well enough," said Mrs. Tipping, solemnly; "there's nothing to dislike in them. Seems to me they must have cost a lot of money, that's all—I suppose I may make a remark!"

Flower changed the subject, and turning to Miss Tipping began to speak in a low voice of their new home. Miss Tipping wanted a sort of Eden with bar improvements, and it was rather difficult to find.

They had discussed the matter before, and the wily skipper had almost quarrelled with his bride-elect over the part of the country in which they were to live, Miss Tipping holding out for the east coast, while Flower hotly championed the south. Mrs. Tipping, with some emphasis, had suggested leaving it until after the honeymoon, but a poetic advertisement of an inn in Essex catching her daughter's eye, it was decided that instant inspection should be made.

They travelled down from Fenchurch Street, accompanied by Dick and Mrs. Tipping, the skipper, who was painfully on the alert for any chance of escape, making a great fuss of his foot, and confessing to a feeling of unusual indisposition. He sat in one corner of the carriage with his eyes half closed, while Miss Tipping, with her arm affectionately drawn through his, was the unconscious means of preventing a dash for liberty as the train steamed slowly through a station.

The nearest station to the Rose of Essex was five miles distant, a fact which (owing perhaps to the expensive nature of newspaper charges) did not appear in the advertisement.

"It's a nice little place," said the landlady of the Railway Hotel, as they asked her opinion over lunch; "there's a little land goes with it. If you want to drive over, I'd better be having something got ready."

Mrs. Tipping, who halved the duties with Flower, she doing the ordering and he the paying, assented, and in a short time they were bowling rapidly along through narrow country lanes to their destination. The skipper noticed with pleasure the lonely nature of the country, and his heart beat fast as he thought of the chances of success of a little plan of escape.

So far as appearance went, the inn was excellent. Roses clustered round the porch and hung in fragrant bunches from the walls, while three or four sturdy lime trees in one corner threw a grateful shade over a rustic table and settles. Flower, with a grateful sigh, said that it was the very thing. Even Mrs. Tipping, after a careful inspection, said that they might do worse; Dick, with an air of professional gravity, devoted most of his attention to the cellar, while the engaged couple walked slowly round the immense garden in the rear exchanging tender whispers.

"We'll think it over and let you know," said Mrs. Tipping to the landlord.

"There's been a lot after it," said he slowly, with a glance at his wife.

"And yet it ain't gone," said the business-like Mrs. Tipping, pleasantly.

"I'm going to take it, mar," said Miss Tipping, firmly.

Mrs. Tipping sighed at her haste, but finding her determined, went down the cellar again, accompanied by Dick, for a last look round. Captain Flower, leaning heavily on Miss Tipping's arm, limped slowly to the carriage.

"Tired?" she enquired, tenderly, as he sank back in the cushions.

"Foot's painful," he said, with a faint smile. "Good gracious!"

"What's the matter?" asked Miss Tipping, alarmed by his manner.

"I've left my pipe in the garden," said Flower, rising, "the one you gave me. I wouldn't lose it for the world."

"I'll get it," said Miss Tipping, springing out of the carriage. "Whereabouts did you leave it, do you think?"

"By the bee-hives," said Flower, pale with excitement, as he heard Mrs. Tipping and Dick coming up from the cellar. "Make haste; somebody might take it."

Miss Tipping darted into the house, and immediately afterwards the Tippings ascended from the cellar, attended by the landlady.

"Driver," said Flower, sharply.

"Sir," said the man, looking round and tenderly rubbing his back.

"Take that to the lady who has just gone in, at once," gabbled Flower; "hurry up."

For want of anything better, he handed the astonished driver his tobacco-pouch, and waved him to the house. The lad descended from his perch and ran to the door just as Dick Tipping, giving vent to a sharp cry, was rushing out. The cry acted on the skipper like magic, and, snatching up the whip, he gave the horse a cut in which was concentrated the fears of the last fortnight and the hopes of his future lifetime.

The animal sprang forward madly just as Dick Tipping, who had pushed the driver out of the way, rushed out in pursuit. There was a hard white road in front and it took it at a gallop, the vehicle rocking from side to side behind it as Flower played on it with the whip. Tipping was close behind, and the driver a good second. Flower, leaving the horse to take care of itself for a time, stood upright in the carriage and hurled cushions at his foremost pursuer. The third cushion was long and limp, and, falling on end in front of him, twined itself round his swift-moving legs and brought him heavily to the ground.

"He's winded," said Flower, as he saw the coachman stop and help the other man slowly to his feet; "shows what a cushion can do."

He clambered onto the seat, as a bend in the road shut the others from his sight, and gathering up the reins, gave himself over to the joyous feeling of his new-found liberty as they rushed through the air. His ideas of driving were elementary, and his mode of turning corners was to turn them quickly and get it over; but he drove on for miles without mishap, and, the horse having dropped to a steady trot, began to consider his future movements.

"They'll be setting the wires to work, I expect," he thought, soberly. "What a comfortable old world this must have been before they invented steam and telegraph. I'll go a little bit farther, and then tie it up to a tree."

He made what he considered an endearing noise with his mouth, and the startled animal at once bounded forward with the intention of getting out of hearing. A gentle incline favoured the pace, which was now so considerable that the skipper, seeing another craft approaching him, waved his hand towards it warningly.

"I wonder who ought to get out of the way?" he said, thoughtfullly; "I s'pose the horse knows."

He left it to that able quadruped, after giving it a little bang on the flank with the butt end of the whip to keep its faculties fresh. There was a frenzied shout from the other vehicle, a sudden violent stoppage, with the crashing of wood, and Flower, crawling out of the ditch, watched with some admiration the strenuous efforts of his noble beast to take the carriage along on three wheels.

"Look what you've done!" roared the driver of the other vehicle, foaming with passion, as he jumped out and held his plunging horse by the head. "Look at my gig, sir! Look at it!"

Flower looked, and then returned the courtesy.

"Look at mine," he said, impressively; "mine's much the worst."

"You were on the wrong side of the road," shouted the other.

"I was there first," said Flower; "it wouldn't have happened if you hadn't tried to get out of my way. The course I was on I should have passed you easily."

He looked up the road. His horse, trembling violently, was standing still, with the wreck of the carriage behind it. He stooped mechanically, and picking up the whip which was lying in the road said that he would go off for assistance.

"You stay here, sir," said the other man with an oath.

"I won't," said the skipper.

His adversary made no reply, but, having by this time soothed his frightened horse, took his whip out of its socket and strode towards him with the butt raised over his head. Flower arranged his own whip the same way, and both men being new to the weapon, circled round each other two or three times waiting for a little instruction. Then the owner of the gig, whose temper was rising every second, ran in and dealt the skipper a heavy blow on the head.

The blow dispelled an idea which was slowly forming there of asking the extent of the damage, and, if it were not too much, offering to make it good. Ideas of settlement vanished; ideas of honour, morality, and even escape vanished too; all merged in the one fixed idea of giving the other man a harder blow than he had given.

For a minute or two the battle raged fairly equally; both were securing a fair amount of punishment. Then, under a heavy blow from Flower, his foe went down suddenly. For a second or two the skipper held his breath with fear, then the other man raised himself feebly on his knees, and, throwing away his whip, staggered to his feet and, unfastening the reins, clambered unsteadily into his gig and drove off without a word.

The victorious skipper looked up and down the lonely road, and shaking his head sadly at the noble steed which had brought him into this mess, tenderly felt his bruised and aching head, and then set off as fast as his foot would permit up the road.

He looked about eagerly as he went for a place of concealment, fully aware of the inability of a lame shipmaster to outdistance horseflesh. Hedges and fields bounded both sides of the road, but half a mile farther along, on the right-hand side, the field stretched away upwards to meet a wood. Towards this wood Captain Flower, having first squeezed himself through a gap in the hedge, progressed with all speed.

He sat on the trunk of a fallen pine to regain his breath, and eagerly looked about him. To his disappointment he saw that the wood was of no great depth, but was a mere belt of pines running almost parallel with the road he had quitted. With the single idea of getting as far away from the scene of his crime as possible, he began to walk through it.

The wood was very still, and the shade grateful after the heat of the sun. Just beyond, the fields were shimmering in the heat, and he pricked up his ears as the unmistakable sound of wheels and hoofs came across the silent fields. He looked round wildly, and seeing a tiny cottage standing in a bit of a clearing, made towards it.

A little old man twisted with rheumatism rose as he stood at the open door and regarded him with a pair of bloodshot, but sharp, old eyes, while an old woman sitting in a Windsor-chair looked up anxiously.

"Can I come in?" asked Flower.

"Aye," said the old man, standing aside to let him pass.

"Hot day," said the skipper, taking a seat.

"No, 'tain't," said the old man.

"Not so hot as yesterday," said Flower, with a conciliatory smile.

"It's 'otter than it was yesterday," said the old man. "What ha' you done to your face?"

"I was climbing a tree," said Flower, with a laugh, "and I fell down; I've hurt my foot, too."

"Served you right if you'd broke your neck," said his amiable host, "climbing trees at your time o' life."

"Nice cottage you've got here," said the persistent Flower.

"I wish you 'ad to live in it," said the old man.

He took a proffered cigar, and after eyeing it for some time, like a young carver with a new joint, took out a huge clasp-knife and slowly sawed the end off.

"Can I sleep here for the night?" asked Flower, at length.

"No, you can't," said the old man, drawing at his cigar.

He smoked on, with the air of a man who has just given a very clever answer to a very difficult question.

"We ain't on'y got one room besides this," said the old woman solemnly. "Years ago we used to have four and a wash-place."

"Oh, I could sleep on the floor here," said Flower, lightly. "I'll pay you five shillings."

"Let's see your money," said the old man, leaning forward.

Flower put the sum in his hand. "I'll pay now," he said, heartily.

"The floor won't run away," said the other, pulling out an old leathern purse, "and you can sleep on any part of it you like."

Flower thanked him effusively. He was listening intently for any sounds outside. If the Tippings and the man in the gig met, they would scour the country-side, and almost certainly pay the cottage a visit.

"If you let me go upstairs and lie down for an hour or two," he said, turning to the old man, "I'll give you another half-crown."

The old man said nothing, but held out his hand, and after receiving the sum got up slowly, and, opening a door by the fire-place, revealed a few broken stairs, which he slowly ascended, after beckoning his guest to follow.

"It's a small place," he said, tersely, "but I daresay you've often slept in a worse."

Flower made no reply. He was looking from the tiny casement. Through an opening in the trees he saw a couple of figures crossing the field towards the wood.

"If anybody asks you whether you have seen me, say no," he said, rapidly, to the old man. "I've got into a bit of a mess, and if you hide me here until it has blown over, I'll make it worth your while."

"How much?" said the old man.

Flower hesitated. "Five pounds for certain," he said, hastily, "and more if you're put to much trouble. Run down and stop your wife's mouth quietly."

"Don't order me about," said the old man, slowly; "I ain't said I'll do it yet."

"They're coming now," said Flower, impatiently; "mind, if they catch me you lose your five pounds."

"All right," said the other. "I'm doing it for the five pounds, mind, not for you," added this excellent man.

He went grunting and groaning down the narrow stairs, and the skipper, closing the door, went and crouched down by the open casement. A few indistinct words were borne in on the still air, and voices came gradually closer, until footsteps, which had been deadened by the grass, became suddenly audible on the stones outside the cottage.

Flower held his breath with anxiety; then he smiled softly and pleasantly as he listened to the terms in which his somewhat difficult host was addressed.

"Now, gaffer," said the man of the gig, roughly.

"Wake up, grandpa," said Dick Tipping; "have you seen a man go by here?—blue serge suit, moustache, face and head knocked about?"

"No, I ain't seen 'im," was the reply. "What's he done?"

Tipping told him briefly. "We'll have him," he said, savagely. "We've got a mounted policeman on the job, besides others. If you can catch him it's worth half a sov. to you."

He went off hurriedly with the other man, and their voices died away in the distance. Flower sat in his place on the floor for some time, and then, seeing from the window that the coast was clear, went downstairs again.

The old woman made him up a bed on the floor after supper, although both he and the old man assured her that it was unnecessary, and then, taking the lamp, bade him good-night and went upstairs.

Flower, left to himself, rolled exultingly on his poor couch, and for the first time in a fortnight breathed freely.

"If I do get into trouble," he murmured, complacently, "I generally manage to get out of it. It wants a good head in the first place, and a cool one in the second."

CHAPTER XVI

He was awake early in the morning, and, opening the door, stood delightedly breathing the fresh, pine-scented air.

The atmosphere of the Blue Posts was already half forgotten, and he stood looking dreamily forward to the time when he might reasonably return to life and Poppy. He took a few steps into the wood and, after feeling for his pipe before he remembered that Miss Tipping was probably keeping it as a souvenir, sat on a freshly-cut log and fell into a sentimental reverie, until the appearance of a restless old man at the door of the cottage took him back to breakfast.

"I thought you'd run off," said his host, tartly.

"You thought wrong, then," said Flower, sharply, as he took out his purse. "Here are two of the five pounds I promised you; I'll give you the rest when I go."

The old man took the money and closed his small, hard mouth until the lips almost disappeared. "More money than sense," he remarked, cordially, as the skipper replaced his purse.

Flower made no reply. Some slices of fat bacon were sizzling in a pan over the wood-fire, and the pungent smell of the woods, mixed with the sharpness of the morning air, gave him an appetite to which, since his enforced idleness, he had been a stranger. He drew his chair up to the rickety little table with its covering of frayed oil-cloth, and, breaking a couple of eggs over his bacon, set to eagerly.

"Don't get eggs like these in London," he said to the old woman.

The old woman leaned over and, inspecting the shells, paid a tribute to the hens who were responsible for them, and traced back a genealogy which would have baffled the entire College of Heralds—a genealogy hotly contested by the old man, who claimed a bar sinister through three eggs bought at the village shop some generations before.

"You've got a nice little place here," said Flower, by way of changing the conversation, which was well on the way to becoming personal; "but don't you find it rather dull sometimes?"

"Well, I don't know," said the old woman. "I finds plenty to do, and 'e potters about like. 'E don't do much, but it pleases 'im, and it don't hurt me."

The object of these compliments took them as a matter of course, and after hunting up the stump of last night's cigar, and shredding it with his knife, crammed it into a clay pipe and smoked tranquilly. Flower found a solitary cigar, one of the Blue Posts' best, and with a gaze which wandered idly from the chest of drawers on one side of the room to the old china dogs on the little mantel-shelf on the other, smoked in silence.

The old man brought in news at dinner-time. The village was ringing with the news of yesterday's affair, and a rigourous search, fanned into excitement by an offer of two pounds reward, was taking the place of the more prosaic labours of the country side.

"If it wasn't for me," said the old man, in an excess of self-laudation, "you'd be put in the gaol—where you ought to be; but I wouldn't do it if it wasn't for the five pounds. You'd better keep close in the house. There's some more of 'em in the wood looking for you."

Captain Flower took his advice, and for the next two days became a voluntary prisoner. On the third day the old man reported that public excitement about him was dying out, owing partly to the fact that it thought the villain must have made his escape good, and partly to the fact that the landlord of the Wheatsheaf had been sitting at his front door shooting at snakes on the King's Highway invisible to ordinary folk.

The skipper resolved to make a start on the following evening, walking, the first night so as to get out of the dangerous zone, and then training to London. At the prospect his spirits rose, and in a convivial mood he purchased a bottle of red currant wine from the old woman at supper, and handed it round.

He was still cheerful next morning as he arose and began to dress. Then he paused, and in a somewhat anxious fashion patted his trousers pockets. Minute and painful investigation revealed a bunch of keys and a clasp-knife.

He tried his other pockets, and then, sinking in a dazed fashion into a chair, tried to think what had become of his purse and loose change. His watch, a silver one, was under his pillow, where he had placed it the night before, and his ready cash was represented by the shilling which hung upon the chain.

He completed his dressing slowly while walking about the room, looking into all sorts of likely and unlikely hiding-places for his money, and at length gave up the search in disgust, and sat down to wait until such time as his host should appear. It was a complication for which he had not bargained, and unable to endure the suspense any longer, he put his head up the stairway and bawled to the old man to come down.

"What's the matter now?" demanded the old man as he came downstairs, preceded by his wife. "One would think the place belonged to you, making all that noise."

"I've lost my purse," said Flower, regarding him sternly. "My purse has been taken out of one pocket and some silver out of the other while I was asleep."

The old man raised his eyebrows at his wife and scratched his chin roughly.

"I s'pose you've lost my three pounds along with it?" he said, raspily.

"Where's my purse?" demanded the skipper, roughly; "don't play the fool with me. It won't pay."

"I don't know nothing about your purse," said the other, regarding him closely with his little bloodshot eyes; "you're trying to do me out o'my three pounds—me what's took you in and 'id you."

The incensed skipper made no reply, but, passing upstairs, turned the bed-room topsy-turvy in a wild search for his property. It was unsuccessful, and he came down with a look in his face which made his respected host get close to his wife.

"Are you going to give me my money?" demanded he, striding up to him.

"I've not got your money," snarled the other, "I'm an honest man."

He started back in alarm, and his wife gave a faint scream as Flower caught him by the collar, and, holding him against the wall, went through his pockets.

"Don't hurt him," cried the old woman; "he's only a little old man."

"If you were younger and bigger," said the infuriated skipper, as he gave up the fruitless search, "I'd thrash you till you gave it up."

"I'm an honest man," said the other, recovering himself as he saw that his adversary intended no violence; "if you think I've stole your money, you know what you can do."

"What?" demanded Flower.

"Go to the police," said the old man, his little slit of a mouth twisted into a baleful grin; "if you think I've stole your money, go and tell the police."

"Let 'em come and search the house," said the old woman, plucking up spirit. "I've been married forty-two years and 'ad seven children. Go and fetch the police."

Flower stared at them in wrathful concern. Threats were of no use, and violence was out of the question. He went to the door, and leaning against it, stood there deep in thought until, after a time, the old woman, taking courage from his silence, began to prepare breakfast. Then he turned, and drawing his chair up to the table, ate silently.

He preserved this silence all day despite the occasional suggestion of the old man that he should go for the police, and the aggrieved refrain of the old woman as to the length of her married life and the number of her offspring.

He left at night without a word. The old man smiled almost amiably to see him go; and the old woman, who had been in a state of nervous trepidation all day, glanced at her husband with a look in which wifely devotion and admiration were almost equally blended.

Flower passed slowly through the wood, and after pausing to make sure that he was not followed, struck across the fields, and, with his sailor's knowledge of the stars, steered by them in the direction of London.

He walked all that night unmolested, his foot giving him but little trouble, and passed the following day under a haystack, assuaging his hunger with some bread and cheese he had put in his pocket.

Travelling by night and sleeping in secluded spots by day, he reached the city in three days. Considering that he had no money, and was afraid to go into a town to pawn his watch, he did not suffer so much from hunger as might have been expected—something which he vaguely referred to as Providence, but for which the sufferers found other terms, twice leading his faltering footsteps to labourers' dinners in tin cans and red handkerchiefs.

At Stratford he pawned his watch and chain and sat down to a lengthy meal, and then, with nearly eighteen shillings in his pocket, took train to Liverpool Street. The roar of the city greeted his ears like music, and, investing in a pipe and tobacco, he got on a 'bus bound eastward, and securing cheap apartments in the Mile End Road, sat down to consider his plans. The prompt appearance of the Tipping family after his letter to Fraser had given him a wholesome dread of the post, and until the connection between the two was satisfactorily explained he would not risk another, even in his new name of Thompson. Having come to this decision, he had another supper, and then went upstairs to the unwonted luxury of a bed.

CHAPTER XVII

It is one of the first laws of domestic economy that the largest families must inhabit the smallest houses—a state of things which is somewhat awkward when the heads wish to discuss affairs of state. Some preserve a certain amount of secrecy by the use of fragmentary sentences eked out by nods and blinks and by the substitution of capital letters for surnames; a practice likely to lead to much confusion and scandal when the names of several friends begin with the same letter. Others improve the family orthography to an extent they little dream of by spelling certain vital words instead of pronouncing them, some children profiting so much by this form of vicarious instruction that they have been known to close a most interesting conversation by thoughtlessly correcting their parents on a point of spelling.

There were but few secrets in the Wheeler family, the younger members relating each other's misdeeds quite freely, and refuting the charge of tale-bearing by keeping debit and credit accounts with each other in which assets and liabilities could usually be balanced by simple addition. Among the elders, the possession of a present secret merely meant a future conversation.

On this day the juniors were quite certain that secret proceedings of a highly interesting nature were in the air. Miss Tyrell having been out since the morning, Mrs. Wheeler was looking forward anxiously to her return with the view of holding a little private conversation with her, and the entire Wheeler family were no less anxious to act as audience for the occasion. Mr. Bob Wheeler had departed to his work that morning in a condition which his family, who were fond of homely similes, had likened to a bear with a sore head. The sisterly attentions of Emma Wheeler were met with a boorish request to keep her paws off; and a young Wheeler, rash and inexperienced in the way of this weary world, who publicly asked what Bob had "got the hump about," was sternly ordered to finish his breakfast in the washhouse. Consequently there was a full meeting after tea, and when Poppy entered, it was confidently expected that proceedings would at once open with a speech from the sofa.

"Take the children outside a bit, Belinda," said her mother, after the tea things had been removed.

"Got my 'ome lessons to do," said Belinda.

"Do 'em when you come back," said Mrs. Wheeler.

"Sha'n't 'ave time," replied Belinda, taking her books from a shelf; "they'll take me all the evening. We've all got a lot of 'ome lessons to-night."

"Never mind, you take 'em out," persisted Mrs. Wheeler.

"When I want to go out," said Belinda, rebelliously, "you won't let me."

"Do as your mother tells you," commanded Mr. Wheeler, with excellent sternness.

"I want a little quiet," said Mrs. Wheeler; "a little fresh air will do you good, Peter."

"I'll go and smoke my pipe in the washhouse," said Mr. Wheeler, who had his own notions of healthful recreation.

"Take your pipe outside," said Mrs. Wheeler, significantly. "Did you 'ear what I said, Belinda?"

Belinda rose noisily and gathering up her untidy books, thrust them back in a heap on the shelf, and putting on her hat stood at the door commenting undutifully upon her parents, and shrilly demanding of the small Wheelers whether they were coming or whether she was to stay there all night. She also indulged in dreary prognostications concerning her future, and finally driving her small fry before her, closed the street door with a bang which induced Mrs. Wheeler to speak of heredity and Mr. Wheeler's sister Jane's temper.

"Where are you going, Poppy?" she enquired, as the girl rose to follow the dutiful Mr. Wheeler. "I want to speak to you a moment."

The girl resumed her seat, and taking up a small garment intended for the youngest Wheeler but two, or the youngest but one, whichever it happened to fit best, or whichever wanted it first, stitched on in silence. "I want to speak to you about Bob," said Mrs. Wheeler, impressively. "Of course you know he never keeps anything from his mother. He 'as told me about all the gells he has walked out with, and though, of course, he 'as been much run after, he is three-and-twenty and not married yet. He told me that none of 'em seemed to be worthy of him."

She paused for so long that Poppy Tyrell looked up from her work, said "Yes," in an expressionless manner, and waited for her to continue.

"He's been a good son," said the mother, fondly; "never no trouble, always been pertickler, and always quite the gentleman. He always smokes his cigar of a Sunday, and I remember the very first money 'e ever earned 'e spent on a cane with a dog's 'ed to it."

"Yes," said Poppy again.

"The gells he's 'ad after 'im wouldn't be believed," said Mrs. Wheeler, shaking her head with a tender smile at a hole in the carpet. "Before you came here there was a fresh one used to come in every Sunday almost, but 'e couldn't make up his mind. We used to joke him about it."

"He's very young still," said Poppy.

"He's old enough to be married," said Mrs. Wheeler. "He's told me all about you, he never has no secrets from 'is mother. He told me that he asked you to walk out with 'im last night and you said 'No'; but I told 'im that that was only a gell's way, and that you'd give 'im another answer soon."

"That was my final answer," said Poppy Tyrell, the corners of her mouth hardening. "I shall never say anything else."

"All young gells say that at first," said Mrs. Wheeler, making praiseworthy efforts to keep her temper. "Wheeler 'ad to ask me five times."

"I meant what I said," said Poppy, stitching industriously. "I shall never change my mind."

"It's early days to ask you perhaps, so soon after Captain Flower's death," suggested Mrs. Wheeler.

"That has nothing at all to do with it," said the girl. "I shall not marry your son, in any case."

"Not good enough for you, I suppose?" said the other, her eyes snapping. "In my time beggars couldn't be choosers."

"They can't choose much now," said Poppy, in a low voice; "but as you know I'm going to a situation on Monday, I shall soon be able to pay off my debt to you: though, of course, I can't repay you for your kindness in letting me live here when I had nowhere else to go."

"It isn't me you owe it to," said Mrs. Wheeler. "I'm sure I couldn't 'ave afforded to do it whatever Wheeler liked to say if Bob hadn't come forward and paid for you."

"Bob?" cried Poppy, springing to her feet and dropping her work onto the floor.

"Yes, Bob," said the other, melodramatically; "'im what isn't good enough to be your husband."

"I didn't know," said the girl, brokenly; "you should have told me. I would sooner starve. I would sooner beg in the streets. I will go at once."

"I daresay you know where to go, so I sha'n't worry about you," replied Mrs. Wheeler. "You quiet ones are generally the worst."

"I am sorry," murmured Poppy; "I did not mean to be rude, or ungrateful."

"You're very kind," said Mrs. Wheeler. "Is Mr. Fraser up in London?"

"I'm sure I don't know," said the girl, pausing at the door.

"Sure to be, though," said Mrs. Wheeler, significantly; "you won't 'ave to starve, my dear. But, there, you know that—some people's pride is a funny thing."

Miss Tyrell regarded her for a moment in silence and then quitted the room, coming back again from half-way up the stairs to answer a knock at the door. She opened it slowly, and discovered to her horror Mr. Fraser standing upon the doorstep, with a smile which was meant to be propitiatory, but only succeeded in being uneasy.

"Is that Mr. Fraser?" demanded Mrs. Wheeler's voice, shrilly.

"That's me," said Fraser, heartily, as he shook hands with Poppy and entered the room.

"I thought you wouldn't be far off," said Mrs. Wheeler, in an unpleasant voice. "Poppy's been expecting you."

"I didn't know that Mr. Fraser was coming," said Poppy, as the helpless man looked from one to the other. "I suppose he has come to see you. He has not come to see me."

"Yes, I have," said Mr. Fraser, calmly. "I wanted—"

But Miss Tyrell had gone quietly upstairs, leaving him to gaze in a perturbed fashion at the sickly and somewhat malicious face on the sofa.

"What's the matter?" he enquired.

"Nothing," said Mrs. Wheeler.

"Isn't Miss Tyrell well?"

"So far as I'm permitted to know the state of 'er 'ealth, she is," was the reply.

"Mr. Wheeler well?" enquired Fraser, after a long pause.

"Very well, I thank you," said Mrs. Wheeler.

"And Miss Wheeler, and Bob, and the whole pa—— and all of them?" said Fraser.

"All very well," said Mrs. Wheeler.

His stock of conversation being exhausted he sat glancing uncomfortably round the littered room, painfully conscious that Mrs. Wheeler was regarding him with a glance that was at once hostile and impatient. While he was wondering whether Miss Tyrell had gone upstairs for a permanency, he heard her step on the stairs, and directly afterwards she appeared at the door with her hat and jacket on.

"Good-bye, Mrs. Wheeler," she said, gravely.

"Good-bye," said Mrs. Wheeler, in the same way that a free-speaking woman would have said "Good-riddance."

The girl's eyes rested for a moment on Fraser. Then she bade him good-bye, and, opening the door, passed into the street.

Fraser looked at Mrs. Wheeler in perplexity, then, jumping up suddenly as Poppy passed the window, he crossed to the door.

"Good-bye, Mrs. Wheeler," he shouted, and, vaguely conscious that something was wrong somewhere, dashed off in pursuit.

Poppy Tyrell, her face pale and her eyes burning, quickened her pace as she heard hurrying footsteps behind her.

"I just wanted a few words with you, Miss Tyrell," said Fraser, somewhat breathlessly.

"I—I am going on business," said Poppy, in a quiet voice.

"I didn't understand Mrs. Wheeler just now," said Fraser. "I hope you didn't mind my calling?"

"Oh, no," said the girl; "call as often as you like, but this evening I'm busy. Come to-morrow."

This hospitality over-reached itself. "Have you left the Wheelers?" he enquired, suddenly.

"Yes," said Poppy, simply.

"What's the good of telling me to call, then?" enquired Fraser, bluntly.

"They will be pleased to see you, I'm sure," said Miss Tyrell.

"Where are you going?" asked Fraser.

Miss Tyrell made no reply, except to favour him with a glance which warned him not to repeat the question, and he walked beside her for some time in silence.

"Good-bye," she said, suddenly.

"I'm not going," said Fraser, with artless surprise.

"Mr. Fraser," said the girl, reddening with anger, "will you please understand that I wish to be alone?"

"No," said Mr. Fraser, doggedly.

"A gentleman would not have to have half as much said to him," said Poppy, trembling.

"Well, thank God, I'm not a gentleman," said Fraser, calmly.

"If I had a father or a brother you would not behave like this," said the girl.

"If you had a father or a brother they would do it instead," said Fraser, gently; "it's just because you've got nobody else that I'm looking after you."

Miss Tyrell, who had softened slightly, stiffened again with temper.

"You?" she said, hotly. "What right have you to trouble yourself about me?"

"No right at all," said Fraser, cheerfully, "but I'm going to do it. If you've left the Wheelers, where are you going?"

Miss Tyrell, gazing straight in front of her, made no reply.

"Won't you tell me?" persisted the other.

"I'm not going anywhere," said Poppy, stopping suddenly and facing him. "I've got a new berth next Monday, and to-morrow morning I am going to see them to ask them to employ me at once."

"And to-night?" suggested the other.

"I shall go for a walk," said the girl. "Now that you know all about my concerns, will you please go?"

"Walk?" repeated Fraser. "Walk? What, all night? You can't do it—you don't know what it's like. Will you let me lend you some money? You can repay me as soon as you like."

"No, thank you."

"For my sake?" he suggested.

Miss Tyrell raised her eyebrows.

"I'm a bad walker," he explained.

The reply trembling on Miss Tyrell's lips realised that it was utterly inadequate to the occasion, and remained unspoken. She walked on in silence, apparently oblivious of the man by her side, and when he next spoke to her made no reply. He glanced at a clock in a baker's shop as they passed, and saw that it was just seven.

In this sociable fashion they walked along the Commercial Road and on to Aldgate, and then, passing up Fenchurch Street, mingled with the crowd thronging homewards over London Bridge. They went as far as Kennington in this direction, and then the girl turned and walked back to the City. Fraser, glancing at the pale profile beside him, ventured to speak again.

"Will you come down to Wapping and take my cabin for the night?" he asked, anxiously. "The mate's away, and I can turn in fo'ard—you can have it all to yourself."

Miss Tyrell, still looking straight in front of her, made no reply, but with another attempt to shake off this pertinacious young man of the sea quickened her pace again. Fraser fell back.

"If I'm not fit to walk beside you, I'll walk behind," he said, in a low voice; "you won't mind that?"

In this way they walked through the rapidly thinning streets. It was now dark, and most of the shops had closed. The elasticity had departed from Miss Tyrell's step, and she walked aimlessly, noting with a sinking at the heart the slowly passing time. Once or twice she halted from sheer weariness, Fraser halting too, and watching her with a sympathy of which Flower would most certainly have disapproved if he had seen it.

At length, in a quiet street beyond Stratford, she not only stopped, but turned and walked slowly back. Fraser turned too, and his heart beat as he fancied that she intended to overtake him. He quickened his pace in time with the steps behind him until they slackened and faltered; then he looked round and saw her standing in the centre of the pathway with her head bent. He walked back slowly until he stood beside her, and saw that she was crying softly. He placed his hand on her arm.

"Go away," she said, in a low voice.

"I shall not."

"You walked away from me just now."

"I was a brute," said Fraser, vehemently.

The arm beneath his hand trembled, and he drew it unresistingly through his own. In the faint light from the lamp opposite he saw her look at him.

"I'm very tired," she said, and leaned on him trustfully. "Were you really going to leave me just now?"

"You know I was not," said Fraser, simply.

Miss Tyrell, walking very slowly, pondered. "I should never have forgiven you if you had," she said, thoughtfully. "I'm so tired, I can hardly stand. You must take me to your ship."

They walked slowly to the end of the road, but the time seemed very short to Fraser. As far as he was concerned he would willingly have dispensed with the tram which they met at the end and the antique four-wheeler in which they completed their journey to the river. They found a waterman's skiff at the stairs, and sat side by side in the stern, looking contentedly over the dark water, as the waterman pulled in the direction of the Swallow, which was moored in the tier. There was no response to their hail, and Fraser himself, clambering over the side with the painter, assisted Miss Tyrell, who, as the daughter of one sailor and the guest of another, managed to throw off her fatigue sufficiently to admire the lines of the small steamer.

Fraser conducted her to the cabin, and motioning her to a seat on the locker, went forward to see about some supper. He struck a match in the forecastle and scrutinised the sleepers, and coming to the conclusion that something which was lying doubled up in a bunk, with its head buried in the pillow, was the cook, shook it vigorously.

"Did you want the cook, sir?" said a voice from another bunk.

"Yes," said Fraser, sharply, as he punched the figure again and again.

"Pore cookie ain't well, sir," said the seaman, sympathetically; "'e's been very delikit all this evenin'; that's the worst o' them teetotalers."

"All right; that'll do," said the skipper, sharply, as he struck another match, and gave the invalid a final disgusted punch. "Where's the boy?"

A small, dirty face with matted hair protruded from the bunk above the cook and eyed him sleepily.

"Get some supper," said Fraser, "quick."

"Supper, sir?" said the boy with a surprised yawn.

"And be quick about it," said the skipper, "and wash you face first and put a comb through your hair. Come, out you get."

The small sleeper sighed disconsolately, and, first extending one slender leg, clambered out and began to dress, yawning pathetically as he did so.

"And some coffee," said Fraser, as he lit the lamp and turned to depart.

"Bill," said the small boy, indignantly.

"Wot d'ye want?" said the seaman.

"'Elp me to wake that drunken pig up," said the youth, pointing a resentful finger at the cook. "I ain't goin' to do all the work."

"You leave 'im alone," said Bill, ferociously. The cook had been very liberal that evening, and friendship is friendship, after all.

"That's what a chap gets by keeping hisself sober," said the youthful philosopher, as he poured a little cold tea out of the kettle on his handkerchief and washed himself. "Other people's work to do."

He went grumbling up to the galley, and, lighting some sticks, put the kettle on, and then descended to the cabin, starting with genuine surprise as he saw the skipper sitting opposite a pretty girl, who was leaning back in her seat fast asleep.

"Cook'll be sorry 'e missed this," he murmured, as he lighted up and began briskly to set the table. He ran up on deck again to see how his fire was progressing, and thrusting his head down the forecastle communicated the exciting news to Bill.

To Fraser sitting watching his sleeping guest it seemed like a beautiful dream. That Poppy Tyrell should be sitting in his cabin and looking to him as her only friend seemed almost incredible. A sudden remembrance of Flower subdued at once the ardour of his gaze, and he sat wondering vaguely as to the whereabouts of that erratic mariner until his meditations were broken by the entrance of the boy with the steaming coffee, followed by Bill bearing a couple of teaspoons.

"I nearly went to sleep," said Poppy, as Fraser roused her gently.

She took off her hat and jacket, and Fraser, taking them from her, laid them reverently in his bunk. Then Poppy moved farther along the seat, and, taking some coffee pronounced herself much refreshed.

"I've been very rude to you," she said, softly; "but Mrs. Wheeler was very unkind, and said that of course I should go to you. That was why."

"Mrs. Wheeler is—" began Fraser, and stopped suddenly.

"Of course it was quite true," said Poppy, healthfully attacking her plate; "I did have to come to you."

"It was rather an odd way of coming," said Fraser; "my legs ache now."

The girl laughed softly, and continued to laugh. Then her eyes moistened, and her face became troubled. Fraser, as the best thing to do, made an excuse and went up on deck, to the discomfort of Bill and the boy, who were not expecting him.

Poppy was calm again by the time he returned, and thanked him again softly as he showed her her bunk and withdrew for the night. Bill and the boy placed their berths at his disposal, but he declined them in favour of a blanket in the galley, where he sat up, and slept but ill all night, and was a source of great embarrassment to the cook next morning when he wanted to enter to prepare breakfast.

Poppy presided over that meal, and it, and the subsequent walk to discover lodgings, are among Fraser's dearest memories. He trod on air through the squalid roads by her side, and, the apartments having been obtained, sat on the arm of the armchair—the most comfortable part—and listened to her plans.

"And you won't go away without letting me know?" he said, as he rose to depart.

Miss Tyrell shook her head, and her eyes smiled at him. "You know I won't," she said, softly. "I don't want to."

She saw him to the door, and until he had quitted the gate, kept it hospitably open. Fraser, with his head in a whirl, went back to the Swallow.

CHAPTER XVIII

The prime result of Mrs. Banks' nocturnal ramble with Mr. William Green, was a feeling of great bitterness against her old friend, Captain John Barber. Mr. Green, despite her protests, was still a member of the crew of the Foam, and walked about Seabridge in broad daylight, while she crept forth only after sundown, and saw a hidden meaning in every "Fine evening, Mrs. Banks," which met her. She pointed out to Captain Barber, that his refusal to dismiss Mr. Green was a reflection upon her veracity, and there was a strange light in her eyes and a strange hardening of her mouth, as the old man said that to comply with her request would be to reflect upon the polite seaman's veracity.

Her discomfiture was not lessened by the unbecoming behaviour of her daughter, who in some subtle manner, managed to convey that her acceptance of her mother's version of the incident depended upon the way she treated Mr. Frank Gibson. It was a hard matter to a woman of spirit, and a harder thing still, that those of her neighbours who listened to her account of the affair were firmly persuaded that she was setting her cap at Captain Barber.

To clear her character from this imputation, and at the same time to mark her sense of the captain's treatment of her, Mrs. Banks effected a remarkable change of front, and without giving him the slightest warning, set herself to help along his marriage to Mrs. Church.

She bantered him upon the subject when she met him out, and, disregarding his wrathful embarrassment, accused him in a loud voice of wearing his tie in a love-knot. She also called him a turtledove. The conversation ended here, the turtledove going away crimson with indignation and cooing wickedly.

Humbled by the terrors of his position, the proud shipowner turned more than ever to Captain Nibletts for comfort and sympathy, and it is but due to that little man to say that anything he could have done for his benefactor would have given him the greatest delight. He spent much of his spare time in devising means for his rescue, all of which the old man listened to with impatience and rejected with contumely.

"It's no good, Nibletts," he said, as they sat in the subdued light of the cabin one evening.

"Nothing can be done. If anything could be done, I should have thought of it."

"Yes, that's what struck me," said the little skipper, dutifully.

"I've won that woman's 'art," said Captain Barber, miserably; "in 'er anxiety to keep me, the woman's natur' has changed. There's nothing she wouldn't do to make sure of me."

"It's understandable," said Nibletts.

"It's understandable," agreed Captain Barber, "but it's orkard. Instead o' being a mild, amiable sort o' woman, all smiles, the fear o' losing me has changed 'er into a determined, jealous woman. She told me herself it was love of me as 'ad changed her."

"You ain't written to her, I suppose?" asked Nibletts, twisting his features into an expression of great cunning.

Captain Barber shook his head. "If you'd think afore speaking, Nibletts," he said, severely, "you'd know as people don't write to each other when they're in the same house."

The skipper apologised. "What I mean to say is this," he said, softly. "She hasn't got your promise in writing, and she's done all the talking about it. I'm the only one you've spoken to about it, I s'pose?"

Captain Barber nodded.

"Well, forget all about it," said Nibletts, in an excited whisper.

Captain Barber looked at him pityingly.

"What good'll that do?" he asked.

"Forget the understanding," continued Nibletts, in a stage whisper, "forget everything; forget Captain Flower's death, act as you acted just afore he went. People'll soon see as you're strange in your manner, and I'll put the news about as you've been so affected by that affair that your memory's gone."

"I was thinking of doing that the other day myself," said Captain Barber, slowly and untruthfully.

"I thought you was, from something you said," replied Nibletts.

"I think I spoke of it, or I was going to," said Barber.

"You did say something," said Nibletts.

"I wonder what would be the best way to begin," said Barber, regarding him attentively.

Captain Niblett's nerve failed him at the responsibility.

"It's your plan, Captain Barber," he said, impressively, "and nobody can tell a man like you how it should be done. It wants acting, and you've got to have a good memory to remember that you haven't got a memory."

"Say that agin," said Captain Barber, breathing thickly.

Captain Nibletts repeated it, and Captain Barber, after clearing his brain with a glass of spirits, bade him a solemn good-night, and proceeded slowly to his home. The door was opened by Mrs. Church, and a hum of voices from the front room indicated company. Captain Barber, hanging his hat on a peg, entered the room to discover Mrs. Banks and daughter, attended by Mr. Gibson.

"Where's Fred?" he asked, slowly, as he took a seat.

"Who?" said Miss Banks, with a little scream.

"Lawk-a-mussy, bless the man," said her mother. "I never did."

"Not come in yet?" asked Barber, looking round with a frightful stare. "The Foam's up!"

The company exchanged glances of consternation.

"Why, is he alive?" enquired Mrs. Church, sharply.

"Alive!" repeated Captain Barber. "Why shouldn't he be? He was alive yesterday, wasn't he?"

There was a dead silence, and then Captain Barber from beneath his shaggy eyebrows observed with delight that Gibson, tapping his forehead significantly, gave a warning glance at the others, while all four sitting in a row watched anxiously for the first signs of acute mania.

"I expect he's gone round after you, my dear," said the wily Barber to Miss Banks.

In the circumstances this was certainly cruel, and Gibson coughed confusedly.

"I'll go and see," said Miss Banks, hurriedly; "come along, mother."

The two ladies, followed by Mr. Gibson, shook hands and withdrew hurriedly. Captain Barber, wondering how to greet Mrs. Church after he had let them out, fixed his eyes on the carpet and remained silent.

"Aren't you well?" enquired the lady, tenderly.

"Well, ma'am?" repeated Uncle Barber, with severity.

"Ma'am?" said Mrs. Church, in tones of tender reproach; "two hours ago I was Laura. Have you been to the 'Thorn'?"

"What 'Thorn'?" demanded Captain Barber, who had decided to forget as much as possible, as the only safe way.

"The Thorn Inn," said Mrs. Church, impatiently.

"Where is it?" enquired Captain Barber, ingenuously.

Mrs. Church looked at him with deep consideration. "Why, at the end of the cottages, opposite the 'Swan.'"

"What 'Swan'?" enquired Captain Barber.

"The Swan Inn," said Mrs. Church, restraining her temper, but with difficulty.

"Where is it?" said Uncle Barber, with breezy freshness.

"Opposite the 'Thorn,' at the end of the row," said Mrs. Church, slowly.

"Well, what about it?" enquired Captain Barber.

"Nothing," said Mrs. Church, sharply, and proceeded to set supper.

Captain Barber, hugging himself over his scheme, watched her eagerly, evincing a little bewilderment as she brought on a small, unappetizing rind of cheese, bread, two glasses, and a jug of water. He checked himself just in time from asking for the cold fowl and bacon left from dinner, and, drawing his chair to the table, eyed the contents closely.

"Only bread and cheese?" he said, somewhat peevishly.

"That's all," said Mrs. Church, smiling; "bread and cheese and kisses."

Captain Barber tapped his forehead. "What did we have for dinner?" he asked, suddenly.

"Sausages," replied Mrs. Church, blandly; "we ate them all."

A piece of Captain Barber's cheese went the wrong way, and he poured himself out some water and drank it hurriedly. "Where's the beer?" he demanded.

"You've got the key of the cask," said the housekeeper.

Captain Barber, whose temper was rising, denied it.

"I gave it to you this morning," said Mrs. Church; "you were going to do something to it, don't you know?"

"I don't remember," said Uncle Barber, surlily.

"Whatever has happened to your memory?" said Mrs. Church, sweetly.

"My memory," said the trickster, slowly, passing his hand over his brow; "why, what's the matter with it?"

"It doesn't seem quite so good as it was," said the lady, affectionately. "Never mind, my memory will have to do for both."

There was enough emphasis on this last sentence to send a little chill through the captain's frame.

He said nothing, but keeping his eye on his plate attacked his frugal meal in silence, and soon afterwards went upstairs to bed to think out his position.

If his own memory was defective, Mrs. Church's was certainly redundant. When he came hurrying in to dinner next day she remembered that he had told her he should not be home to that meal. He was ungallant enough to contemplate a raid upon hers; she, with a rare thoughtfulness, had already eaten it. He went to the "Thorn," and had some cold salt beef, and cursed the ingenious Nibletts, now on his way to London, sky-high.

Mrs. Banks came in the next evening with her daughter, and condoled with the housekeeper on the affliction which had already been noised about Seabridge. Mrs. Church, who had accepted her as an ally, but with mental reservations, softly applied a handkerchief to her eyes.

"How are you feeling?" demanded Mrs. Banks, in the voice of one addressing a deaf invalid.

"I'm all right," said Barber, shortly.

"That's his pride," said Mrs. Church, mournfully; "he won't own to it. He can't remember anything. He pretends he doesn't know me."

"Who are you?" asked the sufferer, promptly.

"He'll get the better of it," said Mrs. Banks, kindly, as her quondam foe wiped her eyes again. "If he don't, you'd better marry before October."

To say that Captain Barber pricked up his ears at this, indicates but feebly his interest in the remark. He held his breath and looked wildly round the room as the two ladies, deftly ignoring him, made their arrangements for his future.

"I don't like to seem to hurry it," said the housekeeper.

"No, of course you don't. If he said October, naturally October it ought to be, in the usual way," remarked the other.

"I never said October," interrupted the trembling mariner.

"There's his memory again," said Mrs. Banks, in a low voice.

"Poor dear," sighed the other.

"We'll look after your interests," said Mrs. Banks, with a benevolent smile. "Don't you remember meeting me by the church the other night and telling me that you were going to marry Mrs. Church in October?"

"No," bawled the affrighted man.

"Clean gone," said Mrs. Church, shaking her head; "it's no use."

"Not a bit," said Mrs. Banks.

"October seems rather early," said Mrs. Church, "especially as he is in mourning for his nephew.

"There's no reason for waiting," said Mrs. Banks, decidedly. "I daresay it's his loneliness that makes him want to hurry it. After all, he ought to know what he wants."

"I never said a word about it," interposed Captain Barber, in a loud voice.

"All right," said Mrs. Banks, indulgently. "What are you going to wear, my dear?" she added, turning to the housekeeper.

Mrs. Church seemed undecided, and Captain Barber, wiping the moisture from his brow, listened as one in a dream to a long discussion on the possibilities of her wardrobe. Thrice he interrupted, and thrice the ladies, suspending their conversation for a moment, eyed him with tender pity before resuming it.

"Me and Frank thought of October," said Elizabeth, speaking for the first time. She looked at Captain Barber, and then at her mother. It was the look of one offering to sell a casting vote.

"October's early," said the old lady, bridling.

Mrs. Church looked up at her, and then modestly looked down again. "Why not a double wedding?" she asked, gently.

Captain Barber's voice was drowned in acclamations. Elizabeth kissed Mrs. Church, and then began to discuss her own wardrobe. The owner of the house, the owner of the very chairs on which they were sitting, endeavoured in vain to stop them on a point of order, and discovered to his mortification that a man without a memory is a man without influence. In twenty minutes it was all settled, and even an approximate date fixed. There was a slight movement on the part of Elizabeth to obtain Captain Barber's opinion upon that, but being reminded by her mother that he would forget all about it in half an hour's time, she settled it without him.

"I'm so sorry about your memory, Captain Barber," said Mrs. Banks, as she prepared to depart. "I can understand what a loss it is. My memory's a very good one. I never forget anything."

"You forget yourself, ma'am," returned her victim, with unconscious ambiguity, and, closing the door behind her, returned to the parlour to try and think of some means of escaping from the position to which the ingenuity of Captain Nibletts, aided by that of Mrs. Banks, had brought him.

CHAPTER XIX

Opponents of medicine have hit upon a means of cleansing the system by abstaining for a time from food, and drinking a quantity of fair water. It is stated to clear the eyes and the skin, and to cause a feeling of lightness and buoyancy undreamt of by those who have never tried it. All people, perhaps, are not affected exactly alike, and Captain Flower, while admitting the lightness, would have disdainfully contested any charge of buoyancy. Against this objection it may be said, that he was not a model patient, and had on several occasions wilfully taken steps to remove the feeling of lightness.

It was over a fortnight since his return to London. The few shillings obtained for his watch had disappeared days before; rent was due and the cupboard was empty. The time seemed so long to him, that Poppy and Seabridge and the Foam might have belonged to another period of existence. At the risk of detection he had hung round the Wheelers night after night for a glimpse of the girl for whom he was enduring all these hardships, but without success. He became a prey to nervousness and, unable to endure the suspense any longer, determined to pay a stealthy visit to Wapping and try and see Fraser.

He chose the night on which in the ordinary state of affairs the schooner should be lying alongside the wharf; and keeping a keen lookout for friends and foes both, made his way to the Minories and down Tower Hill. He had pictured it as teeming with people he knew, and the bare street and closed warehouses, with a chance docker or two slouching slowly along, struck him with an odd sense of disappointment. The place seemed changed. He hurried past the wharf; that too was deserted, and after a loving peep at the spars of his schooner he drifted slowly across the road to the Albion, and, pushing the door a little way open, peeped cautiously in. The faces were all unfamiliar, and letting the door swing quietly back he walked on until he came to the Town of Yarmouth.

The public bar was full. Tired workers were trying to forget the labours of the day in big draughts of beer, while one of them had thrown off his fatigue sufficiently to show a friend a fancy step of which he was somewhat vain. It was a difficult and intricate step for a crowded bar, and panic-stricken men holding their beer aloft called wildly upon him to stop, while the barman, leaning over the counter, strove to make his voice heard above the din. The dancer's feet subsided into a sulky shuffle, and a tall seaman, removing the tankard which had obscured his face, revealed the honest features of Joe. The sight of him and the row of glasses and hunches of bread and cheese behind the bar was irresistible. The skipper caught a departing customer by the coat and held him.

"Do me a favour, old man," he said, heartily.

"Wot d'ye want?" asked the other, suspiciously.

"Tell that tall chap in there that a friend of his is waiting outside," said Flower, pointing to Joe.

He walked off a little way as the man re-entered the bar. A second or two later, the carman came out alone.

"'E ses come inside 'e ses if you want to see 'im."

"I can't," said Flower.

"Why not?" asked the other, as a horrible suspicion dawned upon him. "Strewth, you ain't a teetotaler, are you?"

"No," replied the skipper, "but I can't go in."

"Well 'e won't come out," said the other; "'e seems to be a short-tempered sort o' man."

"I must see him," said the skipper, pondering. Then a happy thought struck him, and he smiled at his cleverness. "Tell him a little flower wants to see him," he said, briskly.

"A little wot?" demanded the carman, blankly.

"A little flower," repeated the other.

"Where is she?" enquired the carman, casting his eyes about him.

"You just say that," said the skipper, hurriedly. "You shall have a pint if you do. He'll understand."

It was unfortunate for the other that the skipper had set too high an estimation on Joe's intelligence, for the information being imparted to him in the audible tones of confidence, he first gave his mug to Mr. William Green to hold, and then knocked the ambassador down. The loud laugh consequent on the delivery of the message ceased abruptly, and in the midst of a terrific hubbub Joe and his victim, together with two or three innocent persons loudly complaining that they hadn't finished their beer, were swept into the street.

"He'll be all right in a minute, mate," said a bystander to Joe, anxiously; "don't run away."

"'Tain't so likely," said Joe, scornfully.

"Wot did you 'it me for?" demanded the victim, turning a deaf ear to two or three strangers who were cuddling him affectionately and pointing out, in alluring whispers, numberless weak points in Joe's fleshly armour.

"I'll 'it you agin if you come into a pub making a fool of me afore people," replied the sensitive seaman, blushing hotly with the recollection of the message.

"He told me to," said the carman, pointing to Flower, who was lurking in the background.

The tall seaman turned fiercely and strode up to him, and then, to the scandal of the bystanders and the dismay of Mr. William Green, gave a loud yell and fled full speed up the road. Flower followed in hot pursuit, and owing, perhaps, to the feeling of lightness before mentioned, ran him down nearly a mile farther on, Mr. Green coming in a good second.

"Keep orf," panted the seaman, backing into a doorway. "Keep—it—orf!"

"Don't be a fool, Joe," said the skipper.

"Keep orf," repeated the trembling seaman.

His fear was so great that Mr. Green, who had regarded him as a tower of strength and courage, and had wormed himself into the tall seaman's good graces by his open admiration of these qualities, stood appalled at his idol's sudden lack of spirit.

"Don't be a fool, Joe," said the skipper, sharply; "can't you see it's me?"

"I thought you was drownded," said the trembling seaman, still regarding him suspiciously. "I thought you was a ghost."

"Feel that," said Flower, and gave him a blow in the ribs which almost made him regret that his first impression was not the correct one.

"I'm satisfied, sir," he said, hastily.

"I was picked up and carried off to Riga: but for certain reasons I needn't go into, I want my being alive kept a dead secret. You mustn't breathe a word to anybody, d'ye understand? Not a word."

"Aye, aye, sir," said Joe; "you hear that, Will-yum?"

"Who the devil's this?" demanded the skipper, who had not bargained for another confidant.

"It's the new 'and, sir," said Joe. "I'll be answerable for 'im."

Flower eyed the pair restlessly, but Mr. Green assured him with a courtly bow that Mr. Smith's assurances might be relied upon. "He hoped he was a gentleman," he said, feelingly.

"Some of us thought—I thought," said Joe, with a glance at the skipper, "that the mate shoved you overboard."

"You always were a fool," commented the skipper.

"Yes, sir," said Joe, dutifully, and as they moved slowly back along the road gave him the latest information about Seabridge and the Foam.

"The Swallow's just come up in the tier," he concluded; "and if you want to see Mr. Fraser, I'll go and see if he's aboard."

The skipper agreed, and after exacting renewed assurances of secrecy from both men, waited impatiently in the private bar of the Waterman's Arms while they put off from the stairs and boarded the steamer.

In twenty minutes, during which time the penniless skipper affected not to notice the restless glances of the landlord, they returned with Fraser, and a hearty meeting took place between the two men. The famished skipper was provided with meat and drink, while the two A. B.'s whetted their thirst in the adjourning bar.

"You've had a rough time," said Fraser, as the skipper concluded a dramatic recital of his adventures.

Flower smiled broadly. "I've come out of it right side uppermost," he said, taking a hearty pull at his tankard; "the worst part was losing my money. Still, it's all in the day's work. Joe tells me that Elizabeth is walking out with Gibson, so you see it has all happened as I bargained for."

"I've heard so," said Fraser.

"It's rather soon after my death," said Flower, thoughtfully; "she's been driven into it by her mother, I expect. How is Poppy?"

Fraser told him.

"I couldn't wish her in better hands, Jack," said the other, heartily, when he had finished; "one of these days when she knows everything—at least, as much as I shall tell her—she'll be as grateful to you as what I am."

"You've come back just in time," said Fraser, slowly; "another week, and you'd have lost her."

"Lost her?" repeated Flower, staring.

"She's going to New Zealand," replied the other; "she's got some relations there. She met an old friend of her father's the other day, Captain Martin, master of the Golden Cloud, and he has offered her a passage. They sail on Saturday from the Albert Dock."

Flower pushed the tankard from him, and regarded him in consternation.

"She mustn't go," he said, decisively.

Fraser shrugged his shoulders. "I tried to persuade her not to, but it was no use. She said there was nothing to stay in England for; she's quite alone, and there is nobody to miss her."

"Poor girl," said Flower, softly, and sat crumbling his bread and gazing reflectively at a soda-water advertisement on the wall. He sat so long in this attitude that his companion also turned and studied it.

"She mustn't go," said Flower, at length. "I'll go down and see her to-morrow night. You go first and break the news to her, and I'll follow on. Do it gently, Jack. It's quite safe; there's nobody she can talk to now; she's left the Wheelers, and I'm simply longing to see her. You don't know what it is to be in love, Jack."

"What am I to tell her?" enquired the other, hastily.

"Tell her I was saved," was the reply. "I'll do the rest. By Jove, I've got it."

He banged the table so hard that his plate jumped and the glasses in the bar rattled in protest.

"Anything wrong with the grub?" enquired the landlord, severely.

Flower, who was all excitement, shook his head.

"Because if there is," continued the landlord, "I'd sooner you spoke of it than smash the table; never mind about hurting my feelings."

He wiped down the counter to show that Flower's heated glances had no effect upon him, withdrawing reluctantly to serve an impatient customer.

"I'll go down to-morrow morning to the Golden Cloud and try and ship before the mast," said Flower, excitably; "get married out in New Zealand, and then come home when things are settled. What do you think of that, my boy? How does that strike you?"

"How will it strike Cap'n Barber?" asked Fraser, as soon as he had recovered sufficiently to speak.

Flower's eyes twinkled. "It's quite easy to get wrecked and picked up once or twice," he said, cheerfully. "I'll have my story pat by the time I get home, even to the names of the craft I was cast away in. And I can say I heard of Elizabeth's marriage from somebody I met in New Zealand. I'll manage all right."

The master of the Swallow gazed at him in help-less fascination.

"They want hands on the Golden Cloud," he said, slowly; "but what about your discharges?"

"I can get those," said Flower, complacently; "a man with money and brains can do anything. Lend me a pound or two before I forget it, will you? And if you'll give me Poppy's address, I'll be outside the house at seven to-morrow. Lord, fancy being on the same ship with her for three months."

He threw down a borrowed sovereign on the counter, and, ordering some more drinks, placed them on the table. Fraser had raised his to his lips when he set it down again, and with a warning finger called the other's attention to the remarkable behaviour of the door communicating with the next bar, which, in open defiance of the fact that it possessed a patent catch of the latest pattern, stood open at least three or four inches.

"Draught?" questioned Flower, staring at the phenomenon.

The other shook his head. "I'd forgotten those two chaps," he said, in a low voice; "they've been listening."

Flower shifted in his seat. "I'd trust Joe anywhere," he said, uneasily, "but I don't know about the other chap. If he starts talking at Seabridge I'm done. I thought Joe was alone when I sent in for him."

Fraser tapped his chin with his fingers. "I'll try and get 'em to ship with me. I want a couple of hands," he said, slowly. "I'll have them under my eye then, and, besides, they're better at Bittlesea than Seabridge in any case."

He rose noisily, and followed by Flower entered the next bar. Twenty minutes afterwards Flower bade them all a hearty good-night, and Mr. Green, walking back to the schooner with Joe, dwelt complacently on the advantages of possessing a style and address which had enabled them to exchange the rudeness of Ben for the appreciative amiability of Captain Fraser.

Flower was punctual to the minute next evening, and shaking hands hastily with Fraser, who had gone down to the door to wait for him, went in alone to see Miss Tyrell. Fraser, smoking his pipe on the doorstep, gave him a quarter of an hour, and then went upstairs, Miss Tyrell making a futile attempt to escape from the captain's encircling arm as he entered the room. Flower had just commenced the recital of his adventures. He broke off as the other entered, but being urged by Miss Tyrell to continue, glanced somewhat sheepishly at his friend before complying.

"When I rose to the surface," he said, slowly "and saw the ship drawing away in the darkness and heard the cries on board, I swam as strongly as I could towards it. I was weighed down by my clothes, and I had also struck my head going overboard, and I felt that every moment was my last, when I suddenly bumped up against the life-belt. I had just strength to put that on and give one faint hail, and then I think for a time I lost my senses."

Miss Tyrell gave an exclamation of pity; Mr. Fraser made a noise which might have been intended for the same thing.

"The rest of it was like a dream," continued Flower, pressing the girl's hand; "sometimes my eyes were open and sometimes not. I heard the men pulling about and hailing me without being able to reply. By-and-by that ceased, the sky got grey and the water brown; all feeling had gone out of me. The sun rose and burnt in the salt on my face; then as I rose and fell like a cork on the waters, your face seemed to come before me, and I determined to live."

"Beautiful," said Fraser, involuntarily.

"I determined to live," repeated Flower, glancing at him defiantly. "I brushed the wet hair from my eyes, and strove to move my chilled limbs. Then I shouted, and anything more dreary than that shout across the waste of water I cannot imagine, but it did me good to hear my own voice, and I shouted again."

He paused for breath, and Fraser, taking advantage of the pause, got up hurriedly and left the room, muttering something about matches.

"He doesn't like to hear of your sufferings," said Poppy.

"I suppose not," said Flower, whose eloquence had received a chill, "but there is little more to tell. I was picked up by a Russian brig bound for Riga, and lay there some time in a state of fever. When I got better I worked my passage home in a timber boat and landed yesterday."

"What a terrible experience," said Poppy, as Fraser entered the room again.

"Shocking," said the latter.

"And now you've got your own ship again," said the girl, "weren't your crew delighted to see you?"

"I've not seen them yet," said Flower, hesitatingly. "I shipped on another craft this morning before the mast."

"Before the mast," repeated the girl, in amazement.

"Full-rigged ship Golden Cloud bound for New Zealand," said Flower, slowly, watching the effect of his words—"we're to be shipmates."

Poppy Tyrell started up with a faint cry, but Flower drew her gently down again.

"We'll be married in New Zealand," he said, softly, "and then we'll come back and I'll have my own again. Jack told me you were going out on her. Another man has got my craft; he lost the one he had before, and I want to give him a chance for a few months, poor chap, to redeem his character. Besides, it'll be a change. We shall see the world. It'll just be a splendid honeymoon."

"You didn't tell Captain Martin?" enquired the girl, as she drew back in her chair and eyed him perplexedly.

"Not likely," said Flower, with a laugh. "I've shipped in the name of Robert Orth. I bought the man's discharges this morning. He's lying in bed, poor chap, waiting for his last now, and hoping it'll be marked 'v. g.'"

Poppy was silent. For a moment her eyes, dark and inscrutable, met Fraser's; then she looked away, and in a low voice addressed Flower.

"I suppose you know best what is to be done," she said, quietly.

"You leave it to me," said Flower, in satisfied tones. "I'm at the wheel."

There was a long silence. Poppy got up and crossed to the window, and, resting her cheek on her hand, sat watching the restless life of the street. The room darkened slowly with the approach of evening. Flower rose and took the seat opposite, and Fraser, who had been feeling in the way for some time, said that he must go.

"You sail to-morrow evening, Jack?" said Flower, with a careless half-turn towards him.

"About six," was the reply.

"We sail Saturday evening at seven," said Flower, and took the girl's hand in his own. "It will be odd to see you on board, Poppy, and not to be able to speak to you; but we shall be able to look at each other, sha'n't we?"

"Captain Martin is a strict disciplinarian," said Poppy.

"Well he can't prevent us looking at each other," said Flower, "and he can't prevent us marrying when we get to the other end. Good-night, Jack. Next time you see us we'll be an old married couple."

"A quick passage and a safe return," said Fraser. "Good-night."

Poppy Tyrell just gave him her small hand, and that was all. Flower, giving him a hearty grip, accompanied him as far as the door of the room.

He looked back as he gained the pavement, and the last he saw of them they were sitting at the open window. Flower leaned out and waved his hand in farewell, but Poppy made no sign.

CHAPTER XX

In the rising seaport of Bittlesea Captain Fraser, walking slowly along the quay on the fateful Saturday, heard the hour of seven strike from the tower of the old church wedged in between the narrow streets at the back of the town. The little harbour with its motley collection of craft vanished; he heard the sharp, hoarse cries of command on the Golden Cloud, and saw the bridge slowly opening to give egress to the tug which had her in tow. He saw her shapely hull and tapering spars glide slowly down the river, while Poppy Tyrell, leaning against the side, took her last look at London. He came back with a sigh to reality: the Swallow had dwindled to microscopical proportions, and looked dirty; Bittlesea itself had the appearance of a village with foolish aspirations to be considered a port, and he noticed, with a strong sense of pity tempered with disdain, the attentions of two young townsmen to a couple of gawky girls in white frocks.

With a feeling that the confinement of the house would be insupportable, he roamed idly about until the day gave place to twilight, and the red eye of the lightship on the horizon peeped suddenly across the water. Bittlesea was dull to aching point; a shirt-sleeved householder or two sat in his fragrant front-garden smoking, and a murmur of voices and shag tobacco floated out from tavern doorways. He paced up and down the quay, until the necessity of putting a stop to the vagaries of his crew furnished him with a little wholesome diversion.

In their quest for good beer Mr. Green and Joe had left themselves in the hands of the other members of the crew, and had gone off with them in a body to the Cap and Bells, where, in a most pointed fashion, Mr. Green, who had been regarding the fireman's complexion for some time with much displeasure, told the boy to go back to the ship and get his face washed.

"He's all right, ain't you, Tommy?" said the cook, coming to the rescue.

"Boys ought to keep their faces clean," said Mr. Green, impressively; "there's nothing more unpleasant than a face what wants washing. You don't want to grow up like that, do you? Look at it, Joe."

"It might be cleaner," said Joe, thus appealed to, slowly; "likewise it might be dirtier."

"It might be much dirtier," said Mr. Green, emphatically; "anybody with eyes in their 'ed can see that."

There was an awkward pause, during which the fireman, with one eye peeping furtively from beyond the rim of a quart pot, saw both Joe and the cook kick Mr. Green's foot to call his attention to the fact that his words might be misconstrued by another member of the party.

"I 'ate toffs," he said, deliberately, as he placed his mug on the counter.

"They're all right when you know 'em, Charlie," said Joe, who was averse to having the evening spoiled at that early hour.

"A real toff's bad enough," continued the fireman, "but a himitation one—pah!" He buried his face in the pewter again, and laughed discordantly.

"You go aboard and wash you face, Tommy," repeated Mr. Green. "I should think you'd find plenty o' soap in Charlie's bunk."

"Do you know what you want?" demanded the fireman, regarding him fixedly.

"I know what you want," said Mr. Green, with a supercilious smile.

"Oh! Wot?" said the other.

The polite seaman rose to his feet and watched him carefully. "A banjo," he replied.

It was not the reply according to time-honoured formula, and Charlie, who was expecting something quite different, was at no pains to hide his perplexity. "A banjo?" he repeated, slowly, "a banjo—a ban——?"

Light came to him suddenly, and he flew at Mr. Green with his fists whirling. In a second the bar was in an uproar, and the well-meant and self-preservative efforts of Joe and the cook to get the combatants into the street were frustrated by people outside blocking up the doors. They came out at last, and Fraser, who was passing, ran over just in time to save Mr. Green, who was doing his best, from the consequences of a somewhat exaggerated fastidiousness. The incident, however, afforded a welcome distraction, and having seen Mr. Green off in the direction of the steamer, while the fireman returned to the public-house, he bent his steps homewards and played a filial game at cards with his father before retiring.

They sailed for London the following afternoon, Mr. Green taking a jaundiced view of the world from a couple of black eyes, while the fireman openly avowed that only the economical limitations of Nature prevented him from giving him more. Fraser, a prey to gentle melancholy, called them to order once or twice, and then left them to the mate, a man whose talent for ready invective was at once the admiration and envy of his peers.

The first night in London he spent on board, and with pencil and paper sat down to work out the position of the Golden Cloud. He pictured her with snowy pinions outspread, passing down Channel. He pictured Poppy sitting on the poop in a deck-chair and Flower coming as near as his work would allow, exchanging glances with her. Then he went up on deck, and, lighting his pipe, thought of that never-to-be-forgotten night when Poppy had first boarded the Foam.

The next night his mood changed, and unable to endure the confinement of the ship, he went for a lonely tramp round the streets. He hung round the Wheelers, and, after gazing at their young barbarians at play, walked round and looked at Flower's late lodgings. It was a dingy house, with broken railings and an assortment of papers and bottles in the front garden, and by no means calculated to relieve depression. From there he instinctively wandered round to the lodgings recently inhabited by Miss Tyrell.

He passed the house twice, and noted with gloom the already neglected appearance of her front window. The Venetian blind, half drawn up, was five or six inches higher one side than the other, and a vase of faded flowers added to the forlornness of the picture. In his present state of mind the faded blooms seemed particularly appropriate, and suddenly determining to possess them, he walked up the steps and knocked at the door, trembling like a young housebreaker over his first job.

"I think I left my pipe here the other night," he stammered to the small girl who opened it.

"I'll swear you didn't," said the small damsel, readily.

"Can I go up and see?" enquired Fraser, handing her some coppers.

The small girl relented, and even offered to assist him in his search, but he waved her away, and going upstairs sat down and looked drearily round the shabby little room. An execrable ornament of green and pink paper in the fireplace had fallen down, together with a little soot; there was dust on the table, and other signs of neglect. He crossed over to the window and secured two or three of the blooms, and was drying the stalks on his handkerchief when his eye suddenly lighted on a little white ball on the mantel-piece, and, hardly able to believe in his good fortune, he secured a much-darned pair of cotton gloves, which had apparently been forgotten in the hurry of departure. He unrolled them, and pulling out the little shrivelled fingers, regarded them with mournful tenderness. Then he smoothed them out, and folding them with reverent fingers, placed them carefully in his breastpocket. He then became conscious that somebody was regarding his antics with amazement from the doorway.

"Mr. Fraser!" said a surprised voice, which tried to be severe.

Mr. Fraser bounded from his chair, and stood regarding the intruder with a countenance in which every feature was outvying the other in amazement.

"I thought—you—were on the Golden Cloud," he stammered.

Miss Tyrell shook her head and looked down. "I missed the ship," she said, pensively.

"Missed the ship?" shouted the other; "missed the ship? Did Flower miss it too?"

"I'm afraid not," said Miss Tyrell, even more pensively than before.

"Good heavens, I never heard of such a thing," said Fraser; "how ever did you manage to do it?"

"I went to lie down a little while on Saturday afternoon," said Poppy, reflectively; "I'd got my box packed and everything ready; when I got up it was past seven o'clock, and then I knew it was no use. Ships won't wait, you know."

Fraser gazed at her in amaze. In his mind's eye he still saw the deck of the Golden Cloud; but Poppy's deck-chair was empty, and Flower, in place of exchanging glances with her, was walking about in a state equally compounded, of wrath and bewilderment.

"And you had given up your berth in the City?" said Fraser, at length, in concern.

The consciousness of a little colour in her cheek which she could not repress affected Miss Tyrell's temper. "No," she said, sharply.

"Didn't you intend to go, then?" asked the bewildered Fraser.

"I—oh, will you give me my gloves, please, before I forget them?" said Miss Tyrell, coldly.

It was Fraser's turn to colour, and he burnt a rich crimson as he fished them out.

"I was going to take care of them for you," he said, awkwardly. "I came to look after a pipe I thought I'd left here."

"I saw you taking care of them," was the reply.

There was a pause, during which Miss Tyrell took a seat and, folding her hands in her lap, gazed at him with the calm gaze which comes of perfect misdoing and the feminine determination not to own up to it. The room was no longer shabby, and Fraser was conscious of a strange exaltation.

"I understood that you had given notice in the City," he said, slowly; "but I'm very glad that you didn't."

Miss Tyrell shook her head, and stooping down adjusted the fire-stove ornament.

"Didn't you intend to go?" repeated the tactful seaman.

"I'd left it open," said Miss Tyrell, thoughtfully; "I hadn't definitely accepted Captain Martin's invitation. You jump at conclusions so, but of course when I found that Captain Flower had shipped before the mast for my sake, why, I had to go."

"So you had," said Fraser, staring.

"There was no help for it," continued Miss Tyrell.

"Didn't seem like it," said the more accurate Fraser.

His head was in a whirl, and he tried vainly to think of the exact terms in which she had announced her intention to emigrate, and combated the objections which he thought himself justified in advancing. He began to remember in a misty, un-certain fashion that they were somewhat vague and disjointed, and for one brief moment he wondered whether she had ever had any idea of going at all. One glance at the small figure of probity opposite was enough, and he repelled the idea as unworthy.

"I believe that you are sorry I didn't go," said Poppy, suddenly.

"I'm sorry for Flower," said the other.

"He will be back in six or seven months," said Poppy, gently; "that will soon pass away. I shall not be very old to marry even then. Perhaps it is all for the best—I don't like—"

"Don't like?" prompted Fraser.

"Don't like to be hurried," continued Miss Tyrell, looking down.

There was another pause. The girl got up and, walking to the window, gazed out upon the street.

"There is a nice air in the streets now," she said at length, without turning round.

Fraser started. Politeness and inclination fought with conscience. The allies won, but inclination got none of the credit.

"Would you care to go for a walk?" he asked.

Miss Tyrell turned and regarded him with an unmistakable air of surprise.

"No, thank you," she said, in a manner which indicated reproof.

Fraser shifted restlessly. "I thought that was what you meant," he said, indignantly.

"You jump at conclusions, as I said before," remarked Miss Tyrell. "It wouldn't be right."

"I don't see any harm in it," said Fraser, stoutly; "we've been before, and Flower knows of it."

The girl shook her head. "No," she said, firmly.

To her surprise, that ended the matter. The rattle of traffic and the hum of voices came in at the open window; the room seemed unwontedly quiet by contrast. Miss Tyrell sat reaping the empty reward of virtue, and bestowing occasional glances on the fine specimen of marine obtuseness in the armchair.

"I hope that I am not keeping you from a walk," she observed, at length.

"No," said Fraser.

He rose in confusion, wondering whether this was a hint for him to go, and after a supreme mental effort decided that it was, and murmured something about getting back to the ship. Poppy shook hands with him patiently. It is always a sad thing to see a fine young man lacking in intelligence. Some of her pity perhaps showed in her eyes.

"Are you going?" she asked, with a shade of surprise in her voice.

Fraser gazed at her in perplexity. "I suppose so," he murmured.

"Which means that you want a walk, but don't like leaving me here alone, I suppose," said Miss Tyrell, resignedly. "Very well, I will come."

She left him for a moment in search of her hat, and then, putting aside the gloves she was about to don in favour of those he had endeavoured to secrete, led the way downstairs. Her composure was sufficient for two, which was just the quantity required at that moment.

CHAPTER XXI

The summer passed quickly. All too quickly for Captain Barber, who said that it was the shortest he ever remembered. But, then, his memory, although greatly improved, was still none of the best, many things which Mrs. Church fondly and frequently referred to having escaped it altogether.

He even forgot that he was to be married in October, and in these circumstances Mrs. Gibson, Miss Banks, and Mrs. Church put their banns up. This acted as a specific, and Captain Barber, putting the best face he could on the matter, went and interviewed the verger on his own behalf.

The wedding-day found him resigned, but dazed, The morning air was crisp and chill, with a faint odour of dead leaves and the aromatic smell of chrysanthemums which decked the front garden. The house was as clean as a new pin, or the deck of the Foam, which, having been thoroughly scrubbed down in honour of the occasion, was now slowly drying in the sun. Down below, the crew, having finished their labours for the day, were anxiously attiring themselves in their Sunday best.

The grizzled head of Ben popped out at the companion and sniffed heartily at the smell of wet deck. His coat was of black, and his new boots creaked deliciously as he slowly paced the deck and affected ignorance of the little cluster of heads at the forecastle hatch. He went below again, and a murmur, gentle but threatening, rose against Tim.

"You wait," said the youth, sharply.

"If you've made me waste eighteenpence, Timmy," said a stout A. B. named Jones, "the Lord ha' mercy on you, 'cos I won't."

The cook, who was clinging to the ladder with his head level with the deck, gave an excited gasp. "Tim's all right," he said; "look there."

The last words were jerked out of him by reason of the weight of his friends, who were now leaning on him, breathing heavily under the stress of strong excitement. Ben was on deck again, and in an obviously unconcerned manner was displaying a silk hat of great height to all who cared to look. The mate's appearance alone, without the flags which dressed the schooner, would have indicated a festival.

Three or four labourers sunning themselves on the quay were much impressed and regarded him stolidy; a fisherman, presuming upon the fact that they both earned their living on the water, ventured to address him.

"Now, then," said Jones, as he took something reverently from an empty bunk, "who's going up fust?"

"I ain't," said Tim.

"Wot about you, cookie?" said Jones.

"Well, wot about me?" demanded the other.

"I thought p'r'aps you'd like to lead the way," said Mr. Jones, mildly.

"You thought wrong, then," said the cook, shortly.

"It was jist a compliment," urged Mr. Jones.

"I don't like flattery," said the cook; "never did."

Mr. Jones sighed and shook his head irresolutely. The other A.B. patted him on the back.

"You look a fair bloomin' treat," he said, heartily. "You go up fust; you look as though you've slep' in one a'most."

"None o' your larks, you know," remarked Mr. Jones, with suspicious sourness; "no backing out of it and leavin' me there by myself."

There was a chorus of virtuous but profane indignation. It was so indignant that Mr. Jones apologised, and stood for some time regarding the article in his hand with the face of a small child eyeing a large powder. Then he clapped it on his head and went on deck.

The mate was just talking to the fisherman about an uncle of his (born since his promotion) who had commanded a brig, when his voice failed him, and he gazed open-mouthed at a stout seaman who had just come up on deck. On the stout seaman's face was the look of one who sees a vision many miles off; on the stout seaman's head was a high hat of antique pattern which had suffered in the brushing. To avoid the mate's eye he folded his arms and, leaning over the side, gazed across the river. Words trembled on the mate's lips, but they died away in a squeak as a little top-hatted procession of three issued coyly from the forecastle and, ranging itself beside Mr. Jones, helped him to look across the river.

"I never did," said the fisherman. "What are we a-coming to?"

The mate did not stay to inform him. He walked hastily to the quartette and, bursting with rage, asked Jones what he meant by it.

"Mean by wot, sir?" asked Jones, in surprise.

"Top-hats," said the mate, choking.

The four turned and regarded him stolidly, keeping as close together as possible for the sake of moral support and the safety of their head-gear.

"For the weddin', sir," said Jones, as though that explained everything.

"You take 'em off," said the mate, sharply. "I won't let you wear 'em."

"I beg your pardin," said Jones, with great politeness, "we got these 'ere 'ats for the weddin', an' we're a-goin' to wear 'em."

He took the offending article off and brushed it tenderly with his coat-sleeve, while the furious mate looked assault and battery at the other three. Tim, whose hat came well down over his eyes, felt comparatively safe; but the cook, conscious that his perched lightly on the top of his head, drew back a pace. Then he uttered an exclamation as Captain Nibletts, who was officiating as best man, came hurriedly down the cliff.

"Hats?" said the little skipper, disengaging himself from the mate's grasp, as he came on board. "Yes, I don't mind."

"Wot about Capt'in Barber?" demanded the mate, impressively.

"If they was pudding-basins 'e wouldn't mind," said Nibletts, testily; "he's that nervous 'e don't know what 'e's doing hardly. He was raving like a madman for five minutes cos 'e couldn't fasten his collar, and then I found he'd forgot to put his shirt on. He don't care."

He hurried down to the cabin and then came bustling up again. His small face was strained with worry, and the crew eyed him respectfully as he came forward and dealt out white satin favours.

"Cap'in Barber'll be all right with you looking arter 'im, sir," said Jones, with strong conviction.

"That he will," said the cook, nodding.

"There's some whisky in a bottle in my locker, cook," said Nibletts, dancing about nervously; "give the hands one drink each, cook. Only one, mind."

The men thanked him, and with kindly eyes watched him go ashore. The cook went down for the whisky, and Tim, diving into the forecastle, brought up four mugs.

"He must ha' meant another bottle," said Jones, as the cook came slowly up again with a bottle containing one dose.

"There ain't another," said the cook; "he's 'alf off 'is 'ed."

There was a pained silence. "We must toss for it," said Jones, at length; "that is, unless you chaps don't want it."

"Toss," said three voices speaking as one.

Jones sighed, and the coins were produced. The prize fell to Tim, and he leaned against the windlass and slowly poured the yellow liquid into his mug.

"There's more than I thought there was," remarked Mr. Jones, in surprise.

"Bottles is deceiving," said the cook.

"It ain't the fust toss as Tim 'as won," said the third man, darkly.

The ordinary seaman made no reply, but, stepping over to the water-cask, added with great care a little water.

"Here's your 'ealth, chaps," he said, good-naturedly, as he drank, "and may you never want a drink."

"You've never drunk all that, Tim?" said Mr. Jones, anxiously.

Tim shook his head. "There's too much to drink all at once," he said, gravely, and sat, with the mug on his knee, gazing ashore. "It's warming me all over," he mused. "I never tasted sich whisky afore. I'm in a gentle glow."

So was the cook; a glow which increased to fever heat as the youth raised the mug to his lips again, and slowly drained it and handed it to him to wash up.

A little later the men went ashore, and strolling aimlessly up and down the road, passed the time in waiting for the ceremony and making sudden dashes after small boys who were throwing at their hats and hitting their heads.

Seabridge itself was quiet, but Mrs. Banks' house was in a state of ferment. Ladies with pins in their mouths wandered about restlessly until, coming into the orbit of one of the brides, they stuck one or two into her and then drew back to behold the effect. Miss Banks, in white satin, moved about stiffly; Mrs. Church, in heliotrope, glanced restlessly up the road every time she got near the window.

"Now you sit down," said one lady, at length, "both of you. All you've got to do now is to wait for the gentlemen."

It was whispered that Mr. Gibson's delay was due to the fact that he had gone up for Captain Barber, and as time passed a certain restlessness became apparent in the assembly, and sympathetic glances were thrown in the direction of Mrs. Church. Places at the window were at a premium, and several guests went as far as the garden gate and looked up the road. Still no Captain Barber.

"It's time they were here," said Mrs. Banks at last, in a stern voice.

There was a flutter at the gate, and a pretty girl heliographed with her eyes that the parties of the other part were in sight. A minute or two later they came into sight of the window. Captain Barber, clad in beautiful raiment, headed the cortège, the rear of which was brought up by the crew of the Foam and a cloud of light skirmishers which hovered on their flanks. As they drew near, it was noticed that Captain Barber's face was very pale, and his hands trembled, but he entered the house with a firm step and required no assistance.

Of his reception there was never for a moment any doubt. Young matrons smiled and shook their heads at him, middle-aged matrons took him by the hand, while old ladies committed themselves to the statement that they had seen matrimony in his eye for years. He received the full measure accorded to a very distinguished convert, and, taking a chair placed against the wall, surveyed the company with the air of a small boy who has strayed into a hostile alley. A little natural curiosity found vent.

"Now, what first put it into your head to get married?" ask one fair enquirer.

"Mrs. Church," said the ex-mariner, simply.

"Yes, of course," said the matron; "but was it love at first sight, or did it grow on you before you knew it?"

Captain Barber blushed. "It growed on me afore I knew it," he replied, fervently.

"I suppose," said a lady of a romantic turn of mind, "that you didn't know what was happening at first?"

"I did not, ma'am," agreed the Captain, in trembling tones. "Nobody was more surprised than wot I was."

"How strange," said two or three voices.

They regarded him tenderly, and the youngest bridesmaid, a terrible child of ten, climbed up on his knee and made audible comparisons between the two bridegrooms, which made Mr. Gibson smile.

"Time we started," said Mrs. Banks, raising her voice above the din. "Cap'in Barber, you and Mr. Gibson and the other gentlemen had better get to the church."

The men got up obediently, and in solemn silence formed up in the little passage, and then started for the church some two hundred yards distant, the crew of the Foam falling in behind unchallenged.

To this day Captain Barber does not know how he got there, and he resolutely declines to accept Captain Niblett's version as the mere offspring of a disordered imagination. He also denies the truth of a statement circulated in the town that night that, instead of replying to a leading question in the manner plainly laid down in the Church Service, he answered, "I suppose so."

He came out of the church with a buzzing in his ears and a mist before his eyes. Something was clinging to his arm, which he tried several times to shake off. Then he discovered that it was Mrs. Barber.

Of the doings of the crew of the Foam that night it were better not to speak. Suffice it to say that when they at length boarded their ship Tim was the only one who still possessed a hat, and in a fit of pride at the circumstance, coupled, perhaps, with other reasons, went to bed in it. He slept but ill, however, and at 4 A. M., the tide being then just on the ebb, the only silk hat in the forecastle went bobbing up and down on its way to the sea.

CHAPTER XXII

A fine October gave way to a damp and dreary November; a month of mists and fogs, in which shipping of all sizes and all nations played blind man's buff at sea, and felt their way, mere voices crying in the wilderness, up and down the river. The Swallow, with a soul too large for its body, cannoned a first-class battleship off the Medway, and with a thoughtfulness too often lacking at sea, stood by and lowered a boat, whereupon the captain, who had been worrying about his paint, invented, in his surprise, a brand-new adjective for the use of senior officers of the British Navy.

Over three months had elapsed since the Golden Cloud set out on her long voyage; three months during which Fraser, despite his better sense, had been a constant visitor of Poppy Tyrell's, and had assisted her in the search for fresh lodgings to avoid the attentions of Mr. Bob Wheeler, who, having discovered her whereabouts, had chosen to renew his suit.

On two or three occasions the girl had accompanied him on board the steamer, and at such times it was Mr. Green's pleasure to wink in a frenzied manner at Mr. Joe Smith and to make divers bets of pints of beer, which made that thirsty soul half crazy to listen to. He also said that any one with half an eye could see what was in the wind.

"And a very nice couple they'll make, too," said Joe, solemnly.

"An' what about Cap'in Flower?" suggested Mr. Green; "she's evident the young lady he was talking about that night, and Tommy's heard 'em speaking about him once or twice, too."

Joe shuffled uneasily. He was beginning to entertain a considerable regard for his new skipper, dating from the time he discovered that his sinister suspicions concerning him were unfounded. He had moreover conceived a dog-like admiration for Poppy Tyrell.

"That's 'is business," he said, shortly; "judging by what you 'eard in that pub, Cap'in Flower knows where to put 'is hand on one or two more if 'e wants 'em."

He walked off in dudgeon, ignoring a question by Mr. Green as to whose foot kep' the door open, and felt dimly the force of the diction that no man can serve two masters; and, with a view to saving himself worry, dismissed the matter from his mind until some weeks afterwards it was forcibly revived by the perusal of a newspaper which the engineer had brought on board. Without giving himself time for due reflection, he ran up on deck and approached the skipper.

"Golden Cloud's in the paper as overdue, sir," he said, respectfully.

"What is?" enquired Fraser, sharply.

"Golden Cloud, sir; boat Cap'in Flower is on," said Joe, slowly.

Fraser regarded him sternly. "What do you know about it?" he asked.

Joe looked round helplessly. At such moments Willyum Green was a tower of strength, but at the present time he was fooling about helping the ship's cat to wash itself.

"What do you know about it?" repeated Fraser.

"Will-yum told me, sir," said Joe, hastily.

Mr. Green being summoned, hastily put down the cat and came aft, while Joe, with a full confidence in his friend's powers, edged a few feet away, and listened expectantly as the skipper interrogated him.

"Yes, sir, I did tell Joe, sir," he answered, with a reproachful glance at that amateur. "I met Cap'in Flower that evening again, late, an' he told me himself. I'm sorry to see by this morning's paper that his ship is overdue."

"That'll do," said Fraser, turning away.

The men moved off slowly, Mr. Green's reproaches being forestalled by the evidently genuine compliments of Joe.

"If I'd got a 'ead like you, Will-yum," he said, enviously, "I'd be a loryer or a serlicitor, or some-think o' the kind."

Days passed and ran into weeks, but the Golden Cloud was still unspoken. Fraser got a paper every day when ashore, but in vain, until at length one morning, at Bittlesea, in the news columns of the Daily Telegraph, the name of the missing ship caught his eye. He folded the paper hurriedly, and breathed hard as he read:—

"Missing ship, Golden Cloud.

"Rio Janeiro, Thursday.

"The barque Foxglove, from Melbourne to Rio Janeiro, has just arrived with five men, sole survivors of the ship Golden Cloud, which they report as sunk in collision with a steamer, name unknown, ten weeks out from London. Their names are Smith, Larsen, Petersen, Collins and Gooch. No others saved."

In a dazed fashion he read the paragraph over and over again, closely scanning the names of the rescued men. Then he went up on deck, and beckoning to Joe, pointed with a trembling finger to the fatal paragraph. Joe read it slowly.

"And Cap'in Flower wasn't one o' them, sir?" he asked, pointing to the names.

Fraser shook his head, and both men stood for some time in silence.

"He's done it this time, and no mistake," said Joe, at last. "Well, 'e was a good sailorman and a kind master."

He handed the paper back, and returned to his work and to confer in a low voice with Green, who had been watching them. Fraser went back to the cabin, and after sitting for some time in a brown study, wrote off to Poppy Tyrell and enclosed the cutting.

He saw her three days later, and was dismayed and surprised to find her taxing herself with being the cause of the adventurous mariner's death.

"He would never have heard of the Golden Cloud if it hadn't been for me," she said, trembling. "His death is at my door."

Fraser tried to comfort her and straining metaphor to the utmost, said that if the finger of Providence had not made her oversleep herself she would undoubtedly have shared the same fate.

The girl shook her head.

"He shipped before the mast for the sake of being on the same ship as I was," she said, with quivering lip; "it is not every man who would have done that, and I—I—"

"Overslept yourself," said Fraser, consolingly.

Miss Tyrell made an impatient gesture, but listened hopefully as her visitor suggested that it was quite possible Flower had got away in another boat.

"I'll watch the paper every day," she said, brightening; "you miss some at sea."

But nothing came of the watching. The Golden Cloud had had its obituary in the paper in large type, and that was all—a notice to certain women and children scattered about Europe to go into mourning and to the owners to get another ship.

By the end of the couple of months Fraser had given up all hope. He was very sorry for his unfortunate friend, but his sorrow was at times almost tempered by envy as he pondered over the unexpected change which had come over his relations with Poppy Tyrell. The old friendly footing had disappeared, and her manner had become distant as though, now that the only link which connected them was broken, there was no need for further intercourse. The stiffness which ensued made his visits more and more difficult. At last he missed calling one night when he was in London, and the next time he called the girl was out. It was a fortnight before he saw her, and the meeting was embarrassing to both.

"I'm sorry I was out last time you came," said Poppy.

"It didn't matter," said Fraser.

Conversation came to a standstill. Miss Tyrell, with her toes on the fender, gazed in a contemplative fashion at the fire. "I didn't know——" began Fraser, who was still standing.

He cleared his voice and began again. "I didn't know whether you would rather I left off coming," he said, slowly.

Her gaze travelled slowly from the fire to his face. "You must please yourself," she said, quietly.

"I would rather please you," he said, steadily.

The girl regarded him gravely. "It is rather inconvenient for you sometimes," she suggested, "and I am afraid that I am not very good company."

Fraser shook his head eagerly. "It is not that at all," he said hastily.

Poppy made no reply, and there was another long silence. Then Fraser advanced and held out his hand.

"Good-bye," he said, quietly.

"Good-bye," said the girl. She smiled brightly, and got up to see him downstairs.

"I wanted to say something before I went," said Fraser, slowly, as he paused at the street-door, "and I will say it."

Miss Tyrell, raising her eyebrows somewhat at his vehemence, waited patiently.

"I have loved you from the moment I saw you," said Fraser, "and I shall go on loving you till I die. Good-bye."

He pressed her hand again, and walked down the little front garden into the street. At the gate he paused and looked round at Poppy still standing in the lighted doorway; he looked round again a few yards down the street, and again farther on. The girl still stood there; in the momentary glimpse he had of her he fancied that her arm moved. He came back hastily, and Miss Tyrell regarded him with unmistakable surprise.

"I thought—you beckoned me," he stammered.

"Thought I beckoned you?" repeated the girl.

"I thought so," murmured Fraser. "I beg your pardon," and turned confusedly to go again.

"So—I—did," said a low voice.

Fraser turned suddenly and faced her; then, as the girl lowered her eyes before his, he re-entered the house, and closing the door led her gently upstairs.

"I didn't like you to go like that," said Miss Tyrell, in explanation, as they entered her room.

Fraser regarded her steadfastly and her eyes smiled at him. He drew her towards him and kissed her, and Miss Tyrell, trembling with something which might have been indignation, hid her face on his shoulder.

For a long time, unless certain foolish ejaculations of Fraser's might count as conversation, they stood silent; then Poppy, extricating herself from his arm, drew back and regarded him seriously.

"It is not right," she said, slowly; "you forget."

"It is quite right," said Fraser; "it is as right as anything can be."

Poppy shook her head. "It has been wrong all along," she said, soberly, "and Captain Flower is dead in consequence. I never intended to go on the Golden Cloud, but I let him go. And now he's dead. He only went to be near me, and while he was drowning I was going out with you. I have been very wicked."

Fraser protested, and, taking her hand, drew her gently towards him again.

"He was very good to my father," said Poppy, struggling faintly. "I don't think I can."

"You must," said Fraser, doggedly; "I'm not going to lose you now. It is no good looking at me like that. It is too late."

He kissed her again, secretly astonished at his own audacity, and the high-handed way in which he was conducting things. Mixed with his joy was a half-pang, as he realised that he had lost his fear of Poppy Tyrell.

"I promised my father," said the girl, presently. "I did not want to get married, but I did not mind so much Until—"

"Until," Fraser reminded her, fondly.

"Until it began to get near," said the girl; "then I knew."

She took her chair by the fire again, and Fraser, placing his beside it, they sat hand in hand discussing the future. It was a comprehensive future, and even included Captain Flower.

"If he should be alive, after all," said Poppy, with unmistakable firmness, "I shall still marry him if he wishes it."

Fraser assented. "If he should ever turn up again," he said, deliberately, "I will tell him all about it. But it was his own desire that I should watch over you if anything happened to him, so he is as much to blame as I am. If he had lived I should never have said a word to you. You know that."

"I know," said Poppy, softly.

Her hand trembled in his, and his grasp tightened as though nothing should loosen it; but some thousands of miles away Captain Flower, from the deck of a whaler, was anxiously scanning the horizon in search of the sail which was to convey him back to England.

CHAPTER XXIII

Time as it rolled on set at rest any doubts Miss Tyrell might have had concerning the fate of Captain Flower, and under considerable pressure from Fraser, she had consented to marry him in June. The only real reason for choosing that month was, that it was close at hand, though Fraser supplied her with several others to choose from. Their engagement could hardly have been said to have been announced, for with the exception of old Mr. Fraser and the crew of the Swallow, who had gleaned the fact for themselves without any undue strain on their intellects, there was nobody to tell.

The boy was the first to discover it. According to his own indignant account, he went down to the cabin to see whether there was anything he could do, and was promptly provided with three weeks' hard labour by his indignant skipper. A little dissertation in which he indulged in the forecastle on division of labour met with but scant response; Joe said that work was good for boys, and Mr. Green said that he knew a boy who worked eighteen hours a day, and then used to do sums in his sleep to improve his education. The other men set their wits to work then, and proved to have so large an acquaintance with a type of boy that Tommy loathed, that he received a mild chastisement for impertinence to his elders and betters.

It wanted but two days to the wedding. The Swallow was lying in the river, her deck unoccupied except for Mr. Green and the boy, who were smoking in the bows, and the ship's cat, which, with one eye on Mr. Green, was stalking the frying-pan. Fraser had gone ashore on business connected with his wedding-garments, and Poppy Tyrell, with all her earthly belongings in a couple of boxes, sat in the cabin dreaming of her future.

A boat bumped against the side of the steamer, and Mr. Green, looking round, observed the long form of Joe scrambling over the side. His appearance betokened alarm and haste, and Mr. Green, after a brief remark on the extravagance, not to say lordliness, of a waterman's skiff when a hail would have taken the ship's boat to him, demanded to know what was the matter.

"Send that boy below," said Joe, hastily.

"What for?" enquired the gentleman interested, rebelliously.

"You go below," repeated Joe, sternly, "'fore I take you by the scruff o' your little neck and drop you down."

The boy, with a few remarks about the rights of man in general and ships' boys in particular, took his departure, and Joe, taking the startled Mr. Green by the arm, led him farther aft.

"You've got a 'ead on you Will-yum, I know," he said, in a fierce whisper.

"People have said so," remarked the other, modestly. "What's the row?"

For answer, Joe pointed to the cabin, and that with so much expression on his features that Mr. Green, following his gaze, half expected to see something horrible emerge from the companion.

"It's all up," said the tall seaman, poetically. "You can put the wedding-dress away in brown paper, and tell the church bells as there is no call for 'em to ring: Cap'n Flower has turned up ag'in."

"WHAT?" cried the astonished Mr. Green.

"I see 'im," replied Joe. "I was just goin' on the wharf as I passed to speak to old George, when I see 'im talking to 'im. He didn't see me, an' I come off 'ere as fast as my legs could carry me. Now, wot's to be done? You've got the 'ead-piece."

Mr. Green scratched the article in question and smiled feebly.

"On'y two days, and they would ha' been married," said Joe; "bit 'ard, ain't it? I'm glad as I can be as he's safe, but he might ha' waited a day or two longer."

"Did George seem scared?" enquired his friend.

"Wot's that got to do with it?" demanded Joe, violently. "Are you goin' to set that 'ead-piece to work or are you not?"

Mr. Green coughed confusedly, and attempted to think with a brain which was already giddy with responsibility.

"I don't want to do anything that isn't straight and gentlemanly," he remarked.

"Straight?" repeated Joe. "Look 'ere! Cap'n Fraser's our old man, ain't he? Very good, it's our dooty to stand by 'im. But, besides that, it's for the young lady's sake: it's easy to see that she's as fond of him as she can be, and she's that sort o' young lady that if she come up now and told me to jump overboard, I'd do it."

"You could swim ashore easy," asserted Mr. Green.

"They was to be married Thursday morning," continued Joe, "and now here's Cap'n Flower and no 'ead-piece on the ship. Crool, I call it."

"She's a very nice young lady," said the mortified Mr. Green; "always a pleasant smile for everybody."

"He'll come aboard 'ere as safe as heggs is heggs," said Joe, despondently. "Wot's to be done?"

He folded his arms on the side and stood ruefully watching the stairs. He was quite confident that there were head-pieces walking the earth, to which a satisfactory solution of this problem would have afforded no difficulty whatever, and he shook his own sadly, as he thought of its limitations.

"It only wants a little artfulness, Will-yum," he suggested, encouragingly.

"Get hold of him and make him drunk for three days," murmured Mr. Green, in a voice so low that he half hoped Joe would not hear it.

"And then boil 'im," said the indignant seaman, without looking round. "Ah! Here he comes. Now you've got to be astonished, mind; but don't make a noise, in case it fetches the young lady up."

He pointed to the stairs, and his friend, going to his side, saw a passenger just stepping into a boat. The two men then turned away until, at sight of Captain Flower's head appearing above the side, they went off into such silent manifestations of horror and astonishment that he feared for their reason.

"It's 'is voice," said Joe, hastily, as Flower bawled out to them with inconsiderate loudness. "I never thought to see you ag'in, sir; I 'eard you was drowned months and months ago."

He took the captain's proffered hand somewhat awkwardly, and stood closely scanning him. The visitor was bronzed with southern suns, and looked strong and well. His eye was bright and his manner retained all its old easy confidence.

"Ah, I've been through something since I saw you last, my lad," he said, shaking his head. "The great thing is, Joe, to always keep your head above water."

"Yessir," said the seaman, slowly; "but I 'eard as 'ow you went down with the Golden Cloud, sir."

"So I did," said Flower, somewhat boastfully, "and came up again with the nearest land a mile or two under my feet. It was dark, but the sea was calm, and I could see the brute that sunk us keeping on her way. Then I saw a hen-coop bobbing up and down close by, and I got to it just in time, and hung on to it until I could get my breath again and shout. I heard a hail a little way off, and by-and-by I got along-side two of our chaps making themselves comfortable on two or three spars. There were three drowned fowls in my coop, and we finished them on the fourth day just as a whaler hove in sight and took us off. We were on her over four months, and then we sighted the barque California, homeward bound, and she brought us home. I landed at the Albert Docks this morning, and here I am, hard as nails."

Joe, with a troubled eye in the direction of the cabin, murmured that it did him credit, and Mr-Green made a low, hissing noise, intended to signify admiration. Flower, with a cheery smile, looked round the deck.

"Where's Fraser?" he enquired.

"He's ashore, sir," said Joe, hastily. "I don't know when he'll be back."

"Never mind, I'll wait," was the reply. "George was telling me he is to be married on Thursday."

Joe gasped and eyed him closely.

"So I've 'eard, sir."

"And, Captain Barber's married, too, George tells me," said Flower. "I suppose that's right?"

"So I've 'eard, sir," said Joe, again.

Flower turned and paced a little up and down the deck, deep in thought. He had arrived in London three hours before to find that Poppy had left her old lodgings without leaving any clue as to her whereabouts. Then he had gone on to the Wheelers, without any result, so far as he was concerned, although the screams of the unfortunate Mrs. Wheeler were still ringing in his ears.

"I'll go down below and wait," he said, stopping before the men. "Tell Fraser I'm there, or else he'll be startled. I nearly killed poor old George. The man's got no pluck at all."

He moved slowly towards the cabin and Poppy, leaving the men exchanging glances of hopeless consternation. Then, as he turned to descend, the desperate Joe ran up and laid a detaining hand on his sleeve.

"You can't go down there," he whispered, and dragged him forcibly away.

"Why not?" demanded the other, struggling. "Let go, you fool."

He wrenched himself free, and stood gazing angrily at the excited seaman.

"There's a lady down there," said the latter, in explanation.

"Well, I sha'n't eat her," said the indignant Flower. "Don't you put your hands on me again, my lad, or you'll repent it. Who Is it?"

Joe eyed him helplessly and, with a dim idea of putting off the discovery as long as possible, mysteriously beckoned him forward.

"Who is it?" asked the puzzled Flower, advancing a pace or two.

The seaman hesitated. Then a sudden inspiration, born of the memories of last year's proceedings, seized him, and he shook with the brilliancy of it. He looked significantly at Mr. Green, and his voice trembled with excitement.

"The lady who used to come down to the Foam asking for Mr. Robinson," he stammered.

"What?" said the dismayed Flower, coming briskly forward and interposing two masts, the funnel, and the galley between himself and the cabin. "Why on earth didn't you say so before?"

"Well, I didn't know what to do, sir," said Joe, humbly; "it ain't for the likes of me to interfere."

Flower knit his brows, and tapped the deck with his foot.

"What's she doing down there?" he said, irritably; "she's not going to marry Fraser, is she?"

Joe gulped.

"Yessir," he said, promptly.

"Yessir," said Mr. Green, with an intuitive feeling that a lie of such proportions required backing.

Flower stood in amaze, pondering the situation, and a grin slowly broke the corners of his mouth.

"Don't tell Fraser I've been here," he said, at length.

"No, sir," said Joe, eagerly.

"I'll see him in a day or two," said Flower, "after he's married. You understand me, Joe?"

"Yessir," said Joe, again. "Shall I put you ashore, sir?"

He was almost dancing with impatience lest Fraser or Poppy should spoil his plans by putting in an appearance, but before Flower could reply Mr. Green gave a startled exclamation, and the captain, with a readiness born of his adventures of the last year, promptly vanished down the forecastle as Miss Tyrell appeared on deck. Joe closed the scuttle, and with despair gnawing at his vitals sat on it.

Unconscious of the interest she was exciting, Poppy Tyrell, who had tired of the solitude of the cabin, took a seat on a camp-stool, and, folding her hands in her lap, sat enjoying the peace and calm of the summer evening. Joe saw defeat in the very moment of victory; even while he sat, the garrulous Tommy might be revealing State secrets to the credulous Flower.

"Get her down below," he whispered, fiercely, to Mr. Green. "Quick!"

His friend stared at him aghast, but made no movement. He looked at the unconscious Poppy, and then back at the mouthing figure seated on the scuttle. His brain was numbed. Then a little performance on Charlie's part a week or two before, which had cost that gentleman his berth, occurred to him, and he moved slowly forward.

For a moment the astonished Joe gazed at him in wrathful bewilderment; then his brow cleared, and his old estimate of his friend was revived again. Mr. Green lurched rather than walked, and, getting as far as the galley, steadied himself with one hand, and stood, with a foolish smile, swaying lightly in the breeze. From the galley he got with great care to the side of the ship opposite Poppy, and, clutching the shrouds, beamed on her amiably. The girl gave one rapid glance at him and then, as he tottered to the wheel and hung on by the spokes, turned her head away. What it cost the well-bred Mr. Green to stagger as he came by her again and then roll helplessly at her feet, will never be known, and he groaned in spirit as the girl, with one scornful glance in his direction, rose quietly and went below again.

Satisfied that the coast was clear, he rose to his feet and signalled hurriedly to Joe, then he mounted sentry over the companion, grinning feebly at the success of his manoeuvres as he heard a door closed and locked below.

"You pull me round to the wharf, Joe," said Flower, as he tumbled hurriedly into the boat. "I don't want to run into Fraser, and I just want to give old George the tip to keep quiet for a day or two."

The seaman obeyed readily, and exchanged a triumphant glance with Mr. Green as they shot by the steamer's stern. His invention was somewhat tried by Flower's questions on the way to the wharf, but he answered them satisfactorily, and left him standing on the jetty imparting to George valuable thoughts on the maxim that speech is silver and silence golden.

Joe tried a few of the principal points with Tommy upon his return to the steamer, the necessity for using compliments instead of threats to a ship's boy being very galling to his proud nature.

"You be a good boy like you always 'ave been, Tommy," he said, with a kindly smile, "and don't breathe a word about wot's 'appened this evening, and 'ere's a tanner for you to spend—a whole tanner."

Tommy bit it carefully, and, placing it in his pocket, whistled thoughtfully.

"Fill your pipe out o' that, young 'un," said Mr. Green, proffering his pouch with a flourish.

The boy complied, and putting a few reserve charges in his pocket, looked up at him shrewdly.

"Is it very partikler?" he enquired, softly.

"Partikler!" repeated Joe. "I should think it is. He can't think 'ow partikler it is, can 'e, Will-yum?"

Mr. Green shook his head.

"It's worth more than a tanner then," said Tommy, briskly.

"Look 'ere," said Joe, suppressing his natural instincts by a strong effort. "You keep quiet for three days, and I'll be a friend to you for life. And so will Will-yum, won't you, old man?"

Mr. Green, with a smile of rare condescension, said that he would.

"Look 'ere," said the bargainer, "I'll tell you what I'll do for you: you gimme another tanner each instead, and that's letting you off cheap, 'cos your friendship 'ud be worth pounds and pounds to anybody what wanted it."

He gazed firmly at his speechless, would-be friends and waited patiently until such time as their emotion would permit of a reply. Joe was the first to speak, and Tommy listened unmoved to a description of himself which would have made a jelly-fish blush.

"Tanner each," he said, simply; "I don't want friends who can talk like that to save sixpence."

Mr. Green, with a sarcasm which neither Tommy nor Joe understood, gave him the amount in coppers. His friend followed suit, and the boy, having parted with his reputation at a fair price, went below, whistling.

Fraser came on board soon afterwards, and Mr. Green, with his celebrated drunken scene fresh in his mind, waited nervously for developments. None ensuing, he confided to Joe his firm conviction that Miss Tyrell was a young lady worth dying for, and gloomily wondered whether Fraser was good enough for her. After which, both men, somewhat elated, fell to comparing head-pieces.

Joe was in a state of nervous tension while steam was getting up, and, glued to the side of the steamer, strained his eyes, gazing at the dimly-lit stairs. As they steamed rapidly down the river his spirits rose, and he said vaguely that something inside him seemed to tell him that his trouble would not be in vain.

"There's two days yet," said Mr. Green. "I wish they was well over."

Captain Flower, who had secured a bed at the Three Sisters' Hotel in Aldgate, was for widely different reasons wishing the same thing. His idea was to waylay Fraser immediately after the marriage and obtain Poppy's address, his natural vanity leading him to believe that Miss Tipping would at once insist upon a change of bridegroom, if she heard of his safety before the ceremony was performed. In these circumstances, he had to control his impatience as best he could, and with a view to preventing his safety becoming known too soon, postponed writing to his uncle until the day before the wedding.

CHAPTER XXIV

He posted his letter in the morning, and after a midday meal took train to Seabridge, and here the reception of which he had dreamed for many weary months, awaited him. The news of his escape had spread round the town like wildfire, and he had hardly stepped out of the train before the station-master was warmly shaking hands with him. The porters followed suit, the only man who displayed any hesitation being the porter from the lamp-room, who patted him on the back several times before venturing. The centre of a little, enthusiastic knot of fellow-townsmen, he could hardly get clear to receive the hearty grip of Captain Barber, or the chaste salute with which Mrs. Barber inaugurated her auntship; but he got free at last, and, taking an arm of each, set off blithely down the road, escorted by neighbours.

As far as the cottage their journey was a veritable triumphal progress, and it was some time before the adventuresome mariner was permitted to go inside; but he got free at last, and Mrs. Barber, with a hazy idea of the best way to treat a shipwrecked fellow-creature, however remote the accident, placed before him a joint of cold beef and a quantity of hot coffee. It was not until he had made a good meal and lit his pipe that Uncle Barber, first quaffing a couple of glasses of ale to nerve himself for harrowing details, requested him to begin at the beginning and go right on.

His nephew complied, the tale which he had told Poppy serving him as far as Riga; after which a slight collision off the Nore at night between the brig which was bringing him home and the Golden Cloud enabled him to climb into the bows of that ill-fated vessel before she swung clear again. There was a slight difficulty here, Captain Barber's views of British seamen making no allowance for such a hasty exchange of ships, but as it appeared that Flower was at the time still suffering from the effects of the fever which had seized him at Riga, he waived the objection, and listened in silence to the end of the story.

"Fancy what he must have suffered," said Mrs-Barber, shivering; "and then to turn up safe and sound a twelvemonth afterwards. He ought to-make a book of it."

"It's all in a sailorman's dooty," said Captain Barber, shaking his head. "It's wot 'e expects."

His wife rose, and talking the while proceeded to clear the table. The old man closed the door after her, and with a glance at his nephew gave a jerk of the head towards the kitchen.

"Wonderful woman, your aunt," he said, impressively; "but I was one too many for 'er."

Flower stared.

"How?" he enquired, briefly.

"Married 'er," said the old man, chuckling. "You wouldn't believe wot a lot there was arter her. I got 'er afore she knew where she was a'most. If I was to tell you all that there was arter'er, you'd hardly believe me."

"I daresay," said the other.

"There's good news and bad news," continued Captain Barber, shaking his head and coughing a bit with his pipe. "I've got a bit o' bad for you."

Flower waited.

"'Lizabeth's married," said the old man, slowly; "married that stupid young Gibson. She'll be sorry enough now, I know."

His nephew looked down. "I've heard about it," he said, with an attempt at gloom; "old George told me."

The old man, respecting his grief, smoked on for some time in silence, then he got up and patted him on the shoulder.

"I'm on the look-out for you," he said, kindly; "there's a niece o' your aunt's. I ain't seen her yet; but your aunt praises of her, so she's all right. I'll tell your aunt to ask 'er over. Your aunt ses—"

"How many aunts have I got?" demanded Flower, with sudden irritation.

The old man raised his eyebrows and stared at him in offended amazement.

"You're not yourself, Fred," he said, slowly; "your misfortunes 'ave shook you up. You've got one aunt and one uncle what brought you up and did the best for you ever since you was so 'igh."

"So you did," said Flower, heartily. "I didn't mean to speak like that, but I'm tired and worried."

"I see you was," said his uncle, amiably, "but your aunt's a wonderful woman. She's got a business 'ead, and we're doing well. I'm buying another schooner, and you can 'ave her or have the Foam back, which you like."

Flower thanked him warmly, and, Mrs. Barber returning, he noticed with some surprise the evident happiness of the couple for whose marriage he was primarily responsible. He had to go over his adventures again and again, Captain Barber causing much inconvenience and delay at supper-time by using the beer-jug to represent the Golden Cloud and a dish of hot sausages the unknown craft which sank her. Flower was uncertain which to admire most: the tactful way in which Mrs. Barber rescued the sausages or the readiness with which his uncle pushed a plate over a fresh stain on the tablecloth.

Supper finished, he sat silently thinking of Poppy, not quite free from the fear that she might have followed him to New Zealand by another boat. The idea made him nervous, and the suspense became unendurable. He took up his cap and strolled out into the stillness of the evening. Sea-bridge seemed strange to him after his long absence, and, under present conditions, melancholy. There was hardly a soul to be seen, but a murmur of voices came through the open windows of the Thorn, and a clumsy cart jolted and creaked its way up the darkening road.

He stood for some time looking down on the quay, and the shadowy shapes of one or two small craft lying in the river. The Foam was in her old berth, and a patch of light aft showed that the cabin was occupied. He walked down to her, and stepping noiselessly aboard, peered through the open skylight at Ben, as he sat putting a fresh patch in a pair of trousers. It struck him that the old man might know something of the events which had led up to Fraser's surprising marriage, and, his curiosity being somewhat keen on the point, he descended to glean particulars.

Ben's favourite subject was the misdeeds of the crew, and the steps which a kind but firm mate had to take to control them, and he left it unwillingly to discuss Fraser's marriage, of which faint rumours had reached his ears. It was evident that he knew nothing of the particulars, and Flower with some carefulness proceeded to put leading questions.

"Did you ever see anything more of those women who used to come down to the ship after a man named Robinson?" he enquired, carelessly.

"They come down one night soon arter you fell overboard," replied the old man. "Very polite they was, and they asked me to go and see 'em any time I liked. I ain't much of a one for seeing people, but I did go one night 'bout two or three months ago, end o' March, I think it was, to a pub wot they 'ave at Chelsea, to see whether they 'ad heard anything of 'im."

"Ah!" interjected the listener.

"They was very short about it," continued Ben, sourly; "the old party got that excited she could 'ardly keep still, but the young lady she said good riddance to bad rubbish, she ses. She hoped as 'ow he'd be punished."

Flower started, and then smiled softly to himself.

"Perhaps she's found somebody else," he said.

Ben grunted.

"I shouldn't wonder, she seemed very much took up with a young feller she called Arthur," he said, slowly; "but that was the last I see of 'em; they never even offered me a drink, and though they'd ask me to go down any time I liked, they was barely civil. The young lady didn't seem to me to want Arthur to 'ear about it."

He stitched away resentfully, and his listener, after a fond look round his old quarters, bade him good-night and went ashore again. For a little while he walked up and down the road, pausing once to glance at the bright drawn blind in the Gibsons' window, and then returned home. Captain Barber and his wife were at cribbage, and intent upon the game.

With the morning sun his spirits rose, and after a hurried breakfast he set off for the station and booked to Bittlesea. The little platform was bright with roses, and the air full of the sweetness of an early morning in June. He watched the long line stretching away until it was lost in a bend of the road, and thought out ways and means of obtaining a private interview with the happy bridegroom;

a subject which occupied him long after the train had started, as he was benevolently anxious not to mar his friend's happiness by a display of useless grief and temper on the part of the bride.

The wedding party left the house shortly before his arrival at the station, after a morning of excitement and suspense which had tried Messrs. Smith and Green to the utmost, both being debarred by self-imposed etiquette from those alluring liquids by which in other circumstances they would have soothed their nerves. They strolled restlessly about with Tommy, for whom they had suddenly conceived an ardent affection, and who, to do him justice, was taking fullest advantage of the fact.

They felt a little safer when a brougham dashed up to the house and carried off Fraser and his supporter, and safer still when his father appeared with Poppy Tyrell on his arm, blushing sweetly and throwing a glance in their direction, which was like to have led to a quarrel until Tommy created a diversion by stating that it was intended for him.

By the time Flower arrived the road was clear, and the house had lapsed into its accustomed quiet.

An old seafaring man, whose interest in weddings had ceased three days after his own, indicated the house with the stem of his pipe. It was an old house with a broad step and a wide-open door, and on the step a small servant, in a huge cap with her hands clasped together, stood gazing excitedly up the road.

"Cap'n Fraser live here?" enquired Flower, after a cautious glance at the windows.

"Yes, sir," said the small servant; "he's getting married at this very instant."

"You'll be married one of these days if you're a good girl," said Flower, who was in excellent humour.

The small girl forgot her cap and gave her head a toss. Then she regarded him thoughtfully, and after adjusting the cap, smoothed down her apron and said, "she was in no hurry; she never took any notice of them."

Flower looked round and pondered. He was anxious, if possible, to see Fraser and catch the first train back.

"Cap'n Fraser was in good spirits, I suppose?" he said, cautiously.

"Very good spirits," admitted the small servant, "but nervous."

"And Miss Tipping?" suggested Flower.

"Miss who?" enquired the small girl, with a superior smile. "Miss Tyrell you mean, don't you?"

Flower stared at her in astonishment. "No, Miss Tipping," he said, sharply, "the bride. Is Miss Tyrell here too?"

The small girl was astonished in her turn. "Miss Tyrell is the bride," she said, dwelling fondly on the last word. "Who's Miss Tipping?"

"What's the bride's Christian name?" demanded Flower, catching her fiercely by the hand'.

He was certain of the reply before the now thoroughly frightened small girl could find breath enough to utter it, and at the word "Poppy," he turned without a word and ran up the road. Then he stopped, and coming back hastily, called out to her for the whereabouts of the church.

"Straight up there and second turning on the left," cried the small girl, her fear giving place to curiosity, "What's the matter?"

But Flower was running doggedly up the road, thinking in a confused fashion as he ran. At first he thought that Joe had blundered; then, as he remembered his manner and his apparent haste to get rid of him, amazement and anger jostled each other in his mind. Out of breath, his pace slackened to a walk, and then broke into a run again as he turned the corner, and the church came into view.

There was a small cluster of people in the porch, which was at once reduced by two, and a couple of carriages drawn up against the curb. He arrived breathless and peered in. A few spectators were in the seats, but the chancel was empty.

"They're gone into the vestry," whispered an aged but frivolous woman, who was grimly waiting with a huge bag of rice.

Flower turned white. No efforts of his could avail now, and he smiled bitterly as he thought of his hardships of the past year. There was a lump in his throat, and a sense of unreality about the proceedings which was almost dream-like. He looked up the sunny road with its sleepy, old-time houses, and then at the group standing in the porch, wondering dimly that a deformed girl on crutches should be smiling as gaily as though the wedding were her own, and that yellow, wrinkled old women should wilfully come to remind themselves of their long-dead youth. His whole world seemed suddenly desolate and unreal, and it was only borne in upon him slowly that there was no need now for his journey to London in search of Poppy, and that henceforth her movements could possess no interest for him. He ranged himself quietly with the bystanders and, not without a certain dignity, waited.

It seemed a long time. The horses champed and rattled their harness. The bystanders got restless. Then there was a movement.

He looked in the church again and saw them coming down the aisle: Fraser, smiling and erect, with Poppy's little hand upon his arm. She looked down at first, smiling shyly, but as they drew near the door gave her husband a glance such as Flower had never seen before. He caught his breath then, and stood up erect as the bridegroom himself, and as they reached the door they both saw him at the same instant. Poppy, with a startled cry of joy and surprise, half drew her arm from her husband's; Fraser gazed at him as on one risen from the dead.

For a space they regarded each other without a word, then Fraser, with his wife on his arm, took a step towards him. Flower still regarding them steadily, drew back a little, and moved by a sudden impulse, and that new sense of dignity, snatched a handful of rice from the old woman's bag and threw it over them.

Then he turned quickly, and with rapid strides made his way back to the station.

W.W. Jacobs – A Short Biography

William Wymark Jacobs was born on September 8, 1863 in the Wapping district of London, England. An author, humorist and dramatist, Jacobs is best remembered for the enduring classic tale of horror - "The Monkey's Paw".

As a youth, Jacobs grew up near the Wapping docks in London, where his father was a wharf manager. The family's first home was home was a house on a River Thames wharf.

The docklands setting would show up frequently in his later literary output. Jacobs, the wharf rat, and his three siblings lost their mother when they were all still young children. Their father, William Gage Jacobs, remarried and fathered a further seven children with his erstwhile housekeeper Ellen Florey. Although he grew up surrounded by poverty, Jacobs himself received a formal education in London, first at a private prep school and later at the Birkbeck Literary and Scientific Institute (now part of the University of London and known as Birkbeck College).

Jacobs' adult working life began with a clerical position at the Post Office Savings Bank. The job was not a stimulating one but Jacobs put his imagination to good use and started to write short stories, sketches and articles, many of which appeared in the Post Office house publication "Blackfriars Magazine."

Although Jacobs did receive his fair share of rejection slips at the beginning of his career, many works written during this period of clerical employment appeared in the "Idler" and "Today" magazines, both of which were edited by noted humorist Jerome K. Jerome, who had taken a liking to Jacobs' stories.

From 1898, Jacobs also published stories in "The Strand", a popular, monthly fiction and general interest magazine. The arrangement stayed in place for most of his life and many of the works in Jacobs' subsequent collections – including the nautical serialization A Master of Craft (1899-1900) - appeared there first.

Jacobs' first volume of collected works was published in 1896. Many Cargoes, a selection of sea-faring yarns, established Jacobs as a popular writer and humorist with a penchant for authentic dialogue and trick endings (critics of the day referred to him as the "O. Henry of the Waterfront").

A year later he published a novelette, The Skipper's Wooing, and in 1898 and another collection of short stories titled Sea Urchins. These works painted vivid, if imaginatively stretched, pictures of dockland and seafaring London with colourful characters (such as "The Night Watchman", Ginger Dick) that now seem archetypal.

Many of Jacobs' periodical publications and first editions were illustrated with woodcuts and ink drawings, as was still the custom at the turn of the 20th century. The author worked regularly with artists such as E.W. Kemble, who had illustrated Mark Twain's Adventures of Huckleberry Finn and Harriet Beecher Stowe's Uncle Tom's Cabin, and his good friend Will Owen, who eventually became a household name on the strength of his iconic Bisto Kids, Bovril and Lux Soap advertising posters.

By 1899, Jacobs was able to quit the post office and finally begin a career making a living as a full-time writer.

He married the noted suffragist Agnes Eleanor Williams (who had been jailed for her protest activities) in 1900. They set up a household in Loughton, Essex as well as living part of the year in central London. The couple went on to have five children together though their marriage was considered an unhappy one.

The publication of two short novels: At Sunwich Port (a romantic tale of rival sea captains in the fictional seaside community of Sunwich standing in for the actual East England community of Sandwich, Kent) and Dialstone Lane (another small town romance involving intrigue and buried treasure), in 1902 and 1904 respectively, cemented Jacobs' reputation as one of the leading British authors of the new century.

On the foundations of a continuing ability to write for his audience he was readily published though he never strayed too far from what was becoming his familiar, dependable style. There followed a string of further successful publications, including Captain's All (1905), Night Watches (1914), The Castaways (1916), and Sea Whispers (1926). Jacobs published eighteen books in all during his lifetime; thirteen collections and five novels.

As a storyteller, Jacobs is perhaps better remembered for a handful of brief tales of the supernatural than for his popular nautical-themed works. The most famous of these, The Monkey's Paw, originally appeared as part of the 1902 short story collection The Lady of the Barge. It is an economically written story about a shriveled talisman, a monkey's paw that brings grief and horror in the wake of all too literal wish granting. The story has been adapted for other media repeatedly, starting with a one-act play performed at London's Haymarket Theatre in 1903. There have been multiple film adaptations of the story in the modern era; some of us are familiar with its appearance in an episode of the popular animated series, The Simpsons.

Another macabre gem, The Toll-House, was published as part of the collection Sailor's Knots in 1909. Jacob's once again employs a sparse style to tell the story of a group of men who spend the night in a famously haunted house on a dare (a noticeably similar narrative concept was put to use in the much earlier play The Ghost of Jerry Bundler, which had launched Jacobs' parallel career as a dramatist back in 1899 when it was produced at the St. James Theatre in London). Innovative at the time of writing, these sparingly written, atmospheric ghost stories are now familiar classics of the supernatural genre.

Though prolific in his younger years, Jacobs' productivity dropped dramatically after the start of World War I. Yet even in self-imposed semi-retirement Jacobs was still recognized as a leading humorist, ranked alongside such writers as P. G. Wodehouse and George Birmingham. He enjoyed continuing influence and elevated status among his fellow writers as evidenced by these comments attributed to his colleague Henry James:

"Mr. Jacobs, I envy you. You are popular! Your admirable work is appreciated by a wide circle of readers; it has achieved popularity. Mine never goes into a second edition."

James' literary fortunes would, of course, change, but his back-handedly complimentary admiration is compelling evidence of Jacobs' reputation as a writer and humourist both for his audience and his perhaps more admired literary colleagues.

Though Jacobs would create little in the way of new work after 1911, he was still writing. In these later years, seemingly burnt out creatively, Jacobs concentrated more on writing dramatizations and adaptations of his existing stories, including Beauty and the Barge (a film version starring Margaret Rutherford was also released in 1937) and In the Dark (a one act play that is often performed pr published with The Monkey's Paw adaptation).

Though admired by loyal readers throughout his lifetime, Jacobs has been almost completely forgotten since. Critics are at a loss to name a single reason why - Jacobs is universally considered to be a fine and imaginative literary craftsman. But, as critic John Wain suggested in a 1960 essay, perhaps Jacobs' humour may have been too gentle to persist into the cruel and sarcastic modern era, his dry pokes at proletariat hardship no longer suiting the times.

Nonetheless, Jacobs' legacy remains solid: he continued Dickens' (a writer with whom he is also often compared) tradition for sharing working class stories in authentic vernacular. And polished narratives such as The Monkey's Paw set a standard for the clever use of horror in fiction and popular culture that endures to this day. Indeed recently his works have begun to show an increased demand and appreciation in a world that is constantly looking over its shoulder.

William Wymark Jacobs died in a North London nursing home in Hornsey Lane, Islington on September 1st, 1943, just a week before his 80th birthday.

W.W. Jacobs – A Concise Bibliography

NOVELS AND SHORT STORY COLLECTIONS
MANY CARGOES (SHORT STORIES) (1896)
THE SKIPPER'S WOOING (1897)
SEA URCHINS (SHORT STORIES) (1898) aka MORE CARGOES
A MASTER OF CRAFT (1900)
LIGHT FREIGHTS (SHORT STORIES) (1901)
THE LADY OF THE BARGE (SHORT STORIES) (1902)
AT SUNWICH PORT (1902)
DIALSTONE LANE (1902)
SALTHAVEN (1908)
CAPTAINS ALL (SHORT STORIES) (1911)
NIGHT WATCHERS (SHORT STORIES) (1914)
DEEP WATERS (SHORT STORIES) (1919)

SHORT STORIES (INCLUDING THOSE USED IN THE COLLECTIONS ABOVE)
A BENEFIT PERFORMANCE
A BLACK AFFAIR
A CASE OF DESERTION
A CHANGE OF TREATMENT
A CIRCULAR TOUR
A DISCIPLINARIAN
A DISTANT RELATIVE
A GARDEN PLOT
A GOLDEN VENTURE
A HARBOUR OF REFUGE
A LOVE KNOT
A LOVE PASSAGE
A MARKED MAN
A MIXED PROPOSAL
A RASH EXPERIMENT
A SAFETY MATCH
A SPIRIT OF AVARICE
A TIGER'S SKIN

THE SKIPPER OF THE "OSPREY"
SMOKED SKIPPER
STEPPING BACKWARDS
STRIKING HARD
THE SUBSTITUTE
THE TEMPTATION OF SAMUEL BURGE
THE TEST
THE THREE SISTERS
TO HAVE AND TO HOLD
"THE TOLL-HOUSE"
TWIN SPIRITS
TWO OF A TRADE
THE UNDERSTUDY
THE UNKNOWN
THE VIGIL
WATCH-DOGS
THE WEAKER VESSEL
THE WELL
THE WHITE CAT

STAGE
THE GHOST OF JERRY BUNDLER (1899) (In London)

FILM ADAPTATIONS
A MASTER OF CRAFT (1922)
THE MONKEY'S PAW (1933)
OUR RELATIONS, a Laurel & Hardy film, "suggested by" to Jacobs' "The Money Box." (1936)
FOOTSTEPS IN THE FOG, from the short story The Interruption. (1955)